I0831264

Andraya's Freedom

By Cameron R. E. Senek

Drop Forge Publishing
Edmonton, Alberta
Canada

ISBN 978-0-9880242-2-9

Cover Graphics Designed by:
Jennifer Lee Graphics Design

Supporting Graphics Designed by:
Chandra Senek

Drop Forge Publishing
Edmonton, Alberta
Canada

Second Edition, 2013

Dedications

First, I'd like to dedicate this book to Ms. Virginia Beelaert. You opened my eyes to a world I never imagined when you placed that first book in my hands. You watched me, understood where my imagination would take me, and opened my world with a single story. My thanks will forever be yours.

Second, I'd like to dedicate this book to my friend Lonny. Without your help this dream would have remained that, a dream. Thank you for your guidance my friend.

Third, I'd like to dedicate this book to my family and friends. Our adventures have colored my life and made my imagination flourish.

Most importantly, I'd like to dedicate this book to my wife and children. You are an inspiration to see the world through your eyes, and are my dedication to being better than I am.

Chapter 1

In the Age of King William the First

The ground shook as row upon row of soldiers marched across the clearing. The sounds of their advance echoed in the brisk morning air. Armor and weapons rattled causing the animals to cry out in anticipation of the battle to come. Although the massive walls of Czariana, the capitol city of Andraya, loomed before them, the soldiers appeared unfazed by the task at hand.

"So Marcus has returned to Czariana," William, King of Andraya, calmly remarked. His long black hair, slightly grayed at his temples, hung straight in the calm morning sun. The thin gold crown, encrusted with gems as a sign of his station, rested upon his troubled brow. The middle aged king shifted in his armor as he picked out the opposing ruler across the field. The clear morning air, coupled with his half Elvin sight, made his enemy as clear as if he stood knocking at the main gate.

"Yes, milord, it appears that way," the man at his side replied with a grunt.

"You don't sound impressed, Dec," William said.

"He's wearing the armor of an idiot," Declan replied, his gruff voice uncharacteristic of his full blood Elvin heritage. The two men were very close in age but you couldn't tell it by looking at them. Where King William had already begun to show the signs of time,

Declan still looked like a young man. Wearing the armor of a war time general, his calm, calculating demeanor reflected his emotions perfectly.

"He's got a nice horse though," William said trying to goad his general into a reaction.

"It's only good for dog food and impressing women. That thing won't last an hour in battle. Look at how skittish it is. It's his darn riding mount, not a war horse," the general explained. "Bringing that thing to battle is about as wise as wiping your behind with poison ivy."

Stifling a snicker the king turned to his friend, but upon seeing the general's face couldn't hold back and began to openly laugh. "I remember a certain soldier who wiped his behind with poison ivy once and couldn't sit for a week."

"Milord, must you bring that up at this moment?" Declan asked, a frown forming on his fair featured face.

"I'm not the one who brought up poison ivy, Dec," the king replied, getting his laughter under control. His smile was wide on his face.

"But I got you to relax, didn't I?" Declan asked. His stern face softened a bit as he shifted his focus from the battle field to his friend and cousin. "If not, I could tell you of the story of the fish sandwich and your sister?"

"Oh, don't start that. If I start to think about that story I'll never stop laughing," William replied, choking on a laugh as the memory rushed into his mind. Trying to remain serious, he continued, "How are the troops holding up?"

"As expected, they're nervous and excited. They have been training hard to prepare the city for war, and are eager to see if our defenses will hold," Declan replied.

"Don't be modest, Dec; I honestly believe the Kings Way is going to save a lot of lives by the end of this thing," the king said.

"Well, we'll see how it works if things come to that. Now that this bumbling fool," the general said tilting his chin towards Marcus, "has made good on his threats, I find that I am second guessing myself."

"No worries, old friend, our people will come through this victorious. Marcus might be young but we have the wisdom that comes with age." Sighing, King William continued, "Let's just hope the young king has enough sense to listen first, and think before acting. It will keep all of his men alive as well as ours. If not, then all that we can hope for is that his arrogance, ambition and pride force him to make stupid mistakes. Either that or the field is going to flow with blood by the time this is all over."

"Do you really think he will listen?" the general asked.

"Honestly? No, and neither do you," replied the king as a sad look crossed his half Elvin face.

"Not past hello, milord," the large commander replied. "I can just picture the meeting now. 'Hello, King Marcus.' 'Hello, William.' 'King William, *Marcus*, we must be respectful.' 'I have no need to respect you, *William.* You are just a farmer, not a king.' He's young, stupid and eager to impress his new troops. You don't really think he married that horse face for love, do you?"

Swallowing another belly laugh, the king replied, "No I don't. Darn, Dec, you're going to make him think I'm laughing at him!"

“Might I remind you, milord, that you *are* laughing at him? Besides, he’s human, he can’t see this far,” Declan said trying to hold back a grin.

General Declan's reply to King William made several of the soldiers around the two begin chuckling. They knew that their commander’s remark about humans was aimed at them as well as the opposing ruler. All through their training he goaded them on using human inadequacies to drive them harder to achieve his desired outcomes. He was a hard man, but he had earned the respect of every soldier he commanded.

King William, on the other hand, had always been generous, understanding but strong. He never made anyone feel as if they weren’t important, and each soldier who took the oath to protect the kingdom, city, and all the lands’ inhabitants did so with great pride in their leaders. The different approach taken by both men accomplished one thing, a strong unified army dedicated to the protection of their people.

“See what you have done? Now the men are laughing at him too.” Turning to his forces William said loudly, “You men hold firm, and don’t let this joker take your mind from the task at hand.”

Turning once again to the field outside the gates of Czariana, King William looked at the sea of men before the city walls. “What do you figure the numbers are?”

“Thirty thousand horse, fifteen thousand pike, twenty thousand foot soldiers armed with bows. Add to that what looks like one hundred engineers and fifty craftsmen from my initial reports,” a voice said from behind the king.

Turning to meet the new arrival, King William warmly clasped his friend’s outstretched hand and helped him onto the Command

Platform. "Brody, your timing is perfect." The king smiled. "So around seventy thousand then?"

"Yeah, that's the initial number but do you see how the birds fly from the woods? I would say there is anywhere between two or three thousand more support people in the trees. And I got all of those numbers with Human eyes," Brody said sarcastically to Declan. Like the others, Brody wore his armor, emblazoned with the symbols of his office. His once golden brown hair, covered by his helm, showed more graying than even William's. The pommels of his two swords rising above his shoulders showed him to be more than he appeared. Although a scholar, his prowess with a blade was well known throughout the kingdom.

"So then they are most likely wrong," Declan replied undaunted. Ever since the three were children, Declan and Brody always gave each other a hard time. Ignoring the verbal jousting from both of them, William asked, "Do you think the forest could hold another three thousand men?"

"Yeah, but they wouldn't be prepared for battle. Archers would have to rush through their ranks of cavalry and foot soldiers to be in range of the city. Right now only long range weapons could hit us from back there and none of the movement reports tell of such probabilities. A lot of their war engines have been disabled by our saboteurs on their way from Eland," Brody explained.

"It's a good thing that it's hard to hide an army that size on a month long march. At least we took out some of their force on the way here. Any word yet on the villages that crossed their path?" Declan asked.

"Most have been burned to the ground, but the residents should have all taken refuge in their concealed strongholds. Marcus' army would have marched right by most of the people unaware of how truly close by they were. We won't know more until we can get extra information from the field. We should have a better picture of things tonight when they send their reports," Brody explained.

"Well, let's be prepared for the worst then. If the people have been hurt or killed, then Marcus and his father in-law will pay a high price for this vendetta," William said, suddenly very serious.

"They will, milord, they will. But let's get through this first before we take on another battle right now," Declan replied.

"Indeed," King William said as he turned and left the Command Platform, followed by Declan and Brody. They made their way down to the city wall from the top of the gate house turret where the Command Platform was located.

The city of Czariana was nestled at the foot of a gigantic mountain range that separated the Kingdom of Andraya from the Elvin Kingdom of Layeni. The city itself was a wonder to behold but its most prominent feature, the city walls, was what made it the marvel it was. Nearly thirty feet deep, it appeared as if it was a solid wall of rock and mortar. But hidden within its walls, a series of halls and stairways filled its massive structure.

In the very center of the wall, the Gate House turret rose high above the city. This gate house allowed the city gate to be raised and lowered vertically, instead of on a pivot, allowing for a stronger defense of the city. Since the heavy gate wanted to be closed by the pull of gravity, it was harder to break open than a standard drawbridge or doors hung on hinges. It was from here that the three city commanders walked down until they stood upon the wide walls themselves.

Working their way to a small stone building upon the wall, they entered another series of steps going down deep into the wall. At several points on their descent, they came to platforms opening into rooms and hallways that held supplies and medical units and were the main barracks for the cities soldiers. They continued to descend until they reached ground level and, walking to another set of stairs, began to walk deeper into the true heart of the city's defense, the underground caverns.

The caverns were accessed by three stairways throughout the city. The first was within the city walls, as was being used by the king and his advisors. A second was located behind the Royal household in the private gardens, and a third in the heart of the city. All three could be barricaded from the inside, allowing for a final line of defense against attack.

William spoke words of encouragement and shook hands with anyone who reached for him on their way down. William had earned his seat of rule decades before, but when he became king he changed things. It was true; he was just a farmer before his life was shattered by Marcus' father, Corland Lianthus. But when he became ruler he gave the people of Andraya a voice to decide their own fates.

Now the people of Andraya voted for a king every 5 years. It was only because they had earned the trust of the people that his family was Royalty in Andraya. That alone made William proud. But to see what his people had made of their kingdom during his time as leader truly made his chest swell.

The three men finally made it to the main gate of the underground cavern. It was the main reason Czariana was built at this location and, to William, it was the womb that would keep his people safe in the battle to come.

Chapter 2

In the Age of King Corland the Fourth

"Hey guys, you gotta come check this out!" an excited seven year old Brody called to his friends.

"What did you find now, Brode?" Declan asked, rolling his eyes. Everything was incredible to Brody. He was always finding something "amazing", even if it was only a snail or a lizard. Declan, on the other hand, looked at his full blood human friend with patience born of age. Well at least that's what he thought. As a fifteen year old full blooded Elf, Declan was no more mature than Brody. But the number of years seemed to afford him greater stature, in his mind at least if in no one else's.

Hearing the sarcasm drip from his friend's voice, William, who himself was ten, chuckled and called out, "Where are you, Brody?"

"Over here, guys, come on!" the youngest of the three replied. Brody waved his hand from behind a bush catching William and Declan's attention. The difference in age was always good for an argument between Declan and Brody. So, in a fashion that only a child could truly appreciate, they agreed that they were all ten years old to keep the divisive subject at bay.

When William and Declan finally rounded the bush, they found Brody peering intently into a large hole in the ground.

"What's that, Brode?" Declan asked.

"It's a really deep hole!" the youngster replied.

"Wow, I never knew this was here!" Declan said in honest awe. "This really is amazing."

"Yeah, I've never seen this opening before either and I thought we knew every part of this forest," William whispered, gazing into the darkness below them. "I wonder how deep it is?" he asked in amazement.

Declan quickly grabbed a nearby stone and threw it down the hole. After a second or so, they heard the distinctive sound of rock striking rock. "That sounds deep!" he said.

"Do you really think so, Dec?" Brody asked, still staring into the hole hoping to see something.

"Yeah I bet it is. I wonder if anyone lives down there," Declan replied.

"Well there's only one way to find out, guys, let's go down," William replied.

"Gee, fellas, I want to but it's nearly dark and I don't want to get into trouble. You know how mom yells," Brody said.

"Yeah, and if we cause you to be late she'll yell at us, too," William agreed. "Okay, tomorrow we will meet with ropes and torches. Then we'll go down to see what you've found, Brody."

"I bet there's treasure down there," Brody said with his regular enthusiasm.

With that, the three boys headed back to town discussing their plans for the following day.

The next day all three boys arrived at the town well, where they met every day to start their adventures. They had brought food, ropes, torches, and a surprise from Declan.

"Is that a real sword, Dec?" William asked

"Yep, my father gave it to me before he left with this quarter's shipment. He said I am the man of the house while he is gone and I have to keep mother safe. I thought we might need it on our trip," he said, secretively looking over his shoulder. "Did you guys tell anyone?" he asked.

"Not me."

"Nope, me neither."

"Good, let's keep it that way. I want this to be a surprise for my father when he comes home. Let's go!" Declan exclaimed, as the three boys ran towards the mountains that rose high behind the village.

The three boys quickly found the hole and, after securing a rope to a nearby tree, they began to climb down into the darkness. When they reached the ground, they pulled out a flint and set about lighting the first torch.

Once they became accustomed to the torch light, the boys couldn't believe their eyes. The cavern seemed to go on forever around them, even extending as far back as to go under the mountain. They noticed almost instantly that the sounds of the world above had muted, as if they had entered a world all their own. Unlike the other caves they had explored in the mountains above, this one was fairly dry, without the constant sound of dripping as there always was in the others. In fact, the lack of noise from above and the regular sounds associated with caves made it eerily quiet.

None of the boys could bring themselves to break the peace and as they started to move into the darkness, they did so silently. After several hours of exploring though, their youthful excitement won them over. Finding their voices, they began to shout as they found new and amazing sights deep in the darkness.

They continued to explore, until William's sensible nature finally won out against his curiosity. Calling out to the others he asked, "Hey guys, I've lost all track of time. Do you know how long we've been down here?"

"I haven't got a clue. Without the sun we could have been here for days and I wouldn't have known it," Declan replied, walking back towards his friend. Brody quickly joined them with concern on his face.

"Do you really think we have been down here for days? My mother will be really angry if I was gone that long," he said, now looking around for his mother, picturing the woman hunting for him with a wooden spoon.

"We would be a lot hungrier if we were here for days, Brode," William replied. "It's okay, but I think we should find our way out and get back home. It might still be fairly late and we would still be in a heap of trouble if it was."

So it was agreed. They all began searching for the way out. They soon got very frightened, as none of them could remember exactly where they came from. Frantically, they searched for the exit, until Declan came up with an idea. Working together, they slowly back tracked, following their footprints in the dust.

Soon, they worked their way back to the cavern opening with their rope still hanging down. Although they had to retrace their steps, they didn't lose too much time and were quickly able to find their way out of the cavern. As they exited, each of them looked around and noticed that it was fairly dim in the forest, which meant that they were all probably late for supper. This realization prompted them to rush back home to avoid the anger of their parents, promising to return the next day.

This was the routine the three boys followed for weeks. Each morning they would meet at the well and then head back to the cavern to continue exploring. With each trip they brought more supplies to their private getaway, making it more like home with each visit.

They stopped using torches and switched to an oil lamp which burned longer and brighter. They would tie long pieces of rope around the stone columns and using a code they created utilizing knots, they always knew where and how far from the exit they were at all times.

They became so familiar with the cavern, soon they could move through the tunnels without any use of a lamp at all. Some side caverns they found had their own light from strange, glowing rocks or fungus along the walls. They called these the daylight rooms. It was here that they would douse their lamps and talk using only the light from the walls.

But one of the most exciting days the boys experienced was when they found that the source of the town well was, in fact, a large underground reservoir. They could sit below the opening and hear all sorts of discussions happening above them.

This find was exciting, but it also made them more cautious. They didn't want to get into trouble for exploring the potentially dangerous cave, but more importantly, they didn't want to share their hidden world with anyone else just yet. To make sure no one heard them, they started to talk to each other with a series of hand signals. This allowed them to remain in constant communication with each other while staying silent. With this new addition, their voices no longer echoed around them when they spoke, adding to the peace of their underground world.

Soon, months had passed since they had found their private getaway. Not only did they know the cavern front to back, but they also created an in depth map of it. This allowed them to keep track of the food stores and supplies they had placed in the smaller sub caverns.

Besides some rodents and small birds, the cave was uninhabited. It truly was their private playground. One day when the cautious nature of Brody caused him ask, what if the roof fell in, the boys decided to check how deep everything really was. By going to the opening they now used daily, they tied a knot at the top of the hole above ground and another inside the cavern near the roof. They also marked how far it was from the roof to the floor and were amazed to find that in the area around the hole the ground was five feet thick! And from the roof to the floor of the cave it was around fourteen feet high.

They used their time in the cavern as best they could. They knew that planting season would soon be upon them. When that happened, all of their time would then be spent working the fields with their parents. The boys knew that when the work started, they wouldn't have free time to explore. So they dedicated their free time to learning everything they could about their underground cavern.

As sure as the sun sets and rises, the weather started to warm, and the boys had to begin helping their families in the fields. Their village had no name; it was just referred to by the people as "the village". No one visited, and so directions were rarely given out, leaving no real need for a name. But like all communities, their village wasn't completely self-sufficient and their major export crop was olives.

During the delicate olive growing season, everyone contributed to the community crops. As such, the young of the village were expected to do their parts as well. But as it was for as long as the boys could remember, the growing season was also the tensest time in the community. The villagers were expected to give a percentage of their harvest to the Royalty as payment for protection and an opening to foreign markets. But the Royalty had been asking for a greater percentage at the end of every season. In addition to that, more markets were being closed to the villagers in an effort to avoid competition with Royal merchants.

It was law in Andraya that no one could sell their crops where an official of the king was selling that same produce. So a market selling olives by a king's representative could not also sell olives by one of the villages in the area. This forced the people to have to go farther and get less for their wares. This combination of increased taxes and decreased revenue opportunities caused the ire of people to grow steadily each year.

Although the boys didn't understand any of this, they knew one thing for certain. Keep your mouth shut and do what you were told if you didn't want to get a beating. But the problem was that this year the tensions were even higher in the community. No one talked, and every time someone did start a conversation it was always about the same thing, the Tithing on Tribute Day. These discussions usually got out of hand and fights would break out. This, in turn, would cause all the work to stop until things could be smoothed over amongst the combatants.

It was always the same argument. The people worked too hard for too little. They had nothing to show for it and the Royalty didn't do enough to earn their share. Rumors had begun to spread that barbarian raiders had attacked some of the northern villages situated on the Artillian Sea. Although there was this increased threat, the king did nothing to protect the people. Instead of defending the villages, the King simply took his share earlier to avoid it being taken in the raids.

The Royals took the best of everything, leaving the people to suffer all alone. Because of this increase in resentment, it was no surprise when things turned to violence.

A man in a carriage came out to the fields accompanied by a couple of Royal Guards. You could tell they represented the king directly from the long purple plumes on their helms. The carriage was unlike anything the boys had ever seen before. The large wood frame was painted gold, red, and purple. The colors were so vibrant; they stood out as absurd in the black and green of the fields. Such extravagance assailed Will's senses as ridiculous.

William asked his father who the man in the carriage was. "That, my son," his father replied, "is the royal auditor. It is his job to determine how much of the crops we must tithe to the king."

The man was meeting with a group of the village elders, including the boys' fathers, when an argument broke out.

"That's outrageous, how can the king ask that much of us?" an elderly man, named Opias, exclaimed. William recognized him as the Grandfather of one of the girls that was his age. Scanning the area he found her watching from a distance as well.

"The king offers you safety and freedom, and asks very little in return," the auditor exclaimed.

"The king is a thief if he expects to take that much from us!" the elderly man yelled again.

"Watch your words old man, or you will be hung for treason. It is not for you to question his Majesty but to do as you're told," the auditor said again.

"Now listen here. You have no right to that much of our crops, and on top of that, to send us to the southwest region of the kingdom for selling. That is so far that the crops would ruin before reaching the market!" another man called out.

"Be warned all of you. This is what the King has demanded, and this is what you shall provide, or you shall suffer the consequences," the auditor yelled at everyone around him.

This seemed to ignite a rage in Opias, who lunged at the auditor, and soon both of them were rolling around in the dirt fighting. It was almost comical to see the king's fat representative being manhandled by the grey haired villager. But the humor quickly ended as the fight was broken up by a guard. The large soldier grabbed the old man by the neck and threw him away, as if he were nothing but a bucket of trash.

Opias landed with a thud and let out a sharp cry as the villagers ran to his side. William wasn't sure what was wrong at first. Watching closely, he saw the expression on the auditor's face turn to fear, and the young man knew something was terribly wrong.

"You killed him! You killed my father!" shouted another of the village elders. He leapt at the carriage but was held back by the other villagers, as the king's men sped away.

The cowardly auditor poked his head out of the carriage window and shouted back at the villagers, "Have the tribute ready, or this will be the result for all of you!"

The carriage bounced away in a cloud of dust, as the boys watched in horror. What none of them truly realized, was that this death would change their lives forever.

Chapter 3

In the Age of King William the First

When King William, Declan and Brody entered the underground complex, William couldn't help but think of their first days of exploration. As he stopped to take in the bustling underground city, it amazed him how different everything was compared to back then. Now extra stone columns were added to support the added weight of the city above. He searched for one of the many original pillars, complete with their rope knot markers, to convince himself it was the same place he knew from his childhood. The original pillars were kept as a historical monument, reminding the people of Czariana of the importance this cavern played in their history.

Shortly after building Czariana's first wall, William, Declan, and Brody returned to the cavern with a small army of engineers and explained their plans. It was from that point on that William designed and commissioned the building of each and every stronghold around the Kingdom of Andraya. This was done to provide the same protection, which the capitol city enjoyed, to all of his subjects. That is why he now hoped his people were safe from harm in those strongholds, and that the death toll of his citizens would remain low.

The cavern was filled with people. Although this particular area of the cavern appeared to be populated by troops and support people, William knew that somewhere down here was his own family. He knew that they would be preparing themselves, and many others, for the dangerous siege of their city.

Leading the way, William strode across the floor to a large door off to the side of the first chamber. This was the War Room. Within it, a scale model of the city and the lands beyond were kept on a large table. It was here the Andrayan commanders would plan their attack, and it was from here the Under City would be governed.

As the three men entered, William caught a glimpse of something hanging at Declan's side. A memory flashed through his mind as if the familiar sword with the tattered scabbard under his cousin's cloak had an important meaning. But he would have to search for that meaning later, for now the council awaited them. A woman at the head of the table quickly approached the trio with her hand extended.

"Milord, what can you tell us of the enemy troops?" she asked, taking the King's hand in hers.

"Well, Minister Reese, they came for a fight, that much is all too clear. From what we were able to see from the Command Platform, there are too many men for a long siege. We think we're in for an open attack. What have you discerned from the field reports?" the king asked.

"We made the same determination ourselves. We will have more information tonight, as I'm sure the Prime Minister has already told you," she replied, nodding towards Brody, "But right now it appears as though Marcus means to destroy us all," Reese said with a sigh, and everyone in the room nodded their agreement.

"Well my friends, this isn't a surprise to any of us, is it? We all knew we would have to face Marcus eventually, better now than to prolong the inevitable. The death of his father and the fall from grace of his family name drove him on this path. We all expected it, but I know we all hoped for a better solution than this," William said to everyone in the room.

"So, Majesty, what do we do?" a mousey man sitting at the war table asked.

"That, my dear Minister Finley, is what we are here to discuss. General Declan, can you please take the lead?" King William asked.

"Yes, milord. Ladies and gentlemen, based on the information from our best estimates, their current numbers are over seventy thousand strong. Be that as it may, over the last several weeks, as this army has been on the move towards Czariana, our agents in the field have given us the following information.

"The forces outside our gate are all loyal to High King Porthanaclies, who is in turn, backing his new son-in-law. Let's face it, Porthanaclies is just happy that someone married his horse fa…I mean daughter. He will do anything for the man that finally chose to marry her." Declan's choice of words brought about a brief chuckle from the room.

"That being said, Marcus surely knew that before he proposed to her and now has to prove his worth to his new kingdom. As King of Eland, it is his position to lead and rule. If Marcus can prove himself, he will replace Porthanaclies as the undisputed ruler within the year. At that time, I believe an unfortunate accident will most likely occur for both his father-in-law and his, um lovely wife.

"Because I believe those are Marcus' motives, I think it safe to say that he is going to attempt to make an example of Czariana and Andraya. He needs to show his new people that it is not anyone who can truly lead. He must crush any thoughts Elanders might have to do what we all did so long ago. We should expect the following, that number one he will not call for Parlay for three or four days. Number two is that anyone who goes out of the walls of this city will be allowed to leave through the enemy ranks. Then when it appears they are going to be allowed to depart freely, Marcus will have them brutally killed as an example. This will be done to attempt to break our resolve and make the people turn on all of us. Third, he will not parlay with civility. He will force us to war by giving us terms we could not possibly accept. Finally, once the Parlay is done and he can say he followed the ancient laws of War properly, he will initiate a full out attack on the city itself."

"So there isn't a hope for peace then?" a woman in long flowing robes asked.

"We didn't say that, Minister Eva. Peace is our first and our greatest hope. But we must accept that the destruction of the Lianthus family name has driven Marcus to this vendetta. We all know how difficult it can be to stop one once it has been declared," Brody replied.

"That brings us to each of you. I would like to hear your reports. How are our people faring in their transition to the under-city?" King William asked. "Minister Reese, let's start with Community Works."

"The entire city has been moved below ground, majesty. All water sources have been secured and all of the causeways to the Royal Court have been retracted. It cannot be accessed unless new bridges are created. The alleys and side streets are all sealed along the Kings Way as well. I can say with the surest confidence that the city has been locked down and is as ready for attack as we can make it," she reported.

"Good. Minister Finley, what can you tell us about food stores?" William asked the small man.

"The entire Department of Agriculture has worked to move all of the livestock into the mountain caves behind the city. My farmers are all minding them and our stocks of feed are in good supply. Each man is also keeping an eye out for anyone stupid enough to try to attack the city from the mountain passes. Only a fool would attempt it with those near vertical cliff faces, but you never know," the minister replied.

"I have also just received a report that the cold rooms are full in the underground complex. Between stored vegetables, preserved fruit, and dried meat we're ready."

"Good work, Minister. I knew I could count on you." William smiled at the shy man. "Okay, now how about Education, Minister Payton?"

"Well unlike the other ministers, my preparations have been easy. We moved all of the citizens into the cavern and set up new school houses in the different zones. Classes will go on and I have instructed the teachers to increase lessons in message running, as you requested, to help increase communications," she replied.

"Excellent. Be sure that your teachers keep a close eye on things. We don't want rambunctious children increasing the tension down here. You may find your Ministry will be of the utmost importance in the days to come. We need those kids to function with us and your guidance will help us achieve that. Minister Eva, what do you have to report?" William asked.

"Like Minister Payton, my preparations haven't been very taxing. I've had volunteers move all of the valuable stonework indoors to avoid attacks, and all of the items of artistic value have been moved to the vaults. There really isn't much more for my department to do," the Minister of Art and Culture replied.

"Thank you, Minister. How about Commerce, Minister Dominic?" the king asked.

"We made sure that any of the merchant caravans that could make it were hurried home and are safely in the cavern or preparing to help with communications. The ones that were too far away from the city were redirected to safe zones outside of the march of the enemy. All of the city's treasure vaults have been locked, and we have secured the doors with large marble blocks as secondary sealing measures. You would need a triple team of oxen to move those blocks," the minister laughed.

"Excellent idea, Minister. You have my thanks. Finally, Minister Tobias, what can you tell us of Development?"

"We've re-established new forges down in the cavern. Some of the work is still being done above ground, but we have made sure the only forges running up there are within quick access of the central city stairway.

"Weapons are at around eighty percent and we have started focusing on long range weapons instead of swords and hand-to-hand weapons. We should be at ninety percent by the time General Declan's estimates for combat come to head," the usually quiet blacksmith replied.

"Thank-you, Master Smith, and my thanks to the rest of you as well. You once again exceeded my wildest expectations. You have handled the preparations well and have proven, once again, that our people choose wisely in your positions. Keep focused on your departments to ensure that everything runs as smoothly as it can and we shall come through this with as little trouble as possible.

"Now if you don't mind I would like to have a few words with Prime Minister Brody and General Declan in private. Good work everyone." And with that the meeting was adjourned and as each person left the room the king smiled and tried to convey confidence. He hoped his words helped belay the fears that he knew were simmering below the surface of their calm demeanors.

Chapter 4

In the Age of King Corland the Fourth

The days after Opias was killed took a strange turn for the villagers. The boys worked twice as hard, as fewer people had time for the crops and more arguments began to occur in the town square. Finally, after a week of steady field-hand drop off, the boys' fathers let them go as well.

"You boys might as well enjoy yourselves for a couple of days," Williams father said. "Once we get the people back into the fields, we will have to work twice as hard to harvest the crop. Regardless of what we give the Royals, the crop has to come in."

And with that, the boys happily went back to their days in the cavern. During their newly restored freedom, they found several small side chambers that were like small personal caves. For some reason these smaller caves were always cold. It was a nice place to hide from the summer heat and the three often spent long hours just resting against the cool rocks talking.

This was how things went for another week and a half until, finally, things began to calm down again. Uracles, who was the son of the dead village elder, never came back to the fields, but when everyone else did, so too did the boys. William worked beside his father most of the time, which was a strangely silent experience. Even when William made an obvious mistake, his father wouldn't as much as look at him. The change in attitude was confusing to all of the village's children. But one thing was for sure, it did make working that much easier. But due to the lack of progress in the fields, they had a lot of work to catch up on.

Again, during this time, all conversations surrounded the upcoming tribute day. The death of Opias was a nagging reminder of how little their lives meant to the Royals. It was clear how the Lianthus family's greed drove them to the callous disregard for all their wellbeing. That disregard was evident in the recent murder of Opias. No one knew for sure if the men who had killed him had admitted their guilt. The one thing they all agreed upon, was that they had to be sure the King knew what had happened. They were convinced that if he knew the truth, an apology and possibly a lowering of the tribute would follow.

Once the harvest was done, the town's Harvest Celebration was held. Unfortunately, this regularly festive occasion suffered from the atmosphere of grief and tension. The effort usually put into the celebration was gone, as if the villagers' spirits had been broken. All said, the boys agreed the evening was a bust.

"My dad was saying that Uracles is going to make trouble when the king shows up for tribute," Declan said.

"Yeah, my dad thinks so too. I heard him talking to mother. He says he doesn't know what to do. He agrees that the king is taking too much this year but to fight trained soldiers is simply insane! Do you fellas think there will be a fight on tribute day?" asked Brody.

"Yeah, it seems inevitable. Everyone is really angry and scared. They all seem as though they are tired of doing all the work while the king makes all the money. My father even said that when raiders come, the king doesn't do anything to protect the villages or help them rebuild. He is taking tribute but not returning anything to the people," William said. "If I were king I would make it so that if you didn't want to pay, you wouldn't have to. If you did, it would be my job to do something when trouble started," William said, puffing out his chest.

"You expect to be king any time soon, Will?" Dec chuckled. "It might just ease things here."

"Yeah, right after you learn how to use that sword you carry," William laughed back.

"I can use it," Declan said defensively, pulling it from its ragged scabbard. Much to Declan's delight, his father said he could keep it after he returned from his trip. His father told him that he had done such a good job protecting his mother while he was away, that Declan had earned the right. The young elf had never been so proud, and no other belonging meant as much to him. He had worked tirelessly to clean the rust from the blade and to hone its edge to a proper one.

"Sure you can, Dec; you can use it to cut your foot off, but you can definitely use it," Brody said, poking fun at their sulking friend.

"Aw, stuff it you two. Someday I'll be able to fight with all weapons, and then the king's men couldn't push our families around," Declan said, angrily returning the Elvin blade to its sheath.

"Well you guys, I'm hungry. I'm going to eat and go to bed. This thing isn't fun anyway," William said as he headed to the food table and back to his hut. Following his lead, Brody and Declan did the same.

William awoke to yelling coming from outside his hut. He threw on his clothes and sandals and ran out to see what the commotion was. He found nearly all the adults and children in the town square. Apparently, yet another argument had broken out amongst the adults. It didn't take long for the young Half Elf to discover the topic was once again the tribute.

"No Uracles, this doesn't make any sense. How can we fight seasoned soldiers? We don't have armor and our weapons serve better for cutting fruit rather than battle," William's father, Domitus, argued.

"Domitus, you always did let people push you around. I say we have no choice but to fight. The king comes and takes more and more from us, and pushes us out of all of the best markets. Our incomes have been dropped so much that I can't even buy shoes for my daughter," Uracles replied.

"I know Uracles, but if we fight we could lose everything, then we won't have children at all. At that rate we probably won't be breathing to enjoy them if we did," Domitus replied to a murmur of agreement from the people around them.

"But they killed my father, Dom, how can I let that go?" Uracles replied, his tone sad at the memory of his loss. The sudden change in emotion from the man surprised William. Everyone could clearly see that it was not just money that worried the villagers. It was the destruction of their community, their families and their way of life that had them up in arms.

"I agree, Uracles, and you, in fact all of us, are owed an explanation for that. Look, let's send an emissary to the king to discuss this first. Then we can measure what we do next," Declan's father, Loran, suggested.

"I can agree with that," replied Uracles. "I'm sorry, everyone, for the pain I have caused you all. I know I didn't do my share during harvest, and I always cause these arguments. The loss of my father has my emotions in a torrent. I will make it up to all of you. I volunteer to go as messenger."

"No, my friend, you would get upset and get yourself into trouble. Is there anyone else who would go?" Loran asked

"I'll go, Loran," Domitus volunteered. Domitus was a full blooded human. It was William's mother, Czaria, from which his Elvin roots came. The thought of her made his heart ache, but now wasn't the time to think about painful memories. "I'll see what can be done."

"But Dom, what about your own children?" Uracles asked.

"We'll watch them while he's away," Loran replied. Loran was William's Elfish uncle, his mother's brother, and was also the village's blacksmith.

The combination of Domitus going to the king and the security that his children would be cared for by Loran seemed to settle the issue. It was agreed that they would word the message to the king carefully, and the following morning Domitus would leave for the Capitol city of Baruth.

Eighteen days passed without word from his father as William and the village waited anxiously for his return. But on the morning of the nineteenth day a panicked scream brought everyone running to the edge of town. There, bloody and bruised, stumbled Domitus. The townsfolk carried him back to his hut where everyone who could fit listened intently to the story he told.

"Who did this to you, Dom?" Loran asked, his wife Nishelle at Domitus' side cleaning the blood, sweat and dirt from his face.

"The king's men," Domitus replied, as he broke into a fit of coughing. "I went to the king and requested an audience. I waited for a day and was finally granted entrance to the great hall. When I went in, I bowed and delivered the message as you instructed me to. I mentioned the death of your father, Uracles, but that didn't seem to faze him. But when I told him that he asked too much of us in tribute, he went mad.

"He started yelling that it was his land, and we were lucky he let us live here at all. He then ordered me thrown out of the city like a dog. I didn't realize that dogs were treated as poorly as this, because they beat me from the castle doors to the city gates. Then after throwing me out of the gates, they beat me some more.

"I dragged myself home and haven't eaten in days. It hurts to breath; I think my ribs are broken. They are coming and they are going to take everything!" Once again his body was wracked with a coughing fit.

"The king said if we cannot survive on what he allows us, then he might as well take the rest. We must prepare; they are coming and I don't think they will be satisfied with just taking the whole crop. I think they are going to destroy our homes, and maybe kill us all." With that, weariness washed over him and he fell unconscious with his head on his pillow.

His words had struck the villagers deeply and as soon as they were sure he was alright, they quickly began to prepare. Weapons were pulled out of hiding and were sharpened. Defenses were raised around the entire village as everyone prepared for attack.

Domitus woke once in a while and spoke strategy with the others. Unfortunately though, he knew as much of war as anyone else in the village, and that was very little indeed. But they all did their best until the day before the Tribute came. Tomorrow they would see if all their hard work would be enough.

Chapter 5

In the Age of King William the First

"Well what do you think?" King William asked his oldest friends.

"They are scared and are using their posts to control it. They are all doing well, all things considered," Declan replied.

"I agree. They have focused on their work to take their minds off of what is waiting out there. Remember the first time we had to deal with battle on this ground? Nothing could have prepared us for what we faced, but back then we didn't know what to expect. We do now," Brody added.

"Yes, well, the question is even with all of these defenses can we still protect our people?" William asked.

"We have all introduced ideas in the creation of this city. Dec's Kings Way, your creation of the outer wall, my long range ballistae. Those few defenses will make the difference, never mind the small ones we still have in reserve," Brody replied.

"Let's not forget Chloe is out there. Your little sister and her Rangers won't let anything happen to us in here," Declan reminded the king. "They have already been busy studying the enemy and although the information they have sent us is limited, we are gaining the upper hand with every minute that passes. With all the thought we have put into this kingdom, why question it now?" Declan asked.

“Because now is the time that those concepts have to work. Like you said, our families thought they were prepared but none of them could even imagine what was coming. I don’t want that to happen again,” William said, looking down at the replica of the city on the table before him.

“Will, go to your family. They are in the Royal Cavern already, I think. Well, everyone but Emma, who I heard was running herself ragged confirming food stores and making sure everyone is safe in the underground city. She’s been doing my job as prime minister, making sure all the ministries are doing their parts,” Brody laughed. “Go rest a while; you know that what Declan said about Marcus making us wait is true. We won’t see battle for a couple of days yet. We can discuss city defenses later.”

“Okay, you’re right. I’m going to get some rest. We will meet in three hours to discuss any new information we receive,” William said, walking away.

‘*That’s the way it’s always been.*’ William thought to himself as he walked, ‘*Declan the protector, Brody the compassionate and me the leader.*’

The position of leader always seemed to be thrust upon him. Even when they were children, people always seemed to follow him where he went.

Then when the rule of the kingdom changed, he was voted king by the people. As such, he had been re-elected every time the vote was held. In fact, no one ever ran against him, except for that one time Marcus put his name on the ballot. Marcus lost with the only votes being cast for him coming from the Baruth region, the former capitol city of Andraya, and a Lianthus family stronghold. If it wasn’t law that the current ruler must run for re-election, he wasn’t sure if anyone would rule the lands of Andraya at all. Well, better him than Marcus, he hoped.

Without realizing it, William had walked the entire length of the underground complex and had arrived at the Royal Cavern. He stepped through the door and was instantly greeted by two of his children.

"Daddy's home!" exclaimed a little girl as she rushed into his arms.

"Yes little one, for a short time at least. Where is your mother?" He asked.

"She is out helping the people get to safety," Ashton, his second son, replied.

"I thought as much. Is Logan with her?" he asked.

"Yes, Father. He won't leave her side, even though she has half the castle guard with her," the boy replied.

"Good. How about you, Ash, how are your duties coming?" the king asked the boy.

"Our family has been settled and I am preparing for my shift with the runners" Ashton said proudly.

"That's great, son. I am very proud of you," William grinned, giving his son a warm hug. "Alright, since she is out, I'm going to rest. I think we are going to have a long night ahead of us. Can you please have one of the cooks bring me something warm? Soup, if they have some ready."

"Yes father, right away," Ash said, striding from the room.

William chuckled to himself. '*He's all duty that one. More like his Aunt Chloe every day.*' The king sat down and started pulling off his boots with the help of his daughter, Czaria, when his supper was brought to him.

"Your soup, milord," the cook announced as she entered his quarters.

"That was fast, Violet. I'm glad that you didn't make it especially for me. I'd hate to have bothered you," he replied, sitting at the table to eat.

"Well it was already made, but I did make it especially for you, milord. I know you like a warm bowl when things get stressful. I just had it simmering until now." She smiled down at him.

"Darn it Violet, how many times do I have to tell you that you don't have to cook anything special for me. I can eat what is being served to everyone else," the king grumbled.

"Milord, can I give you some advice?" the heavy cook asked, stopping at the door.

"As long as you don't punctuate it by hitting me with your wooden spoon, go ahead," the king replied with a grin.

This evoked a loud belly laugh from the heavy cook as she looked him in the eye, something no other servant ever did. "Then listen to the advice and I won't have to. Majesty, you spend so much time trying not to be different from the people that it makes you stand out from us even more. That is why the people trust you. You don't want to be their ruler to rule them, but you accept being their ruler to protect them.

"But right now, the people need a king. No one here knows what to expect, and they all have to believe that you do. Otherwise, the terror people feel would drive this place to madness," she said.

Thinking about what he had been told, William was about to respond when the large woman cut him off. "Now, eat your soup before it gets cold. I'm not bringing you another one on that account," she said laughing her way out the door.

William just shook his head and smiled eating his soup. Violet had been with him from the beginning of his time, leading the people of Andraya. It was because of that history that she had a special place in his heart. He ate his soup with the help of Czaria, who was named after the city, which was in turn named after his deceased mother.

At times, the king would lose himself in the wisps of steam coming off the top of the soup. His mind would go from tactics, to governance and, more than once, to the flash of Declan's strange sword. But as soon as he would let his mind wander too far, he would be brought back by the grunts of his daughter, waiting for another spoonful of soup.

"Well, little one, it's time for a sleep. Do you want to have one with me?" he asked the two year old.

She shook her head no, but when he picked her up and laid her down on the bed beside him, she just placed her two favorite fingers in her mouth and sucked them until she fell asleep.

William woke with a start, not realizing he had fallen asleep. Making sure Czaria was still sleeping on the bed beside him, her arms above her head in the position she took every time she was in a deep slumber, he moved out of the bed.

He quickly walked out of the bed chamber and was surprised to see his wife and oldest son sitting at the table talking quietly. They stopped and smiled when they saw him enter the room.

"I see you've taken a younger woman to your bed." His wife smiled at him.

"Yes, well, she seems to help me fall asleep. A couple of minutes listening to her suck her fingers and I was out cold," he laughed.

"You've been under a lot of stress, Father," his eldest son replied.

"Yeah, that's what everyone keeps saying. Have you two been able to rest today?" he asked them.

"No, we just did a final sweep of the city and everyone is down below. We have already had the men lock the garden entrance and Declan went to make sure everything was braced for the worst. He said that when the blacksmiths all come in, they will then lock off the city center access point, leaving only the front gate access open," Logan replied. With his mother's auburn hair and his father's commanding presence, the young prince seemed destined to follow in William's footsteps. He had a passion for the city, but it seemed to end at its gates. Either way, the people would have to choose him as a successor if he was going to hold the title "King" someday.

"I knew he wouldn't rest," William sighed. "Well, it looks like the city is as ready for battle as it can be. We think that it will be a couple of days yet before Marcus calls for a parlay, trying to escalate our citizens' fear. With our people down here carrying on with their lives, though, we should be able to hold off a large part of the anxiety he is hoping to create.

"We've got the soldiers running half shifts, just monitoring the enemy movement right now. We can have them to full strength in a moment's notice, since they have all been moved to the wall barracks. We don't want Marcus to have information about our true numbers yet."

"How are the wall defenses?" the queen asked, as she gently stroked her husband's hand. William looked up at her and saw the life sparkle in her green eyes. Emma had been with him through it all. She had given him his children, carried the burdens of a Kingdom on her shoulders, and still looked to William as beautiful as ever.

"The long range ballistae and catapults are ready. All we need now is to give the order. What word do we have on the archers, Logan?" the King asked.

"They are all stationed along the Kings Way or at posts behind the walls. When the time comes they will be in position to attack. The wall units are also prepared, but like you said, they are hidden in the barracks to keep our numbers concealed from the enemy. We have also been practicing your three man archer teams. Do you think they will work?" the young man asked.

"It should. It worked for Declan, Brody and I, like I've told you before. It should allow our people to be better protected and it will stop them from tiring too quickly," the King replied.

"I agree father. It seems to increase the amount of time our people can continue to fire without rest. All of the practice seems to prove exactly what you and the Uncles have been saying," Logan said, smiling.

"So your father hasn't lost his mind then?" William asked with a cocked eyebrow.

"Well, some of your ideas make me wonder sometimes, but no, this one seems to bear up well," the youth jibed.

"I'll remember that, young man. I'm glad it's working though; we may need those battle formations once this thing is all over," William said with a sigh.

"You're going to take this further when the siege is over then?" his wife asked, looking concerned.

"Yes. For too long, when kingdoms have fought against one another, the Royalty would either reap the rewards or scurry back to their holes. The problem is that it's always the people who truly get hurt. Reports of destroyed homes and crops have been coming in already," William explained.

"Right now, the people in those villages are questioning why they pay taxes. Where were we to protect them? Logic dictated that we bring Marcus and his troops to our strongest city. Unfortunately, that doesn't change that the villagers' lives along Marcus' route have been completely shattered.

"Hopefully everyone listened when we told them to store important, personal items in the fortresses with them. If they did that, then all we need to do is help them rebuild. If they didn't, then heaven help me, I don't know how I can ever make them whole. I could give them all the money in the world, but burned memories are impossible to replace," the king said as the weight of the situation etched itself deeply on his face.

"I know, my love, and you will find a way to help everyone affected. But now you had better find your men and make the rounds. The people need to see you," Emma replied.

"Yes, you're right. Logan will you join me?" William asked his son.

"Sure, father," the youth said, getting up from the table.

"Get some sleep, Emma. You have secured the lower fortress. You need to be rested as well for the battle ahead," William said.

"Yes, dear, I know. I'll lay down with the baby to catch some sleep," she smiled.

"Good," replied William, as he and Logan left the Royal Quarters. "How is your mother holding up?" William asked.

"She's fine father. She coordinated with the citizens, placing their important belongings in the store houses, where they will be protected. She made sure that everyone had a comfortable home down here and has begun the food rationing. We will have enough stores for a year, so long as nothing too drastic happens," Logan replied.

"Well, I don't plan for this to last that long," William said. "If all goes well, we should be able to finish this up in a day or two after the first arrows fly. I want the Night Hawk to double their patrols on the East and West areas of the city. If we can catch a night raid and secure them without Marcus knowing, we will have been given our chance to end this quickly."

"I will see to it immediately, Father. I'll take the first watch myself. I'm glad you've taken to my team so quickly," Logan said with a smile.

"To be honest son, if it wasn't you suggesting it, I would have passed it off as too dangerous. Having an entire branch of the army that no one sees, performing their duties all from the rooftops and shadows, is a little intimidating," William replied to his son with a look of concern.

"I know, Father. But the Night Hawk are soldiers like the rest, they just allow us to see more of what people don't want us to see. We have been able to stop three assassins, numerous thefts and even a rape. I think we have proven ourselves," Logan said, sounding hurt by his father's doubt.

"You have indeed my son, and I am very proud of how you have led them. That, on top of your daily duty as Archery Captain, has been spectacular. No, it's not the Hawks themselves that worry me, but their future. Someday, you will have to choose between the Hawks and the Archers. If you choose the Archers, we will have to find someone trustworthy to lead the Night Hawk. Let's face it son, a group of trained warriors, working in the shadows, could easily begin to infringe on the rights of our people. Rights we don't have the right to take away from them. If a tight hand isn't on the reins of the Hawks, our city could be thrown into chaos," the king replied.

"Yes, I've thought of that as well. I know the ideals you stand for, and I know what our people have come to expect of our kingdom. I will do my best to choose my commanders with wisdom and to weed out anyone too ambitious for such an important post," Logan said to his father.

"I know you will, son; I trust you with all our lives. Perhaps though for this war you should consider taking full time command of the Hawks. Choose someone within the ranks of the Archers to succeed you in their command. How about Shade? He's your second, could he handle it?" William asked.

"Sure he can father, but why wouldn't I just keep both of my posts?" Logan asked.

"Well, they are both very important divisions of our army and require a lot of attention. Second, they operate at different times of the day. You need to rest too, son. This is a very important time for our city. I need you to keep your mind clear.

"Finally, that sort of promotion during a time of war will give everyone an added feeling of security and pride. Shade taking command of the Archers would tell the people here is just another one of the many people qualified to protect them. That and his pride would help lead them in the upcoming battle," the king concluded.

"That makes sense, Father. I feel I could do both, but nothing you said really has a point worth arguing against. I will do just as you asked. Would it also be prudent for me choose a second for the Night Hawk?" Logan asked.

"Who do you have in mind?"

"Charlie. She is one of the female members of the Night Hawks. There are few amongst my members who are her equal and none are her better," Logan replied.

"A female commander? We don't have many in our ranks. Does she have the respect of your forces?" William asked

"Yes, except for a few hot heads, but that isn't anything I can't handle," Logan shrugged.

"Alright, do it if you think she is the best person for the position. Think it through first, though; remember those hot heads could cause us a lot of grief if you have to crack down on them in the middle of battle," the king said seriously.

"I will, Father. Is there anything else you need me for right now? I should really go and make the changes you requested," Logan asked.

"No that's fine, be careful out there, son." William smiled at his eldest.

"I will, Father; it is our duty to serve," the young man replied, and with a small salute and a smile he turned and walked away.

William watched as the young man walked from him. He was thin and tall like an elf but that was where his quarter blood ended. Each of his children had Elvin characteristics but their dominant human sides prevailed. With Ashton, it was his facial features that showed the sharp edges of the elves. Czaria, on the other hand, had a magic in her voice. When she sang any living creature would calm and tension would melt away. '*If only I could have sung like that as a child*,' he thought sadly to himself.

Chapter 6

In the Age of King Corland the Fourth

The sun rose over the village, bright and clear, as if preparing to bear witness to the events of the day. The men were up earlier than that, watching the surrounding area to make sure they weren't ambushed in the night. Many were visibly tense, walking amongst the huts that made up the homes of the villagers.

But their vigilance wasn't required as nothing stirred outside the village all night. Domitus was among the men in the city square preparing for what would come that day.

"By the laws of war, Corland must parlay. We will discuss with him what we are feeling and what we have been experiencing. He is a ruler; he must have enough sense to see what is happening to us," he said to all assembled.

"We could only hope, but I am more afraid that his greed is what is driving him, and not his sense," Loran replied.

"Your concerns are warranted, but we will pray for peace. We must not fight if we can avoid it," another villager responded.

"I agree. So it will be a delegation of three of us. Those who wish to volunteer step forward. I think both Uracles and I should stay out. He has been wronged by the loss of his father, and as for me? Well my bruises can attest to my feelings of the King. That way we keep this as far from Vendetta as possible," Domitus recommended.

Everyone nodded their agreement, including the unusually quiet Uracles.

Declan, Brody and William all watched the meeting with great interest.

"Do you think there will be fighting?" Brody asked.

"No, I don't think so. The King just has to hear how we are left with so little and common sense will tell him what to do," William replied.

"Yeah, but what if he doesn't care?" Declan asked. "You heard them, he could be greedy and take what he wants and do to all of us what he had done to your father. This worries me."

"What should we do then?" William asked.

"I don't know, Will. But we need to do something; I hate not being prepared." Declan shook his head. "Maybe we should tell them about the cavern?" he suggested.

"What good would that do? Brody asked.

"Maybe we could protect the other kids down there. That would allow our parents to focus on the king and his men," Declan replied.

"That's a good idea, Dec," William said. "Let's go to my father and tell him now." And with that the three boys ran to the town square, where the meeting had just ended and everyone was parting ways to prepare.

"Father, we have something we want to talk to you about," William said when they reached his side.

"Not now son, we have a lot of important preparations to make," Domitus replied.

"Please father, it's important," William pleaded.

Domitus sighed and sat down. “Alright son,” he said, “what is it?”

William went into a full description of what he and his friends had been doing over the last couple of months. He explained how they had mapped the entire cavern and that they even found the town well in the middle of it. He then went on to explain Declan’s idea, about hiding all of the village children in the cavern to allow the adults to focus on dealing with the king and his men. Domitus listened quietly and after they were done thought for a moment about their idea.

“It’s really that big?” He asked.

“It's so huge we could fit everyone in the village in it,” Declan replied. “In fact, we could probably fit three or four villages in it.”

“Why didn’t you tell anyone about this before?” Domitus asked.

“We found it before the busy season and once the growing season came, we had too much work to do. Then when all of this happened with the king, it didn’t seem so important,” William replied “And, well, it was our secret hiding place.”

Domitus smiled, “Yes, we used to have a secret hiding place in the mountains, where we now store food. Okay, this is good news. I will talk to the others. Prepare yourselves for the children. It will be up to you to protect them all.”

The three young men quickly set off to prepare for their role in the protection of the village. As noon came, they had prepared torches, ropes and food for everyone they expected down in the cavern.

Shortly after the noon meal, a man who was acting as a scout came running into the village. “The king is coming and he has a lot more men than usual!” He exclaimed.

“Alright, everyone prepare for the meeting. Boys get the kids to your secret place. Everyone else prepare for the worst,” Uracles yelled. His quiet patience of the morning seemed to now be filled with aggression and tension.

William, Declan, and Brody led all of the town’s children to the opening of their cavern. One by one they began moving the village young down into the cavern. Those too small to climb were placed in large baskets and, working together, the older children lowered them down to safety. Soon, they had all of the village young down in the darkness. Declan lowered himself inside, and William covered the rope and opening with bushes to try to hide their only way out of the underground cave.

Then he, Declan, and Brody all picked up their short bows, and leading the children into the cavern, they came to a safe quiet corner. Here they told several of the other older children to keep the kids as quiet as possible. They explained that they shouldn’t be heard, but that they needed to make sure to avoid any possible detection from above. They also warned everyone not to leave the chamber as getting lost was a very real possibility.

They then headed towards the town well so they could eavesdrop on as much of the villagers conversations as they could.

When they arrived at the opening from which the village got their water, they could hear the people above talking angrily. Apparently, the parlay had already been concluded and their options were to yield or die.

“We can’t give them what he’s asking. Now that he has his sight set on this year’s entire crop, we will starve before winters end,” one woman said.

“She’s right; we need to stop this from going any further. If we don’t do something now, they will continue to come and take all that they want. I say, this stops now!” another voice boomed above them.

“This doesn’t sound good,” Brody said to the others.

William and Declan could just nod, as they kept their ears open to the sky above them.

“So it’s decided then?” William recognized his father’s voice. “We fight them.” Many voiced their agreement, some louder than others, but none of the boys could hear a dissenting voice above them. All three of them flashed worried looks at one another. They knew that their parents were now facing a danger unlike any of them had experienced in their lives.

When the plans for defense began, all three boys listened intently. They had never heard such things discussed in the village before. Like most communities, a routine was established in the lives of the villagers. This routine was passed down for so many generations that the people had long ago even forgotten what it took to go beyond those roles. Each person had a job to do and they were expected to do it. That was how things got done in the community. Sometimes arguments or the occasional fist fight broke out amongst townsfolk. But more often than not, those who fought were quickly dealt with and the combatants often made up shortly after.

But these weren’t fellow villagers they were facing. These were men with swords that had fought side by side for years, who were now advancing on the once quiet village. Worse, though, were the soldiers who were led by a man who didn't care about the village people. He had no reason to hold back.

As with most communities, the villagers watched as over the years the government slowly took away more and more of their rights, belongings, and crops. Thinking there was nothing they could do, they spent their days grumbling, but waiting for someone else to do something about it.

Since ruin had come to their door step, it was no longer possible for the people to sit back and watch their government do as it pleased with their lives. Now that they had to fight, the air became thick with fear. Although they were doing their best to contain that fear, the people of the village were on the verge of hysteria. The question the boys worried about the most was, how do you stop a mad man?

Chapter 7

In the Age of King William the First

The next couple of days passed by as everyone had expected them to. The Eland army built their camp which reached from one side of the semi-circular city walls to the other.

Word came from the Rangers that gave detailed information about the villages that fell in the wake of the enemy army. Most were nothing more now than smoldering ruins in the wake of the Elanders' advance. The good news was that all of the people had listened to the warnings delivered by the Rangers. They had all wisely taken refuge in their hidden fortresses. Thankfully, not a single Andrayan was hurt in the enemy advance.

Having an army of wood folk, commanded by his sister Chloe, was once again proving itself to be an asset to the Andrayans. Not only did they manage dangerous creatures attacking villages, but they acted as law and order in the kingdom. Be that as it may, the role they played now was even more important.

It was reported that the people whose protective locations were in caves were dry and warm. Unfortunately though, those villages without such natural formations were hiding deep in tunnels dug by hand. The news being delivered by the Rangers told of people who were cold and unhappy. The Ranger reports also indicated that the enemy troops appeared to be rebuilding their siege engines. It seemed that Marcus would have catapults at his disposal regardless of the destruction to the ones he tried to bring with him.

William sent messages back to his sister to relocate the homeless people to surrounding communities. He was sure that the citizens of Andraya would open their homes to their neighbors during a time of need such as this.

Ever since the attack on the village when they were children, the protectors of Andraya were always cautious. Brody, Declan, and William, with the help of the Master Smith Tobias, designed all of the city's defenses with the utmost care. Their ideas were then implemented by several very talented engineers, and the citizens who chose to make Czariana their home.

The people of Andraya had always worked with William to make the kingdom a better place. After the way their previous king treated them, William was a welcome change to most. No matter what the decisions he made were, his people always followed him. The only time he sensed hesitation from them was when he announced the creation of the Night Hawk at Logan's urging. It was that reminder of the nervous acceptance from the people of Czariana that reminded William to keep a firm hand on his son's creation. He too worried about the abuse of such power in the future.

All of the information being communicated from the city was done by flags. Large flag poles were located around the city and each could accommodate multiple pennant style flags. These flags symbolized words or numbers, which were used to relay orders to the Rangers in the field. The Rangers would then reply using lamps that would flash responses to the city at night. They would relay their messages from random positions in the forest behind the enemy soldiers so they wouldn't be captured.

These communication strategies helped ensure information could flow to the troops in the field, but the communication structure created inside the city was also in full flow. Trumpeters were used to communicate information over long distances within the city walls. Yet none of the communication systems were more utilized than that of the Runners.

Scores of children were employed to run messages back and forth within the city walls. Based out of the schools, the fees paid for the costs of the children's education and a portion was given directly to the runners as wages. The idea came into practice years ago, before William had become king, and had refined itself since.

The time spent waiting for the opening Parlay was tense for everyone. Each person who had a stake in creating the defenses worried over their part. This nervous tension was shared by the city's head engineer, Owen Surehand. Pacing the top of the city wall, he watched the enemy rebuild their war engines far off in the distance. As he watched, he attempted to calculate their attack range as best he could. His goal was to ensure those engines would be attacked and destroyed by his own machines before they could damage the city behind him.

Owen's job was to find a way to make everything the city's leaders imagined a reality. It was Owen who took Declan's design of a box canyon and designed the city around it, creating the Kings Way. The long causeway, leading from the main gate to just short of the Central Garden, was designed to end sieges with as little bloodshed as possible. Of all of his creations, Owen, like everyone else involved, worried about the Kings Way the most.

Another of the city's engineers and craftsmen, Nathan Glass, was fine tuning his own addition to the city's defenses. Nathan was a glassmaker by trade, but his keen mind also helped him develop many of the city's defenses as Owen's apprentice. Although he was a part of the city's corps of engineers, his background in glass blowing was also what brought on his greatest accomplishment, the long range viewer. By aligning several lenses, he had fashioned a device that allowed the long range gunners to better aim their weapons at their targets. His invention had increased the accuracy of the launch crews so much that the Ministry of Defense created a sub branch of the Gunners called Hawk Eyes. These men and women were awarded the title if their target accuracy was above 90%.

It was also due to the Hawk Eye designation, that the Night Hawks derived their name. Each member of the Night Hawk team was picked from the Hawk Eyes' ranks. As well as being Hawk Eyes, they also had to be as proficient with a crossbow or bow as they were with the long range weapons, and they had to be able to score an 80% at night.

Archers in Andraya were easy to come by since the growing cycle of crops was broad enough to allow for a lot of down time. To fill that time most of the Andrayan people took up archery as a hobby. This was openly endorsed by King William, who decided that having a large militia of people in the kingdom, who could come to their neighbor's aide, was good for kingdom security. To encourage the practice, he created the Tax Carnival at Czariana.

Each fall the people of the kingdom brought a tenth of their crop to the capitol as taxes to support the Andrayan army. The week in which this tax was delivered was when the Tax Carnival was held. The carnival was where the citizens could enjoy dancing, visiting, and feasting, as well as the annual Archery Tournament. Everyone was welcome to join the tournament, which was divided into several different divisions. Each division was awarded a champion, and each champion would move up to the next class until only five competitors remained. Those five people were each offered a place in the army and would again compete to see who the Champion Archer was that year.

The Champion Archer would earn a choice, to either take home their village's share of the taxes, or to give their village "preferred seller" status for a year. As a preferred seller, citizens could sell their crops at the best market in the kingdom without paying fees for the placement.

This way every man, woman, and child was encouraged to learn to yield a bow. The people who accepted the offer to join the Army then went through vigorous additional training. It was this training that prepared them for combat with all the weapons of the battlefield. Successfully completing the additional training was a requirement before they could be awarded the title, "Soldier of Andraya".

William, Declan, and Brody were on the castle walls discussing the latest reports when Logan ran up to them. "Father, Uncles, you have to come with me. I have something important to show you," he said between breaths.

Curious what the young man was so excited about, the three men followed him down from the castle wall and through the empty city streets. Finally after walking deep into the city, they turned down a dark alleyway and stopped when they came to a small door.

"What is this about son?" William asked.

"Just wait in here and you will soon see," Logan grinned, as he ushered the three men into the dimly lit room.

His excitement was difficult to avoid and soon the three men couldn't help but feel the energy in the air. Something big was coming and by Logan's reaction, it was something good.

Shortly after he left, Logan returned followed by a young woman and six other people, three of which William recognized as Night Hawks. The other three were bound, gagged and blind folded. William noticed they looked a little worse for wear. Whoever these men were, they didn't come willingly.

"Gentlemen, I would first like to introduce you to Commander Charlie Bennet, second in command of the Night Hawk. She is also the commander responsible for fulfilling your wishes, Father," the young man grinned. Charlie saluted her seniors.

Commander Bennet was an attractive girl. Her eyes were dark and her braid hung down her back with a heavy weight attached to the end. It didn't take an academic to know this woman was quite adept at the martial arts. William had arranged for the strange battle techniques to be taught to all the Night Hawk members, at Logan's request. He was so impressed with the form of hand to hand combat, that each of his personal guards was also trained martial artists. The weighted braid looked innocent enough, but in the control of a skilled warrior it was a deadly weapon.

"His majesty exaggerates, my lords," Charlie explained. "My men and I were on patrol when we noticed these men moving towards the city wall. We haven't confirmed it yet, but we believe they are from the enemy camp." When the words hit William's ears, he felt numb. This was indeed what he was hoping for.

Charlie continued, "We took to the shadows immediately and watched as these three made their way into the city, using the sewer grate we left open. Once they entered, I sent word to Prince Logan about the breach and had our men tail them.

"When the Prince found me, we had been watching them for nearly an hour. That's when he told us he wanted them caught and detained silently. He said you had some idea for such an opportunity and that these men were important to your plans,." she explained.

"You're right Commander; their successful entrance into the city is just what we needed," William replied. "Logan is this site secure?"

"Yes Father, it's designed for this kind of thing," Logan replied.

"Good. I want to talk to one of them," William said, as one of the men was brought forward and his gag was removed.

"I ain't sayin' nothin'," the enemy soldier blurted.

"That's fine with me," William replied. "You see gentlemen, because I have an image to maintain, I cannot take part in the unpleasantness that is about to befall you. The free citizens of Andraya are sensitive to coercion being used on prisoners. I have no stomach for it myself, but we employ several people who are skilled in finding out what it is we want to know. In fact, this very room was created just for that purpose alone."

"I don't believe nothin' comin' out of your mouth!" replied the man in front of William. "King Marcus has told all of us how you and your people are cowards. You don't have the guts to hurt us in cold blood." The sneer on the man's face was almost enough to make Declan smash him in the face, but William's cool smile froze the general in his place.

"You're right, as is your king. Oh, not about Andrayans not having the guts to do what it takes to remain free. No, we are quite capable of marching into your kingdom, burning it to the ground, and salting the remains to rid ourselves of a threat. You see, we have suffered under the Lianthus family before, and we will not do so willingly again.

"But he is correct in saying that I don't enjoy the kind of things that are going to be done to you to get information. That is why, as Royalty, I don't do anything I don't want to. I delegate those duties to someone else. My general here alone would enjoy gutting you and playing string games with your entrails. Unfortunately, his attention is needed at the gate to deal with your fool king and his soldiers outside. No, instead, you will be left with others to make you talk. You will not eat, or sleep until you tell us what it is you have been sent here to do. You will not know night from day, and you will never know if each other are dead or alive, as you will be separated and dealt with individually.

"You see, if Marcus continues this siege much longer you will starve to death. And let's say that he has the remotest of chances to take the city walls. You three are going to be hidden so deeply, within the city itself, that you will never be found in time. You, like your king, will rue the day you ever set foot in our kingdom. I will personally see to it. The only way to ease your difficulties is to help us get through this as quickly as possible. Now, if you will excuse me, I have a war to win!" William said, and signaled to be let out of the room.

Logan quickly opened the door and William left followed by Brody, Declan, Logan, and Charlie.

"What are your orders, Father?" Logan asked.

"First thing, I want that sewer grate closed and secured. We no longer need to supply the enemy an access point into the city. As for the prisoners, I don't want them fed for the next two days. A cup of water after three. I also want no more sleep than a half hour at a time, and I want them startled awake when their sleep is broken. Also, don't do any physical damage to them. Threaten them into talking, have men scream where the prisoners can hear them. Let them think that their cohorts are being tortured and that they are next. Hopefully they will give us what we need quickly. I will do what is needed to protect our people, but we will not become animals and carve them up for any reason. Andraya stands for freedom, dignity and honor. We will not stain that noble cause for any self-justified reason," the king explained.

"What about non-invasive techniques?" Declan asked.

"Certainly. So long as they won't be damaged, or maimed. But let's give their imaginations a chance to save us that effort. The one that spoke is apparently of low intelligence, so it shouldn't take much. Marcus isn't going to make a lot of headway in the next couple of days, anyway. Let's just use the little time we have before we do anything drastic," William replied.

Logan nodded his understanding and began barking orders as the kingdom's leaders walked away.

"Do you think this will work?" Brody asked.

"I don't know. Either way we can guess that they were either here to deliver information to the enemy, to sabotage our defenses, or both. When the time is right, we will give Marcus signs that his men have been successful and try to use that against him," William said, as the three walked back towards the city gate.

Chapter 8

In the Age of King Corland the Fourth

The mumbling outside of the well stopped and the boys wondered what had happened. Their questions were answered when a loud voice bellowed above them. "What have you decided villagers? Either you hand over the entire crop as an act of contrition, or I put you all in chains and take it," the voice yelled.

The mumbling started again, but only briefly, as Uracles' voice was heard replying, "King Corland, you have taken more and more each year from us, and offered nothing in return. Your men killed my father, and still we came to you with an olive branch trying to work this out. You had one of our people beaten to a bloody pulp, and still we sat down to entreat you to wisdom. It is obvious that you have no wisdom left, but only greed. We will not give over freely; we will fight for what is ours." He yelled to the cheers of the townspeople.

"Then so be it, you fools. Soldiers forward!" replied what the boys guessed must have been the king's voice. From this point, the boys had no clue what had happened. The sound of marching feet on the packed earth was heard, yelling started, and a clash of weapons followed. Then women started screaming, men crying out in pain and all the while the terror rose in the boys bit by bit.

"William, what are we going to do?" Brody asked.

“What we were told to do. We are going to protect the young, and if things get bad, we are taking them out of the kingdom to protection,” William replied.

“But Will, they aren’t doing well,” Declan said.

“No, and a couple of ten year olds aren’t going to make a difference either,” William said. “Dec, you are the strongest guy I know, besides the adults. You could probably help a little, but not enough to change what’s going on. Do you hear the stomping out there, the cries? There are a lot of soldiers and our families are going to be badly hurt. Let’s just hope that all they have to deal with is being hurt,” William said.

Although they hated to say it, both Brody and Declan knew that Will was right. The three sat on the floor of the cavern and listened to the battle above. The cries for help and agony rang for the rest of the day, until night fell and the village noises were reduced to rough talk and whimpers.

"I can’t do this anymore!” Declan said, panic in his voice.

“Dec, if we go up there we can get caught!” William said, trying to calm his cousin down.

“I don’t care, Will. I have to see what’s happened to my parents. I can’t sit here not knowing,” Declan said again, heading back to the opening.

“Okay fine, but we’re coming with you,” William said. “Let’s go check on the others and let them know what’s going on before we go, though. Their parents are up there, too.”

Declan agreed, and all three went back to the children. They made sure everyone was alright and moved out of the cavern to see what had happened.

They climbed out of the hole and slowly worked their way to the village edge. Without making a sound, the three of them moved behind a hut and looked towards the only source of light in the village they could see. Cautiously, they looked towards the light and saw a large bon fire burning in the town square. Unfortunately, though, they couldn't see any of their fellow villagers anywhere near them. Instead, all they saw were soldiers in heavy armor, with long swords at their sides pacing around, laughing and talking near the fire. The three boys searched to see if they could find anyone that they knew. They became concerned that the lack of familiar faces was due to their entire village being killed in the battle. They scanned the area, and finally Brody excitedly grabbed William's arm. Using their sign language he explained to Will and Declan to look across the square, away from the fire. Declan and William searched where Brody pointed and described and saw a large mass of huddled people on the ground.

Carefully, they worked their way around the village in the darkness until they got closer to their defeated families. When they got close, they searched all the dirty faces, struggling to see their parents. William saw his father, who was once again bloody. Brody found his mother tending to his father's wounds, but Declan couldn't find either of his parents.

They moved away from the village until they felt safe enough to whisper.

"I couldn't see my mother or father," Declan said.

"Neither did I," William replied, "but I'm sure they're okay. Your father is a giant; he wouldn't be hurt I'm sure." He tried to assure his friend.

"I need to know if they're okay or not. I'm going back to find him," Declan said.

"Dec, it's too dangerous, you'll get caught," Brody said, visibly shivering with fear.

"I don't care. I need to know if they're okay or not," the young boy said, and moved back towards the village. Brody and William went with him, staying in the shadows as long as they could.

Suddenly, there was a crash in the bushes around them. Just barely stifling cries of surprise, the boys dropped to their stomachs and blended into the grass as best they could.

"That wasn't much of a workout," a gruff voice said.

"Yeah, but at least we saw some action. Anyway, we've been going through some of the huts, and we found some interesting stuff the Commander said we could keep," another voice replied.

"Sure, that's great and all but I wanted action. Besides that big guy, no one was really a challenge and one well-placed arrow was all it took for him." The three boys on the ground flashed looks at one another. The only really big person in the village was Declan's father, the town blacksmith. This didn't sound good.

"So what's the plan for the survivors?" a third voice asked.

"King said to put them in the huts as cells for now. He will decide what to do with them when he returns from the tribute tour," one of the men replied.

"So he goes out and has fun and all we get is guard duty?" the third voice whined.

"Quiet down!" warned one of the men in a rough whisper. "Do you want the king to hear you and turn his attention your way? Besides, there are a couple of good looking women in that bunch; we might be able to find some fun here too," one of the voices laughed. He was joined with laughter from the others as their voices faded into the darkness.

When the boys were sure they were alone again, they hid under a bush and fought back tears. "Did you hear what they said about 'the big guy'?" Declan asked. "They killed my father," he said whimpering.

"Now hold on Dec, they didn't say that. Sure they said he was hit with an arrow but that doesn't mean they killed him," Brody said.

"What else could it mean?" Declan said, tears running down his face.

"Look Dec, you and Brody stay here. I'm going to get into the village and talk to someone. I'll try to find out what happened to your father. But you guys have to promise to stay here. It will be easier for one of us and you are too upset to do it without getting caught," William said.

The others were afraid, but both agreed, that again, what he said made sense. And so it was, that William moved slowly towards the village edge, hoping to be able to speak to someone who could tell him something.

Avoiding the sound of soldiers' voices, Will crept forward, sliding through the deep grass. Moving silently, he edged himself as close as he could to where the villagers were being guarded.

Hut by hut he moved towards the knot of townspeople. Stopping at each hut that he went by, he poked his head in the window to see if anyone was inside. But none of the homes of his fellow villagers were occupied. Finally, he came across a dark figure lying on the floor of one of the huts near the bonfire.

Quietly he slid in through the window to check on the large shape, hoping that it was Declan's father and that he was indeed okay. But when he got close enough he noticed the armor on his chest and the huge wound across his temple. The man's chest wasn't rising or falling, so Will guessed he was a dead soldier. This brought a small feeling of pride in his people to the young half elf. He slipped back out of the hut as quietly as he could.

Once back in the shadows, he finally worked his way to where he could see everyone bunched before the bonfire, holding each other for comfort. He scanned the faces until he caught the attention of one of the adults. The man, whose daughter was a couple of years younger than Will, recognized him immediately. He raised a hand slightly signaling William to stay where he was.

As William watched the man, suddenly there was a crash, and a soldier stumbled in front of him. William quickly rolled against one of the huts and buried his face in the dirt to hide. A bunch of soldiers laughed as the drunken man fell against the wall opposite Will.

"Ah, you fools would fall too if you had as many stitches in the back of your head as I do. That broad hit me with that hammer hard!" he shouted, laughing in his drunken stupor. Stumbling back to his feet, he began weaving back into the village, drinking as he went.

William's eye followed the soldier as he moved on. Remaining in the shadows as best he could, he made eye contact with the villager who anxiously waited to see what happened to the boy. When he saw Will, the man signaled the youth with his hands. He seemed to be saying return to the children. Will thought it over then attempted to signal his question back. Acting as if he was a blacksmith, he beat on a pretend anvil with an invisible hammer. He looked at the man, who seemed confused. This time Will pretended he had really broad shoulders, and pointing at his elf shaped ears, began to again hammer the invisible anvil.

Suddenly, understanding crossed the man's face, followed by a look of sadness. He shook his head and lowered it in respect. So it was true, Declan's father was dead. Stifling a whimper, William held his hand over his heart and bowed slightly. He then traced the outline of a woman's curves and pain shot through him as the man responded the same way as he had for Declan's father. Both his Uncle and Aunt were dead and now he had to tell his cousin.

Again showing a sign of respect to the man, he slowly merged with the shadows, melting into the darkness. He didn't know how he was going to do it, but he knew he was going to have to tell the devastating news to Declan. One of his best friends was now an orphan.

Chapter 9

In the Age of King William the First

By lunch the next day, William was ready to call Parlay on his own, but he knew that was what Marcus wanted. By forcing the townspeople to acknowledge the enemy army, they would be saying they were scared. William knew that Declan wouldn't allow Marcus the satisfaction. In fact, William knew that if he did anything that gave the enemy an ounce of pride, his best friend would go berserk.

'*No*,' William told himself, '*I will just have to bide my time.*' With that, he moved out of the Royal Quarters and made his way to the war room. On his way, he stopped by everyone he saw and gave them a kind word of encouragement or did his best to stem the fear he knew had taken root in his people.

The funny thing was that the longer Marcus waited, attempting to increase the level of fear in the people, the less frightened they became. In fact, the citizens had all been able to make themselves at home in the underground fortress amazingly quickly. Everyone seemed to be their old selves. Merchants sold their wares. Children darted to and fro playing in the open areas. Men met and talked about the coming war, and the women met and talked about the goings on in the community.

Thinking about everyone acclimating to their temporary homes brought the king's memory to his own family. Last night, after he came home from his meeting with the enemy spies, he was welcomed by his wife and two younger children. Ash was reading in the corner, while Czaria was playing in the bedroom with her mother. William walked into the room to see his daughter flopping herself down on the cushions and giggling, only to get up and do it again.

Emma smiled when she saw William, then turning back to the baby she said, '*Czaria, you're crazy.*'

To which Czaria replied, '*I not cazy, I funny.*' she said flopping herself onto the bed again. This brought a full belly laugh from William, who then spent the rest of the night laughing with his family.

William walked into the war room and found that the ministers were already there having a quiet meeting. They all rose as he entered, but he motioned for them to remain seated.

"Is there a problem?" he asked

"Not yet, Majesty," replied Minister Dominic, "but the possibility exists for one."

"What's wrong?" William asked, sitting down at the table.

"We have been hearing dissenting voices at the Moles Head," the Minister of Commerce replied. The Moles Head was the name the community gave the make shift pub in the underground cavern. The person running the pub was the owner of the Lion's Mane, one of the fancier taverns in the city. He decided that a place where people could relax would make things seem a little more normal, and so far it seemed to be working. Several other taverns had opened around the under city as well. Knowing people spoke openly while drinking, William had the ministers pay extra attention to these establishments. Not only that, but it was a great way to measure the outlook of the people.

"What have you been hearing?" the king asked the ministers.

"Well twice now we have had the constables break up potential fights, and each one was caused by the same topic. The dissenters are saying that you should just attack the enemy army and get the fight over with," Minister Eva reported.

"I see. Are the people who are involved different each time or do we have a couple of bad apples?" William asked.

"Well there were different people but they seem to chum around with one another," Dominic replied.

"Alright, well this is what I want you to do. Hold town meetings throughout the under city as quickly as you can. I probably won't be there as I'm keeping a close eye on the enemy's movements. Ask the people to voice their concerns openly and take a vote. If the people agree that we should attack, then I will take it under advisement and will attack within two days. If they vote to wait and allow us to follow our current strategy, then we will do so," William said.

"Your Highness, that seems to me to be both disrespectful to the chain of command and a waste of time," Minister Reese piped up.

"Oh, and what do you mean, Minister?" William asked.

"Well you are the commander of this kingdom. You, the prime minister and the general have never led us astray. We shouldn't allow a couple of troublemakers to bring your judgment into question," she said.

"Thank you Minister; your confidence honors me. But why would it be a waste of time?" William asked.

“Simple, everyone in the city agrees with me. You are leading us well and haven’t given any of us any reason to question you. The vote will be in favor of following you nearly unanimously,” she explained.

“That is also good to hear, Minister, since you all have your finger on the pulse of our community better than I. But that is as good a reason to hold an open vote now as any. It will allow the people to have their voices heard, and odds are, things will go our way. But if the people call for us to attack, I’m not worried. I have a feeling Marcus will call the Parlay soon. Remember, he is young, strong headed, and arrogant. He isn’t going to wait us out. So if we have to commit our troops to war based on the vote, then the odds are, it will still be on our planned time table,” William said, as he smiled at the council.

Everyone in the room chuckled and agreed that the king was probably right. They just needed to keep the people engaged and things would go smoother for the community at large.

“Majesty?” Minister Tobias said, his booming voice carrying across the room.

“Yes, Master Blacksmith, what’s on your mind?” William replied.

“Well majesty, I have to admit your understanding of the nature of our people is very good. But, I have to ask, how many times have you held council votes because you knew it would belay our fears or increase morale?” the large man asked.

“About the same number of times I called for a vote that I was sure I would win,” the king said, grinning at the man across the table from him.

“I’ll remember that the next time we vote,” the blacksmith said with a loud chuckle, causing everyone to start laughing with him.

“All right everyone, if you don’t mind I would like to head top side to see what’s going on,” William said, walking to the door. Everyone in the room bowed low to him, and as he left, he heard the discussion on the town meeting plans begin behind him.

William then made his way up the stairs only to be met by his second son.

“Father,” the young man said, “Logan has been asking for you. He said he has some information.”

“Where is he?” William asked.

“He is at the western catapult, checking on Shade and the Archers,” Ashton explained.

“Thank you, Son; as you were,” the king said, as he continued up to the city walls. He walked the long wall towards the western end of the city. There he found Logan discussing drills with Shade, who seemed to be following everything Logan said with the greatest attention.

William couldn’t help but feel proud, both of the loyalty his son had earned from his men, but also with the pride he could see on Shade’s face. Shade was Brody’s only son in a family of four children. Like his father, he was soft spoken and didn’t have a lot of confidence, but when given a task, he kept to it with open minded determination.

When the two young men saw the king approach, they saluted and waited for him to join them. “Relax gentlemen. Shade, you look well,” the king smiled at the young man.

“Thank you, sir, and you look as calm as usual,” Shade grinned at the king.

“Well I’m glad I look like it, because goodness knows all I have is the look of calm. Did I interrupt something important?” William asked.

“Not at all father; Shade was just explaining some ideas for drills he had and I was just saying how good they sounded. The Archer Commander has been very busy improving my abandoned post,” Logan laughed.

“Oh I wouldn’t say improving, sir, just putting my personal stamp on it, so to speak,” Shade grinned.

“That’s great, Captain. Well if you have a moment to spare, gentlemen, Ashton told me you had something to report?” William said to Logan.

“Just give us a second, okay Shade?” Logan asked his friend who nodded his approval and went to check the arrow supplies on the wall.

“How’s he doing?” William asked.

“Do you really need to ask?” Logan replied. “He’s made for this kind of thing; he just needs to be more forceful. He’s allowed a couple of ambitious soldiers too much leeway, and now he is going to have to come down hard on them to bring things back in line. He can do it, and once he does things should be back to normal again. He just needs to do it quickly,” Logan replied.

“Good. Brody is really proud. I’m glad you took my advice and gave him the promotion,” William said. “But now, you have word from our guests?”

“Yes, one finally broke just before we were planning to feed them. He said they were sent to find a way to sabotage our defenses any way possible. Then they were instructed to find a way to get more men into the city to help open the gates.

"He was so happy to see a hot plate in front of him and to hear the screams stop that he openly discussed what he knew. He said that when they were ready, they were to signal the enemy by swinging a torch within sight of the main force outside," Logan explained.

"Did you have them separated during the questioning?" William asked.

"Yes, they have been in separate rooms since you last saw them. We had a couple of guys screaming like they were being tortured, as you commanded," the young man laughed, causing his father to chuckle with him.

"Good work, Logan. Keep them separated. Now that they have eaten, they know one of them spoke. I don't want them together to cause trouble. Place them in cells within a couple of minutes from one another as a precaution to ensure they can't communicate," William commanded.

"Now that we know what Marcus wanted to be done, I want you to talk to the master gunner about sabotaging one of his Ballistae. That way, when he goes to fire the weapon, the missile will just fall to the ground outside the gates," William continued. "Tell him to only slightly damage it, just in case we need to repair it quickly. I'll think of some way to let the enemy forces into the city."

"Do you think that's a good idea, Father?" Logan asked.

"I trust Dec's Kings Way design. Now go and finish your discussion with Shade. I'll talk to you later," William said, and turning, he headed out to find his advisers.

'So, we have been given our chance to end this quickly,' William thought to himself. '*Thank God for that.*' He sighed. Knowing that the Kings Way might be the only chance of ending the battle with the fewest casualties concerned him. He was sure Marcus wouldn't be reasonable no matter what he told his ministers. War was coming, and it appeared the only way to end it swiftly, might be to allow the enemy into his beloved city.

Chapter 10

In the Age of King Corland the Fourth

After William told Declan about his parents' death, the young man walked off into the darkness, leaving Brody and Will alone. They decided the leave him be, since he would need some time.

William and Brody returned to the cavern and told everyone what they had found. Talking about it openly seemed to be more than he could take, and finally after the roller coaster evening they had all experienced, Will began to cry. William's little sister, Chloe, came to him and they hugged, as everyone in the cave began to whimper around them.

After some time, they finally composed themselves as best they could and the questions started. "What do we do now?", "Where do we go?", and "What will we eat?" William calmed everyone down and took control as best he could.

"There is enough food here with us to last a couple of days," he said, "but we will have to be careful, so everyone only eat a little of what we have. We may need more time than we expect to get somewhere safe. Second, we have no home here; we will have to go on to safety somewhere else. Our parents knew this to be a possibility, and so we have to carry on. Six or seven days from here, through the mountains, is Parinth, an Elvin village outside of Andraya. We will be safe there from King Corland and his men. I think it would be best if we leave right away, though. We can use the darkness to our advantage," William said.

"Who made you the leader?" asked a boy named Jacob. "I'm the oldest here, I should lead."

"Well what's your plan, and then we can choose," Brody said.

"What do you mean choose? I am the oldest and so everyone should follow me," the young man replied.

"I see. So you would replace King Corland, then, as the leader without reason?" A voice came from the darkness. The cavern went quiet as Declan slowly emerged from the shadows. You couldn't see his eyes in the darkness, but everyone was sure he had been crying.

"I'm nothing like King Corland," Jacob replied.

"Really? You refuse to tell us why we should do as you say, except that you're stronger and older than us. So, *King Jacob,* tell us what you will have us do," Declan continued.

"I am not the king. I just think as the oldest you should all listen to me," Jacob said, getting visibly angry.

"I tell you what then, Jake. We can do this one of three ways. One, you lead and those who follow can do as you say, those who don't can choose their leader and follow them. Two, you can stay here by yourself and everyone leaves with an agreed upon leader. Three, you and I fight, and when I beat you into the floor, you will follow who ever I tell you to. Take your pick," Declan said, stepping closer ominously.

William quickly stood between the two. "Dec, you're hurt and angry. I know you think this is right, but think about it. We need to work together, not against one another. We're a bunch of kids, and if we are going to survive, we need to do something."

Declan turned to his oldest friend. "I vote William as the leader. If he says we go to Parinth, then I'm going. If he says that I'm not to fight you, then I won't. That is," Declan said dangerously, "unless you want to press the issue, *Jake*."

"I vote for William, too," Brody said, trying to help calm the situation down. Following his lead, the other children began to voice their votes as well. When the vote was taken, everyone except for Jacob's two brothers voted for William.

"Then it's done. William we've chosen you, what is it you want us to do?" a young girl named Emma said.

William blushed, but in the darkness no one noticed. "Well, I still think Parinth is our best bet. We need to move out now, before light, to avoid being seen by the soldiers. Let's go to the entrance and get going to where we can rest without being caught in the morning," he said, trying not to sound bossy. He didn't want to be accused of being King William.

The children started to follow William, Declan, and Brody to the opening. No one looked back to see if Jacob or his brothers were coming, but whatever their decision, Will wasn't going to force them. Once they were at the opening, Brody and Declan climbed out and stood watch. Then one by one the children followed them. Those who needed help were pulled up and out and those too small to climb were once again placed in the baskets used to lower them.

Finally, when only a few people were left, Jacob and his brothers came to the rope. "I still think I should lead," Jacob said.

"Look Jake, I'm not going to fight with you right now. If we get everyone to safety, you want to have it out, fine. We can fight and then leave it at that. Otherwise, if you can't contribute, we don't need you making things harder." William sighed, "Do you really think I want to be the one who has to get us all to Parinth?"

"Fine, we'll deal with this later," Jacob said, "and trust me; the two of us will deal with this." He then pushed his way to the front of the line and climbed up the rope, followed by his brothers.

"You're doing a good job, Will," Emma said, coming up next to him. "Don't let that bully scare you. We need to get to safety. But Will," she said hesitantly.

"Yes Emma, what is it." William replied.

"What about our parents?" she asked, and he just now noticed how close to tears she was.

"I don't know yet Em, but our village will be freed. Corland will pay for Declan's parents' death, and the pain he caused all of us. I'll see to it, one way or another." The anger in his voice caught them both by surprise, but it seemed to calm Emma's emotions some.

Without saying anything else, she took her place on the rope and climbed out of the cavern. Will was now the last person in the hole. He looked around and made sure that no one was left behind and then climbed out into the night air. Silently, he promised himself this would not be the last time he visited this place.

Chapter 11

In the Age of King William the First

William was in the council room discussing routine management of the citizens' needs with the council in the morning. The town meeting had been a success. Several people were unhappy with being "caged underground", in their words, but most people said they trusted William's choices. That was good for now, but he knew if this dragged on too much longer that more and more people would turn against him. He was already questioning if he had done the right thing by not meeting Marcus' people on the battlefield, before so many people lost their homes.

Unfortunately, now wasn't the time to reassess his decisions. He turned his attention back to ration reports and education plans, when Ashton burst through the door.

"What is the meaning of this interruption, Son?" William barked, rising from his seat.

"I apologize, father, but I must speak to you. It's about Gida," the young man said. The look on William's face shifted instantly.

"Everyone, I must leave. Please continue the meeting without me. Minister Brody, General Declan, please come with me," he said to his best friends. All of them left the room quickly, following Ashton.

"What's all this talk about Gida?" Declan said, as they climbed the stairs to the top of the city wall.

"That is a code I instructed the runners to use. When Czaria was first learning to speak, we were talking about her grandparents, but she couldn't say Grandma. Instead, she started to call her Gida. So Emma's mother adopted the name as her title, and we have used it ever since." William explained.

"Okay so what does your mother-in-law have to do with us?" Brody asked.

"Well, nothing. But there was a Gida on my side of the family as well, my mother. Her name was Czaria," William replied.

"So the code word Gida means something that is affecting Czaria, i.e. Czariana, is occurring?" Declan said.

"That's right," William grinned.

"So why not just use your daughter?" Brody asked.

"Few people remember my mother. She died when I was a child, remember? Czaria, my daughter, was just a little too easy to figure out, and I don't want anyone to panic," William explained, as they reached the door at the top of the wall.

"Panic about what?" Declan nearly shouted in frustration.

"About that," William grinned, pointing out over the wall. There, in an opening amongst the tents below, a pavilion was set up, and above it flew the red trimmed, white flag of Parlay.

"I'll be a son of a..." started Declan. "So the little bugger finally decided he's waited long enough, huh? Three days of waiting. Not bad, I'll give him a little credit. Its two days longer than I thought he would last."

"Alright, so when did they raise the flag?" Brody asked Ashton.

“Ten minutes ago, by the look of the hour glass. We started it when we saw the flag go up,” Ashton said, pointing to an hourglass on a wooden crate.

“Ten minutes, so fifty more until the meeting. Okay men, we’ve discussed this into the ground, but let’s go over it one more time,” William said.

“Simple enough, they are to turn back and pay for the damage they have done,” Declan said.

“That, and they must never approach the kingdom in aggression ever again,” Brody said.

William nodded his agreement. Ashton looked at them in amazement. “You’re all kidding right? Father? Uncles? Do you really think he is going to have come all this way just to turn back because you tell him too?”

The three men laughed. “Ashton, we could offer him every gold piece, every inch of land, and it wouldn’t stop him from attempting to destroy this city and everyone in it,” Brody replied.

The color drained from Ashton’s face. “But why?” he whispered.

All three men stopped laughing and became serious, understanding the young man’s fear. “Ashy,” William said, putting his arm around his sons shoulders, “Marcus hasn’t come here for a simple transgression that needs to be resolved. He has come because of a Vendetta he has called against your Uncles, me, and anyone who follows me.”

“The Vendetta? You mean because of how you became king, taking Andraya from his father?” Ashton said, a look of understanding crossing his face.

"Yes, Son, and he has a personal debt to settle with your Aunt Chloe. Unfortunately for Marcus, he doesn't know that your Aunt is sitting out there, in the forest somewhere, waiting for the role of her Rangers in this battle," Declan replied.

"So what would you have me do?" Ashton said, turning very serious and standing at attention.

"That's my boy," William smiled. "Go down below and quietly explain to the council what is happening. Have them call another batch of town meetings tonight. Also, send word to the Runners that they aren't to report this below until I say so."

"Alright, Father, good luck," Ashton said, as he turned and headed down the steps.

Sighing, William turned to his best friends. "Brody, call together the command staff. I want word quickly sent through the ranks that this is to remain quiet until we announce it tonight. Also, have the gunnery sergeants prepare their men. I want round the clock shifts taken on all the long guns, and a quarter of the troops are to be on shift at all times. Everyone is at ready, gentlemen, as of now. When the call goes out, I want our people at their posts where they belong," William said, giving his orders.

Brody saluted and quickly left to have the banner communicators call his command staff together. The flag for all quiet was already flying high from the turret located at the center of the city gates.

"Well, Will, it's almost time," Declan said with a large calming sigh.

"Will? Dec, you haven't called me Will since before I was proclaimed king," William smiled.

"Yeah, well, I don't figure you need reminding of who you are at this moment," Declan replied.

"No, that I certainly do not," William said, as both men walked down the steps towards Czariana's main gate, their enemy waiting on the other side.

Chapter 12

In the Age of King Corland the Fourth

William stared at himself in a rain barrel. After six years, his appearance had changed, a lot. His foster parents told him how much of a man he had become, but he didn't see a man. Once again, he saw a kid trying to be a man. Sure his ears were a little longer, and his shoulders were broader, but he still didn't see anyone special. Ever since the escape from their village, William couldn't help seeing himself that way. All of the children from his village still came to him for support, advice, and leadership. The problem was that by doing so, they just made him feel more of an outsider in their new home.

The Elvin people of Parinth had been very good to William and the other children. Everyone was given a home and was protected by someone, even though most of the children were human and the villagers of Parinth were all elves. Well, almost everyone went to a home. Declan, although politely, refused to stay with anyone. He lived in the hay loft above the Smithy and worked hard for the blacksmith. Everyone in the village understood why; the ringing of the steel reminded him of his father and so no one pushed him.

The villagers were so outraged by what happened, they sent word to their own ruler, King Tianvor, about it. The Elvin king promptly came out to the village to get the whole story. William was awed by the Elvin ruler. King Tianvor was kind, generous and only took what the people felt he deserved, and everyone felt he deserved as much as they could offer. His style was an inspiration, and William would spend hours listening to stories of how he ran his court.

In an effort to help with hunting and protection of the village, every boy and girl from William's village learned to shoot with a bow. Needless to say, having the long lived elves as teachers went far, and soon each child could wield a bow with great prowess. Many children, including William, Chloe, and Brody also learned Elfish, how to play musical instruments, as well as reading and writing. Declan, on the other hand, studied every weapon he could. Fortunately for him, the blacksmith was a weapons master, and had many visitors that were happy to pay for weapons with lessons to the youth. Even though the blacksmith wouldn't dare insult Declan by assuming the role as parent, they had an unspoken bond as such. Declan treated him with respect and worked hard for him, and Beorn did everything he could to make the young man smile. Unfortunately, it was a difficult task, but that didn't stop the Elvin smith from trying.

Life was good in Parinth, but William never forgot the promise to free their village. Once last year, he, Declan, and Brody went back to their old village to see what had become of it. They were horrified to see their friends and families chained and imprisoned, working daily in the olive fields for Corland.

This treatment enraged them, especially when they saw the women being manhandled by the guards. Brody's normal calm quite nature almost shattered into feral anger when he saw his mother being groped.

Year after year, the children grew and became stronger. The youngest, the ones who were too young to even know their parents, didn't have much to do with the older refugees. Their new families were their families for as long as they could remember, and everyone agreed this was for the best.

But still, even with all the progress, William always felt his role as leader of the refugees kept him from totally being welcomed into the village. He explained this once to his foster parents, and they laughed, saying everyone in the village enjoyed having him as part of the community. He said he knew they treated him that way, but he felt he disrespected the elders with his position. His foster father just smiled and told him that it was because he held the mantle of leadership with such integrity that the elders approved.

"William, what are you doing?" He heard Brody's voice as the young man came running up. "We finally get a day off, and you're sticking your head in a bucket. What is with you and buckets?" Brody laughed. The joke caused William to laugh as well.

When he was a boy, William used to run around his families hut with a water bucket on his head. On more than one occasion, he would bump into the wall, fall on his behind, and would start crying. This kept happening until one day his father came to him and said, '*William if you're going to wear that on your head, let me cut holes in it so you can see.*' To which started William wailing in reply, '*But if you cut holes in it, it won't be a bucket anymore.*' His father had no choice but to accept such basic logic. That would indeed be the case, and so he left his son to run into walls with a bucket on his head.

Thinking of his father caused a painful shot to run though Will's heart, and he quickly turned his attention to his friend.

Grabbing his bow and a full quiver of arrows, Will joined Brody as they set out to find Declan. For the next three days, the boys and Chloe were given permission to go hunting in the woods together. They couldn't wait to set out, as camping was one of their favorite pastimes. Each boy knew the mountain side, like they knew their long missed underground cavern.

As Brody and Will hunted through the village, they came across Jacob and his brothers cleaning the stables. Years earlier, Declan and Jacob finally got into the brawl Jacob had threatened Will with in the cave. The two boys got into a violent fist fight, with Jacobs ever present brothers cheering him on. Chloe, who was with Declan at the time, quickly ran to find help when Jacob threw the first punch.

The two boys rolled in the dirt pummeling each other, when suddenly, Declan got the better of his opponent. Rolling on top of him, he was going to call an end to it when Jacob's brothers jumped in. The three of them ganged up on Declan, beating him without mercy.

Finally, Chloe returned with Brody and William hot on her heals, but it was too late. Jacob and his brothers had run away, leaving a bloodied Declan in the mud. Declan was taken by adults for medical attention, but things looked grim. It was by sheer determination and all the talents of the village healers that he survived, so brutal was the attack.

Once Declan was taken to the healers, an Elvin hunting party went in search of the three runaways. Once they were found, they were brought back before a ruling tribunal of the village elders.

"Jacob, Mitchell and Taymor, we the village elders have come to a ruling in what you have been responsible for," spoke the leader of the village, Narooth. "Never, have our people seen such an act of hatred within our village. Your anger and vitriol was clear in the amount of damage you chose to inflict upon young Declan.

"It is the decision of this council that you are to be exiled from Parinth. You will never be welcome here or anywhere within the Elvin kingdom of Layeni." Everyone in the room gasped. The severity of the punishment shocked everyone within earshot.

"Master Narooth," William said stepping forward, "may I speak?"

"Yes, young William, you are recognized as a leader among your people and we will hear you," Narooth replied.

"Master, what these three have done is indeed beyond deplorable. It is disgusting and now my cousin struggles for his very life. But Master, I ask that you and the council reconsider.

"They need to be punished, and my rage at what they have done wants to erupt in vengeance. But we know that anger is not the answer," William said, looking at the three ruling members in turn. "You've all taught us that punishment must fit the crime, and should we lose Declan," William said choking, "Then I would wish to see these three sent away.

"But as my cousin struggles for his life, I think these three should struggle as well. Not only to survive, as an exile would force them, but for their own souls. I ask that you not send them away, but instead find a way for them to earn their place back amongst us. If Declan can heal physically, then I would hope they could heal spiritually."

The three eleven leaders looked at each other and nodded their agreement.

"Young William, you speak as a true leader of men. We agree with you, and I have determined another sentence," Narooth said with a bow to the young half elf.

"Jacob, thank the words and council of young William, for it has saved you and your brothers. Instead of banishment, I order that you live on the outskirts of town. You shall be responsible for toiling each day to earn your continued stay amongst us. The three of you shall earn your redemption by hard work. Melchist," he said to the village's law man, "see to it that their punishment is carried out."

The tall elf nodded to the tribunal, and leading the boys out, set the punishment in motion.

Months passed as Declan fought his way back to health. When he was strong enough, he demanded that he be allowed to go back to work with Beorn at the smithy. Working day and night till exhaustion, he healed himself with determination and the ever present eye of the Master Smith himself. That is, except for his voice. Instead of his normal, melodic Elvin voice, he spoke with a gruff, almost growl like one. It was the only remaining sign that the fight even took place.

Jacob never spoke to any of them after that. His shame was so great that he couldn't even look at them. This, coupled with the loneliness of their existence, was enough for Declan to let his hatred of the three go.

Finally, William and Brody found Declan and Chloe. The four walked into the forest talking excitedly as they went. Chloe was three years younger than William and normally they didn't do much together, but the older they got the more the two of them seemed to grow closer. But it wasn't just their relationship that was the reason for Chloe joining the trio, but rather her love of the forest. Most of her time was spent learning about it from the Elvin elders who treated nature as if it was a member of the family.

Chloe always had a problem with towns and villages. The smaller the location, the better, as far as she was concerned. In fact, the place she considered paradise was a small clearing in the woods where she could sit for hours and listen to the wind in the trees. One night, she even confided in William that the cavern where they all had hidden when they were children made her feel like she was in a box. She said all that stone was too much for her to handle and she was glad to get out when they did.

After marching for hours, they found a spot to setup camp. They staked out their lean-to's and set a fire. They then spent the evening quietly talking about their hopes and what they wanted to accomplish with their lives. For Chloe, it was the dream of becoming a Druid, an Elvin wizard of the forest. The elves had different forms of wizards, from Druids to High Elf Clerics, each specializing in a lifetime of study.

For Brody, it was design and engineering. He loved to see a problem and picture the solution. Nothing was more exciting than taking that picture from his mind's eye and making it take form before him.

William, on the other hand, had no dreams of what he wanted to become. Farming, he guessed, but even at that he wasn't sure. All he knew was he wanted to make things grow, where there was nothing before.

Declan wanted to be a soldier. He wanted conquest and victory. But above all, he wanted to protect his loved ones.

After talking for a few hours, Chloe said she was tired and headed off to her lean-to. The others bid her good night and stayed to talk.

"Will?" Declan said, turning to his friend.

"What Dec?" he replied.

"Are we ever going home?" the young man asked.

"Sure, in a couple of days; you ready to go already?" William asked.

"No, not Parinth, but home. Our Village," Declan said.

"Oh, there. Yeah, some day, but I don't know what we are going to do when we get there," William said.

"You mean now that it is a slave camp," Declan said.

"Yeah, I don't know how we are going to free them all, and take it back from Corland," William replied.

"Well I've been thinking, and maybe we could ask King Tianvor for help," Declan said.

"I've thought of that too, but do you know what that might cause? It's one thing for countrymen to fight against a king, that's called a rebellion. But for two kings to fight against each other gets innocent people killed," William said.

"Sure, but innocent people get killed all the time. Look at what happened to..." Declan started but he couldn't finish his sentence.

"I know, Dec," William replied softly, "But I've been thinking about this a lot, and if you listen to the stories the minstrels tell, great wars are fought between kingdoms, but it's always the people who suffer in those stories.

"What would happen if King Tianvor declared war on King Corland? They would go to war, and as King Tianvor moved towards the castle of King Corland, he would have to hurt a lot of people along the way. He would do it to stop them from attacking from the rear, and to make life difficult for Corland after he left.

"Then what happens after they fight? Corland might survive, rebuild his army and then he would attack King Tianvor. All of the people in Layeni would get hurt and so on and so on. Innocent people in both kingdoms would become the victims, just because of what Corland did to our parents. We can't let that happen Dec, we just can't,." William said in a near whisper.

"I never thought of it like that," Brody admitted, who had privately wondered the same things Declan had.

"Yeah, me neither Brode," Declan added.

"I didn't either until the last minstrel came through town and told the tale of the forty year war. I started to think about all the people who died in the different battles of the different towns. It was then that I realized, the only people who are likely to survive a war are the people who lead from the back of the army. Just like I bet King Corland did when he attacked our village," William explained.

All three of them were quiet for a long time thinking over what they had just discussed. The difficulty of what they all wanted weighed heavier on Brody and Declan than it did before. William was just as lost after vocalizing his concerns as he was when he kept them to himself.

Suddenly, some nearby bushes started to move. All three grabbed their knives and jumped to their feet. They listened as a strange grumbling, snorting sort of sound started to come from the moving bush. Terror overtook them as they watched the foliage. All of their training with the Elvin elders told them that it could only be one kind of animal, a wild boar. There was no way they could kill a boar with just their belt knives, and Declan's sword was by his bedroll in his lean-to. The rooting, snorting noises from the bush grew louder and then with an echoing roar, something burst from the greenery. William, Declan, and Brody all yelled and ran in separate directions. Brody climbed up a tree, Declan leapt for his sword, and William tripped and rolled over to see the wild animal bearing down on him.

Only when he took a second look, did he notice that it wasn't a boar bearing down on him at all. It was too tall. Suddenly, the roaring changed to what sounded like laughter. Coming to his senses he jumped to his feet, ran over to the beast and pulled a blanket off its head. Instead of a boar, at his feet he found his sister, laughing and rolling around holding her stomach.

All three of the boys went from fear, to anger, to laughter as their emotions washed over them. Soon, they were all wrestling with the still laughing Chloe. She was now laughing so loud she was snorting like a pig, making all of them laugh even harder.

The next day the four of them decided to go hunting on their own. Each of them took a direction and decided to meet back at camp later in the day. William took his bow, belt knife, and a short sword with him.

He stealthily moved through the woods searching for tracks of some prey, when he came across a muddy spot with a fresh rabbit track. He smiled as he moved silently in the direction of the track, keeping his eyes open for more signs.

He felt he must be getting closer as the signs of the rabbit started getting more pronounced. He found some leaves with chewing marks. Soon he saw a broken twig on the ground, and now an indention in some plumy grass. He continued forward, watching for the signs taught to him by his foster parents, when suddenly, he sensed something near him. Only moving his eyes he scanned the forest before him. He was looking for any indication that his prey was near. Scanning back and forth keeping his ears keen to the sounds around him, he saw movement!

The lower branches on a shrub on his left moved a bit. He slowly lifted his bow in front of him, preparing to take the shot. Suddenly, the rabbit burst from the bushes darting past him. Pushing aside the adrenaline rush, William quickly raised his bow and aimed ahead of his prey. Releasing the string, the bow made the anticipated twanging noise as the arrow flew from his fingers and landed on target.

Will went over and claimed his prize. He then tied the rabbit to his belt with his prey snare and headed back to camp.

The others had done as well, he found when he returned. Declan had bagged a grouse, Chloe had two squirrels, and Brody, who preferred fishing, had a small trout. Everyone was drunk with the joy of a good day, and each set about cleaning their game. That night, they dined on wild potatoes, grouse, and Cooney stew, with a helping of squirrel and fish. Well, everyone but Chloe, who pointed out that she hated fish. Then for desert, they were welcomed with a surprise from Brody, who found a large bush of ripe strawberries, and shared them with his friends.

Everyone was full, tired, and content. Once again they lay by the fire talking about life, and laughing about the night before. Chloe was again the first to call it a night and, after a warning from the others about not trying a repeat performance, she went to her lean-to for some sleep.

The others were too tired and relaxed to talk any longer, so they just enjoyed the night sounds, keeping to their thoughts. Suddenly, there was a grunting sound from the bushes. All three of them jumped up and grabbed their bows which were at their sides, since they were too lazy early in the day to put them away.

Declan then called out, "Man, Chloe, once was funny but this is stupid."

Still the noises in the bushes kept getting louder and more violent, "Chloe you're not going to get us this time," Brody said, starting to get a bit scared. "Cut it out," he said more loudly.

"What are you guys yelling about?" Chloe's voice came from behind them, in her lean-to. Fear over took all three boys. If Chloe was behind them, what was in front of them?

Each boy stared at the bushes not able to move, when suddenly, a large boar burst into the clearing. Unlike the night before where all three of them split, they were all frozen in their tracks. The boar stood there eyeing all three, grunting and stomping the ground.

Then out of the fear drenched darkness Brody spoke, "Guys I have eyes on him." He said as he raised his bow, the arrow tip next to Declan's ear.

Taking his lead, Declan then raised his and bumped Williams arm saying, "So do I."

Finally William understood, and raised his bow slowly as the enraged animal began getting louder and more aggressive, "I have him too." William breathed.

"3 – 2 – 1, guys," Brody whispered. The others could only guess what he meant as suddenly the boar flew into motion and charged the three. A twanging sound came as Brody's arrow flew, followed by Declan's, and close behind came Williams. Three thuds pounded into the raging animal as all three arrows made impact. Brody's first to hit caught the beast in the hind quarters which staggered it. Declan's caught it in the neck, landing deep, and Williams arrow landed in the only location he had a clear shot of, its snout. With a crash the animal fell to the ground and slid to a stop at William's feet.

Still thrashing the beast tried to get up, but out of nowhere Chloe jumped in front of her brother and dropped a sword through its heart, stopping the rampage.

All four of them dropped to the ground staring at the boar, panting in their fear. Suddenly, a cheer burst from Brody and scared all of them back to reality. Like last night, they quickly went from fear to anger to laughter as the celebratory shout released all the tension in the clearing. All of them got to their feet and started patting each other on the back, as each of them started doing a victory dance. They talked about their successful kill for hours until the sun began to rise on the horizon.

They then retired and slept as exhaustion overtook them. William awoke to the sun far over head and the sounds of fat frying. He got out of his bed roll to find Brody and Chloe warming left overs. They welcomed him over, and when Declan finally woke he joined them. Excitedly, they all discussed the events of the night before as they ate. "You know, I want to show this thing to the others," Brody said.

"Yeah me too, no one would believe us without it,." Chloe exclaimed.

"Okay, so let's tie its legs and we'll carry it between us on a stick," William suggested. Everyone liked that idea, and so, ending their camping trip early, the four of them began the long hike home.

The trip home seemed to take forever since they were all so excited to show the villagers what they had done. Finally, after a couple of hours they came into the village, causing a stir of excitement.

Soon everyone ran up to see their trophy hanging between Declan and Will, its tongue lolling out the side of its mouth. Beorn, Lydia, and Bachand ran up to the boys.

"Boys, what did you do?" Lydia exclaimed. Her reaction puzzled the young group. Quickly they began to wonder if they had done something wrong by killing the animal.

"They killed a boar, Lid; I thought that much was clear," Beorn said with a grin on his face.

"Yes, but they're just children. They know better than to go out hunting boars. Did you know about this Bachand?" She demanded of William and Chloe's foster father.

"No, I did not. And I have to admit, you two," he said, turning to William and Chloe, "if this was planned, I'm a bit concerned about such recklessness." His words quickly turned their pride to shame.

"We are getting ahead of ourselves, here, people," Beorn yelled over the din of the crowd. "Let them explain" And with that, all four excitedly told the story of the trip. When they got to the part about the boar, everyone was spell bound; each person who listened was silent. No one interrupted, and when they finally got to the part where Chloe finished the boar, the crowd let out a collective sigh of relief. Everyone listened with breathless anticipation, as if they were all there with them, sharing the danger. Such a ferocious and angry beast was not one to be taken lightly, and many of the most seasoned hunters could relate to what was being told to them.

When the story was over, a nervous cheer went up from somewhere in the crowd, as Brody had done the night before. Soon it was taken up by everyone else all around them, as most of the village quickly came to recognize what they had accomplished. Watching the excitement around him, William finally knew how they were going to free their village. He knew how and that now was the time.

Chapter 13

In the Age of King William the First

William and Declan stood before the city's main gate, preparing to face yet another Lianthus. Their lives had become an almost constant drama since their former king turned his attention towards their village. Today was yet another page in that bitter history. Even though they faced Marcus and not his father, Corland, they were sure it made no difference.

William looked up to the top of the gate and nodded to the soldiers watching him. A yell of 'Open the gate!' was heard and almost instantly the loud clang of metal on metal began to echo through the air.

Most gates opened inward on hinges. Some lowered like a draw bridge. But it was Brody who thought a gate that could be raised and lowered vertically would offer more protection.

Long ago, while they were designing the cities defenses, Brody made an argument. "*Think of it this way*," he said to everyone planning the layout of the new city, "*a gate on hinges can be smashed open with battering rams; a draw bridge can be lowered by disconnecting the chains or cutting the ropes. But a gate that naturally wants to be closed can't be opened by force. It must be opened by lifting it straight up.*"

The argument was well received, and the designs for the city walls took on a new feature. The engineers added a large central turret above the main gate, to act as the gate house. They later added the command platform to allow the city's commanders a clear view before the walls. It was also from here that the city's banner communications were flown. As soon as the gate was high enough for them to exit without having to stoop, William and Declan walked out. The gate raised a little more allowing plenty of space to re-enter before the loud noise of the lock clanked behind them.

The two men walked towards the tent followed by six Knights in full armor. There stood a similar group, wearing the Dragon crest of Eland, waiting for them. Marcus, accompanied by one of his generals and six equally heavy armored knights at his back, made up the Eland Delegation.

"At least he is following the rules of Parlay so far," Declan whispered.

"Yes, that's a hopeful sign," William responded.

Soon, they stood before Marcus' company and waited, as it was customary for the attacking leader to speak first. They stood there, staring at each other, for what felt like hours before the young man finally spoke.

"Hello William," he said

"King William, King *Marcus*, we must be respectful," William replied, stifling a laugh

"I have no need to respect you, *William*. You are no king as far as anyone with an ounce of royalty would know," he replied.

"Told you," grunted Declan.

"What was that?" Marcus barked.

"My general was just commenting that we expected as much," William replied, locking eyes with the young man.

"Keep your dog quiet, *William*," Marcus said, emphasizing the word while staring directly at Declan.

"Is that how you look at your general then, Marcus? As a dog?" William asked.

"Servants perform their roles as assigned. My general knows how to follow a born leader," Marcus responded, full of pomp and arrogance.

William watched the general for any sign of emotion but nothing crossed the man's face. '*Yes this one has seen a lot of battle,'* William thought to himself.

The general's appearance was very interesting and very telling. His height was average for humans but his girth caught the king's attention. His solid, square form and heavy facial hair made William believe Marcus' general was a half dwarf.

William was sure that there weren't any Dwarvin villages or strongholds in Eland. He had been in the kingdom many times in the past and had never heard of one. But to the north of Eland was a vast range of mountains that separated the southern kingdoms from the frozen north and hordes of Barbarian tribes.

It was within these giant mountains that the Golden Kingdoms, ruled by the Gem Stone Kings, were located. The inhabitants were, of course, Dwarves who mainly kept to themselves and rarely, if ever, ventured into the outside world. The story of the solid man before him peaked his interest. William made a mental note to find out more about this intriguing man, should the opportunity arise.

"Well now, shall we discuss what it is you have come to our door about, or do you wish to just tell us you decided to camp in our glade?" William asked politely.

"No, by all means, let us sit so we can get to the end of this meaningless ritual," Marcus replied. This confirmed to Declan and William that Marcus was just going through the motions. He had no intention of honoring the code of war.

All four leaders entered the tent. As they did, each of the twelve knights took their positions. Facing their opponents, forming a line on either side of the opening, they prepared to wait. Inside were a small table, two chairs, and a pot of tea sitting on a brazier.

When both of the kings were seated, their generals stood at their right shoulders and listened. An older man came forward quickly when the kings looked settled and poured the tea for them. He first poured for Marcus, instead of William as was custom, a blatant sign of disrespect.

"So Marcus, why have you come to Andraya in force?" William asked sipping his tea first, his own act of disrespect.

Marcus never noticed, but the old man did, who lowered his head in shame. This was one of the signs William was hoping to see. As a sign of impudence, the old man had been ordered to ignore protocol and to serve Marcus first. William was sure that Marcus wouldn't earn the loyalty of his own men, if he continued to act the way he had so far.

"You know why I am here, William. I came to take back my father's kingdom, and to take your sister into custody," Marcus replied.

"I see. Well Chloe isn't in the city, I'm afraid, so I can't help you there. As for your claims on Andraya and Czariana, I can't help but remember that the people didn't want you. Or did you forget your attempt at unseating me a couple of years ago?" William asked, again sipping his tea, watching Marcus' face closely.

"I remember that farce you called an election. What a fool's game you play here, William. A true leader is born, not chosen by commoners," Marcus boomed.

"Really? Well how, pray tell, do you deal with a person who should have never led in the first place?" William asked in as sincere a voice as he could muster. "Like your father." He instantly saw the verbal slap land as he wished.

"All Royals are born to lead by God's own design. My father was a great leader until you and your *people* murdered him," he yelled.

"We never murdered anyone, Marcus. Your father fell at the end of the battle that freed Andraya from the Lianthus tyranny. Your father was the one who attempted to take the low road during our fight. My sister just reacted," William calmly explained.

"Your sister is a cut-throat!" Marcus yelled.

William sighed and leaned back in his chair, replacing the teacup on the saucer. "And your father was a coward. Look, this isn't getting us anywhere. What are your demands?"

"The Royalty of Eland demands the surrender of your capital city, Czariana, without condition. You and the leadership shall be locked up in the dungeons in Lytton. The people of Andraya shall fall under the rule of Eland and will tithe to it rather than any government of its own.

"Furthermore your sister shall be tried and executed for her crimes against royal blood. Finally, the city of Czariana will be razed to the ground and all memory of it shall be wiped out of existence," Marcus said with an evil grin on his face.

"I see. Well so long as you're being reasonable Marcus," William said, rolling his eyes. He turned to Declan who shook his head.

"Under advisement of my general and my own conscience, the people of Andraya decline your demands and make a counter offer instead," William replied.

Cocking an eyebrow in interest, Marcus replied, "And what would this offer be?"

The old man seeing William's cup was empty quickly got to his feet and began to pour more tea for the king.

"You and your troops shall return to Eland, leaving behind a royal representative. They shall account, on your behalf, for the damage you have done to the people of Andraya during your march to Czariana. After a thorough audit of the damage, your agent shall return to Lytton. At that time, you shall reimburse the Andrayan people for their losses." Hearing what William said seemed to startle the old gentleman who visibly shook, spilling some tea.

"Are you alright, father?" William asked.

"No milord. May I speak?" The man said to both kings. William nodded and Marcus shrugged.

"Neither of your demands are proper for a true Parlay. You both requested things that were impossible for the other to accept. You are not even attempting to find a peaceful solution," he said in shock.

Marcus laughed loudly and shook his head, prompting William to answer. "Elder, this parlay is only to satisfy the Rules of War set out by our ancestors centuries ago. Your king isn't here to resolve a simple dispute. He came here for a Vendetta, and so of course his demands were designed to be unreasonable. He doesn't care if we accept or not; he wants revenge.

"We, on the other hand, knew this was going to be the case. We have made it clear that our people have been wronged by your king's actions. For that wronging, we demand retribution in the form of payment for their loss. The people who have been hurt must be made whole. We Andrayans refuse to accept that only royalty should be allowed to keep their lives from being shattered. All the people of Andraya deserve the same," William explained.

A loud lazy clapping echoed in the tent as Marcus slowly leaned forward in his chair.

"That's just what I would expect from a fool such as you. You were never meant to lead, William. You were born a peasant, and as such, you think like one. The people are here at our whim only. They serve the royalty and owe us for their lives, not the other way around," Marcus said dispassionately.

"So do you accept our offer?" William asked calmly.

"The people of Eland decline your offer. These discussions are at an end. Tomorrow we go to war," Marcus nonchalantly pronounced.

"I warn you to reconsider, Marcus. Blood does not have to flow because of the past. Your men don't need to die," William said, as he attempted one more time to get through to the arrogant youth.

"My men are warriors; they shall gladly die for their kingdom," Marcus replied, and getting to his feet he swiftly walked to the tent opening followed by his general. "Besides, it is your people who shall die when all of this is over. When we are done, the only memory of this cursed city will be the red stained hillside." And with that he stormed out of the tent.

William got to his feet and turned to the old man. "Elder, I would like to thank you for the tea. I urge you to retreat to a safe location by tomorrow," William said.

"My place is at the young king's side, milord," he replied as William and Declan headed for the door. "But your majesty," he said, stopping William before he walked out, "I thank-you for your concern." To which William smiled weakly and with a nod the two remaining men left the tent and returned to the city gates.

Chapter 14

In the Age of King Corland the Fourth

Everyone knelt in the darkness around the village edge, looking and taking in every detail.

All of the exiled children who chose to return, as well as any volunteers from Parinth, marched the long treacherous path back to their old Village. The elves that accompanied them were shocked at what the exiled children had endured on their trek to Parinth nearly seven years ago. Even the sure footed elves found it difficult terrain. They couldn't even imagine how bad it had been for a band of cold, lost, and desperate children. Their opinions of their adopted friends and children greatly increased.

When they were close to the village, William shut everyone in a large cave, with the opening sealed. The entire group, everyone, spent the whole day in complete darkness.

The idea came from Beorn who was one of the elves that joined them in the liberation of their home.

"Close your eyes," he said to the three boys one night, as they camped during the trip into Andraya. "Now open them and take a look around," he instructed.

Doing as they were told, the boys looked at their surroundings, and they all noticed that a squirrel was sitting on Beorn's shoulder.

"Was that squirrel there the whole time?" Brody asked with amazement.

"Yes it was. What you did was make your eyes more sensitive to the light, by keeping it out of them," the tall blacksmith explained. "The pupils of your eyes open larger to allow more light in when they are starved for it. Just like an owl, the bigger your pupils, the more you can see in the dark."

All day and late into the night they sat, conditioning their eyes for the night raid. Finally, at the agreed upon time, Chloe, who volunteered to keep watch outside, opened the sealed cave letting everyone know it was time to act.

The moon was high as they surveyed the village. Soon the scouts returned, and everyone pooled what they had seen.

"There are eight guards on duty. Those of you we chose as archers follow the scouts and each one of you pick a guard. Aim for their throats, understand? They must die with as little noise as possible. The quieter we can move into position, the less bloodshed there should be. Remember, those are our people down there; we must save them," William explained.

Everyone nodded and the archers followed the scouts to the best locations to take their shots. Then, after hearing the wolf howl from Brody, each person took their shot. Nearly every arrow was fired perfectly and hit their victim. The few that were off target, were backed up by a second archer that quickly finished the job.

Swiftly and silently, everyone surged into the village. Using hand signals, William instructed everyone to take a door. Each hut was now being watched with an archer and a swordsman. The archers drew on the doors, as each swordsman kicked them in and stormed the huts.

Startled sounds came from all of them at once, and from the chaos, erupted sounds of swords being drawn. Several of what used to be homes, were quickly concluded to be the guard houses. Everyone near a guardhouse took defensive positions, as soldiers burst from their huts. As each soldier emerged, they were met with an arrow pointed at them.

"All of you soldiers hold!" William yelled, standing in the center of the village. "You are all surrounded, and each of you has an arrow marked for your heart. Drop your weapons or you shall be shot," he warned.

Several soldiers decided to test their luck and rushed forward. Five twangs, followed by five thuds resonated as the arrows found their marks.

"I warned you, now drop your weapons and lay face down on the ground," William yelled again.

The remaining guards dropped their weapons and laid face down as they were instructed. Several members of William's forces rushed forward, while others kept their bows drawn to ensure no one moved. Each guard was then tied and securely gagged before anyone would breathe easier.

"Search all of the huts and bring everyone into the clearing. Be gentle. These people have seen a lot of pain over the last couple of years," William commanded.

Soon all of the huts were searched, turning up several more soldiers who were promptly restrained and gagged. All of the prisoners inside the huts were chained to the walls, and so Declan and Beorn set to work freeing the captives. By the time the sun began to rise, a scene unlike any the villagers had dreamed could occur was taking place. Tears flowed freely as children were reunited with their parents. Some tears came as others realized their loved ones had died from either the capture of the village or years of hard thankless work.

William and Chloe's father, Domitus, was unfortunately one of them. After the beating he took from the king's guards in the city, and the added wounds from the village capture, he couldn't work the fields, and his heart failed from the labor. Both of them left the village and, leaning on each other for support, cried their pain into the morning air. Soon they were joined by others who all hugged them close to them. With each added person who joined them, the pain seemed to ease from their hearts.

Finally, they all returned and stories were exchanged of what happened. The villagers, who were grateful for freedom, did not speak of their torment. Instead, they chose to drown their memories in their new found freedom. Women would go and find bound guards on the ground and kick and hit them over and over again, taking out unknown violations on them.

What they did say was that when the children had escaped, the king returned. He had decided that instead of killing them all, they would serve him better as slave labor. For the past 6 years they worked every day in the fields, and each year the entire crop was turned over to the king. Rumor had it that Corland was so pleased with the new slave camp, that he found any reason he could to create other such camps in the kingdom.

William saw that further leadership was required and began giving direction to everyone around him.

"Chloe," he said, "take some archers into the forest and hunt for some food." Chloe nodded and calling several others to her, she moved off to do as she was told. "Brody, you and Bachand start taking stock of what supplies we have here in the village.

"Dec, how about you and Beorn create a prison for these parasites?" William said, the loathing he felt for the soldiers thick in his voice. By the end of the day, a large feast was prepared and the soldiers were locked up in the make shift jail. The hut that was converted had been William's home, once. Since their family was dead, he and Chloe decided theirs would be best suited for the purpose. All four sides were manned by a guard to make sure the bound soldiers wouldn't try anything.

Everyone ate and talked for hours. William was pleased to see some of the pain in the faces of the villagers easing. Most had almost instantly been revitalized by the sight of their children. It was those whose children never knew them and decided to stay behind, that seemed to have had their last reason to live torn apart. William took extra care to treat these people with more attention, and they seemed to accept it from him easier than from others. Like them, he too lost someone he loved because of Corland.

That night, the group of scouts he had sent to search for any soldiers they missed, returned. They had tracked two guards that escaped, and both had been found. Neither would surrender and were killed, instead of allowing them to inform the king of the newly freed village. Since most of these scouts were not people from the village itself, William thanked them for their generosity in helping the people they didn't even know.

"William, these are your people, and since you and the other children are now our people, that makes these people ours as well. It's the circle of creation that all Elves believe in," Bachand explained to his foster son. William smiled and hugged the man who cared for him and his sister for all these years. The welcome he found in his stepfather's arms renewed his fresh felt pain, and his tears began to fall anew. The elf just hugged him close and whispered messages of love in the young man's ear. The other scouts stood there, silently placing a hand on his back as an offering of support to the emotional youth.

When William finally composed himself, he led the scouts back to the village and introduced them all. He made sure the scouts had eaten their fill, before telling everyone they should go to bed.

"But where do we go from here, Will?" Brody asked, holding his mother's hand.

"We go on, Brode. If what our friends have said is true, there are other villages like this. They too need to be freed. If all of you will follow me a while longer, we will free Andraya, and Corland Lianthus shall pay for his crimes," William replied to cheers from everyone.

William looked around at the faces he saw. So much had changed in one day. From a village of sorrow to a community of hope and direction, the change was like night and day. '*Yes,*' he said to himself, '*we really can do this!*'

Chapter 15

In the Age of King William the First

"Do you really think this will work?" Declan asked William as the two of them walked the length of the Kings Way, confirming all streets and alleys were blocked and locked.

"Sure," William replied, giving a mobile wall a hard push to make sure it was firmly in place. "I think it will. This road has been measured to hold around 60 to 65 thousand people from one end to the other without horses. If the foot soldiers storm the gates, when the opportunity arises, we should be able to nearly split their forces in two, with the main bulk of horses outside. Then we make our real move," William said.

"And even if the worst happens, and men have to die, then we can use the Kings Way to minimize our losses," Brody said, coming up from behind. "Dec, it's a good design; let's just try it before condemning it to failure. Besides, we have other defenses, and, if need be, we will just have to do it the old fashioned way. Kill as many as we can until they stop coming. If we run low on arrows, then we pluck chickens, heat up the forges and make more. That is why we decided to fight here rather than taking the fight to them. We have a better chance at victory here."

"I know, I know, but Marcus is arrogant, not stupid. Do you really think he is going to fall for an open gate?" Declan asked.

"Wow Dec, you haven't been this unsure since we were kids," Brody replied. "In his eagerness, he might just take it for what it appears, an open present. He sent men in here just for that purpose right? As far as he knows, since he hasn't heard anything to the contrary, his saboteurs were successful. Considering the circumstances, he probably thinks they are just waiting for the right time to open things up. No one has seen the Kings Way in its defensive mode before. Everything behind that gate is going to look very different when they finally get through."

William listened to his two trusted friends as they discussed the effectiveness of their trap. He wished he had Brody's confidence. The Kings Way could be the most efficient bear trap, or death trap for an enemy if it worked well. If it didn't, it would have been a lot of work and planning for nothing, this time. God knows William didn't expect this to be the only attack on Czariana, but once word of the Kings Way got out, it wouldn't be as efficient a defense as it was as a secret.

"Will? William? Hello, King William?" Will's thoughts were broken by a tap on the shoulder. He looked up and saw Brody and Declan looking at him with concern.

"Sorry, guys, I was thinking about the battle." William smiled at them.

"Oh, you have doubts, too?" Declan said, disappointment in his voice.

"Sure I do, but not about the Kings Way. Dec, you designed this corridor perfectly, and the addition of the T at the end of the street, to allow more people to fill in, was a great last minute addition. All of the gates and mobile walls match the rest of the walls perfectly. This is as much a piece of art as it is a defensive trap," William smiled, strongly gripping his friend's shoulder. "If they rush the open gate, it will work one way or the other. If they don't then we are no worse off for building it, and it will remain a secret for the next attack we might face.

"It's the whole battle as it stands. We have contingencies and back up plans galore, and everyone is prepared to do their part. I just want to lose as little life on both sides as possible. The elder fellow in the Parlay tent worries me," William sighed.

"He is on the side he serves, Will," Declan replied, "and he is too old to fight, anyway. He will be alright as will all the people who shouldn't be on the front lines.

"Will, I need you to remember something. This war is between us and them. They aren't worried about our lives in here. You dishonor our people by equating their lives with our enemies. In war, you must value the life of the man at your side, more than the man who wants to kill you.

"Those men and women who protect our gates are not just as important as the men on that field. They are much more important. They are willing to die to protect this city and its people from that horde out there. Remember that, William, or our people will die for nothing," William felt the words from Declan pierce his heart.

"There are soldiers out there that are going to die or be captured because of a personal vendetta. Most of them don't know the real reason for this war," William sighed. "But your words have stung me my friend. You're right, and now my concern should be our people. If Marcus' men don't want this, they can desert. Otherwise, they are the enemy. This Vendetta is lunacy, thank you for reminding me of that, Dec," the middle aged king said as he shook his head.

"That's why we moved against Corland all those years ago, Will," Brody said softly, "These royals who believe they have the right to rule, to order the deaths of others in war, have to be stopped. Andraya has prospered under your rule; we can't allow that to change."

Declan nodded his agreement. "I'm glad you guys are here with me." William said.

"Where else would we be?" Declan replied. "The three of us have always been together; why should that change now?"

William smiled, and the three of them headed back towards the main gate. "All of the forces are ready for the morning then?" William asked.

"Yes; the first line, the archers, are all resting," Brody explained. "We will have the walls manned by swordsmen and pikemen for the night. That way our regular archers will be well rested when the fighting starts. Also, the gunner crews are sleeping in the launch nests, so when they are called upon they will be ready.

"Basically, Marcus' people are going to meet with minimal resistance once they start. Then once we have our people in their proper positions and ready, we will counter. There is no reason for our people to be tired, waiting for the attack. Let their arrows bounce off the clay roofs of the houses. That's the only targets they will hit until we are ready to return volley," he grinned.

"That's a good plan. But you know, most of our troops aren't going to be able sleep anyway?" Declan replied.

"Yeah I know, but at least laying in their beds their bodies will rest, even if their minds cannot," Brody responded.

The others nodded their agreement. In no time at all, they had walked the long street back to the wall, which they climbed, and then continued to the top of the command turret. Looking down over the wall at the number of soldiers before them, they confirmed their calculations.

Once again, William lamented the destruction the advancing army had caused. So much had changed in the plains before his walls. Where once grasslands, with a small creek near the forests edge, filled your view, now was destroyed.

So far, everything was as it had been the day before. Sword and Shield stood closest to the castle walls, followed by pikemen. Archers, made up of a large number of pikemen, were directly behind them followed by cavalry. Then taking up the rear, still out of the range of attack, were four large catapults.

"What do James and Owen say about the catapults?" William asked.

"They have been doing drawings and working out the details with the help of Tobias," Brody replied. "They believe their range is between the archers and the cavalry. Our range is much better; we should be able to fire at them when they are half way to their mark."

"Great. If they get through, though, I want fire teams ready in the city. If they are throwing flaming payloads, then I want their fires taken care of immediately," William said.

"I'll tell Minister Reese as soon as we're done here," Brody replied.

"You're keeping things well under control, Brode. You're almost making this easy," William said.

"My goodness, your majesty, if you keep talking like that, it'll go to my head," Brody grinned.

"Don't let that happen, milord," Declan replied. "If that head gets any bigger, we will have to cut holes in the doorways to get him through." He laughed, and Brody responded by punching the large man in the shoulder.

"Okay, you two, tomorrow this battle is going to take place. Hopefully, the day after is the end. Let's see where it takes us," William said, heading down the stairs.

He was followed by the others to meet and discuss everything once more with the council. They would then go out to the different meeting places in the underground city to inform the people of their next move. The city was so huge, and although everyone was packed fairly tightly down below, it was still such a vast area that a single meeting was impossible. This created the need for the ministers to go out and carry out separate meetings instead.

Tomorrow was the day; there was no doubt about it now. Either Marcus fired the first shot or William would order it, but the city's wait had come to an end.

Chapter 16

In the Age of King Corland the Fourth

It was the end of another busy day for William's ever growing army. They had already freed three villages, counting theirs, from being held captive and he was sure that word would reach the king any day. A week had passed since they started their campaign to free Andraya. Each time they liberated a village, they followed the successful strategy of their first attack and their numbers grew.

They now had a couple thousand people with them. Even though only three villages so far needed freeing from captivity, others were tired of King Corland. William's leadership was freely accepted by most, having proven himself time and again, including to his oldest rival, Jacob. After years of open aggression, Jake's attitude changed when his parents were freed.

The problem with leading this many people, besides the logistics of feeding and giving them shelter, was how slowly they moved. One day while trying to deal with so many new arrivals, Declan came up with an idea.

"Why not split them up?" Declan suggested.

"What do you mean?" William asked.

"I'll take a group to find other villages, Brody and Chloe can take one each. Heck, give a group to Jacob to lead. That way we can spread out and cover more ground. We might just be prepared, by the time Corland hears about us, to face him," Declan explained.

"That's a great idea, Dec!" William exclaimed. "Can you go and find the others so we can talk to them about it?" William asked his oldest friend. Declan turned to go, but William stopped him, "Dec, before you go, are you sure about Jacob? I mean what he and his brothers did to you..."

"I'm over it, and to be honest it works for me. Folks take a gruff elf more seriously than a sing songy one. Look at Beorn. Everyone takes him seriously. That, and," Declan said with a grin, "the girls love the wounded warrior bit." He winked as he turned and left.

William just shook his head at his friend and smiled. He decided to split up the original group, allowing people with more experience to be in each camp, helping their leaders. He also decided that anyone who didn't want to fight should also be split evenly, if they wanted to stay with the moving force. Any who wished could go on to a "friendly" village to wait.

He doubted many would choose to stay behind. The only people who didn't fight were the elderly, and their wisdom was a great resource. The children on the other hand had become great camp messengers. A message could be given to one, and they would rush to deliver it. It was as if he had his own little communication network. You could clearly tell if a young one had a message, as they ran like mad trying to find the recipient. It was due to this urgency that he nicknamed them his runners.

Few would leave the groups, of this he was sure, and Declan's idea would make a lot of sense to most of the people. Some wouldn't be happy, since there was greater protection in numbers. But at this rate, alarms would be raised, followed by a huge force being sent after them, putting an early end to a revolution that had just begun.

Declan soon returned with Brody, Chloe, and Jacob, who was hesitant to be asked to meet with him. He was never close with William after their clash in the caverns. After the fight with Declan, the two hadn't spoken to one another again. Not even after William stood up for him and his brothers at the trial. It was almost as if Jacob had wished more for exile than the daily torment he faced as an outsider.

Once they all settled in, William and Declan told the others the plan. All three agreed that it made more sense than the snail's pace they now moved at. They spoke at length about how to make the entire plan a reality. After dividing all of the villages amongst the five of them, utilizing veterans, elves, elderly, and fighting fit evenly, they brought an end to the meeting. They then sent runners to gather all the other freedom fighters to discuss the plan as large groups. Each person who was assigned certain villages to lead would also be in charge of having a discussion with them about the proposed changes.

Declan, Brody, and Chloe all left after the meeting ended, but Jacob hung behind. When they were alone, Jacob asked the question that was burning in his mind. "Will, why did you choose me?" he asked.

William had expected this and said, "I have a different question for you, Jake. Why wouldn't we choose you?" He asked.

"Well there aren't enough villages to really split into five groups, so why not stick with four?" Jacob replied. "We both know that with our history, I'm the last person you would want to pick. So, again I have to ask, why me?"

"That's a good question Jake," William replied, sitting back down and motioning for Jacob to join him, "The people need to follow those they can believe in. The more second choices we have to make in splitting everyone up, the less confident in those choices the people will be.

"We may have to split things up again if we grow too large. If we do, there may be a problem with confidence in the second group of chosen leaders. So, the more first choices we can offer, the better for morale. Maybe nothing would happen with a second set of leaders, but I don't want to take chances and this is the best way I can think of to avoid that.

"I believe in you Jacob, and I wanted you to have all the trust of your followers I could help you with. By making you a first round choice, everyone will see that you have my confidence.

"I'm afraid this is horribly arrogant sounding, but people have decided to make me their leader. It's always been this way. I always seem to be chosen to lead. Rather than choosing or wanting it myself, it always seems to be my responsibility, and I tell you, Jake, it's not easy. So since I seem to be the elected leader, they have to trust in what I say. So if I say I trust you, then they should trust you.

"But remember, Jake, don't take advantage of this. I'll warn the others of this same thing later. You have been given a command position and that will bring with it trust and respect. Keeping that trust and earning more respect will be completely your responsibility. Break the trust and no one will follow you again," William explained.

"No one has left you, William, how do you know about lost trust?" Jacob asked.

"Because I had to earn yours, Jake, and I know just how hard it is to do that," William smiled at his new commander.

Jacob thought a moment and was about to leave, when he stopped and saluted. William smiled and returned the salute and watched as Jacob walked away.

The meetings went very well. Everyone thought the idea was great and, as such, they quickly prepared for departure. They were all going to go in five different directions, returning to this location in two weeks. It was also agreed that they would stay away from the capitol region as best they could. There was no need to attract the king's attention too soon.

The groups then set out to find more who would join the cause. William was about to call a march for his command, when he heard someone call out to him.

"William!" a girl's voice called behind him. William recognized it immediately; it was Emma. "William, I want to go with you," she said.

"Sure Emma, but why? Declan will be a great leader," he replied.

"I know he will, but where you go, I go," she replied.

Her response drew chuckles from those closest by, causing William to blush a deep crimson. For a while now, he had watched her from afar. Her smile intoxicated him; her auburn hair seemed to flow as if the wind stretched out willowy fingers and caressed it. He could almost drown in her dark eyes, and one could only imagine how her skin felt.

He suddenly became aware of himself and cleared his throat. “Okay, I don’t mind and I’m sure Dec will be okay with it. Did you tell him?” He asked.

“Yes, I told him before I left his group,” she replied with a smile. He smiled back at her and turned to everyone who was watching the two with great interest.

“Okay, people, nothing to see here, let’s move out,” he yelled, and started walking in the direction they were assigned. Emma walked by his side, and although he couldn’t bring himself to look at her for fear of falling flat on his face, he felt like he was walking on air.

Chapter 17

In the Age of King William the First

The morning dawned with the air filled with tension. No one really slept, including William. Of course by extension, neither did Emma. The king was in and out of bed so often, that just as his wife would fall asleep, he would do something that would wake her again. If there wasn't a war already on the horizon, there would be in the Royal Chambers.

"William, you're lucky you have a battle to deal with, because after last night, you almost got a beating from me!" Emma said walking from their bed chamber, and sitting across from him at the breakfast table.

"I'm sorry, dear, I couldn't sleep. I tell you what, have one of the house servants set me up a place to sleep out here. That way you can rest if I have another restless night. Odds are good that I'll be pacing again tonight, anyway. This thing will be over tomorrow, if everything goes well," William explained.

"I know, Will," Emma softened. "Look, you better eat and get up there." She responded.

"Declan and Brody will already be there and this is their command, not mine," William explained. "I'm just going to be on the wall because it's my duty. I'm leaving the implementation of our plans to those who know how better than I."

"Okay, well if you're sticking around, your daughter needs to be changed," Emma said smiling, seeing the droopy bottom of their daughter's diaper as she rolled out of her bed. Will smiled and was about to get up to greet her, when the door to their chamber burst open and in rushed Austin, yet again.

"Father, it's begun!" he panted.

William quickly pulled on his boots and raced behind his son towards the wall access door. He climbed all the way to the gate house door, to find Declan and Brody barking orders.

Looking out over the wall, he saw the commotion below. The racing soldiers looked like an angry hill of ants that had just been kicked over. In the distance, he could see the cavalry moving out of the way of the catapults as they rolled into range. Suddenly, his eye caught sight of something unexpected.

"General, are those?" he yelled down the wall to Declan.

"Yes, Majesty, they are!" boomed the reply from the general as he returned to giving orders to his men.

Fear rose in William's throat as he saw six large Siege towers rolling towards them behind the protective might of the catapults. The towers were massive, covered in Griffon hide to shield the soldiers, who more than likely filled the towers.

If the hides used really were Griffon, there was no way that they could catch fire. That meant that demolition was the only way to stop them from reaching their destination. William watched as Brody came running up with a crew of men. He was issuing orders as they prepared to mount the large flame throwers on the walls. Rushing the walls with ladders; the enemy was already making their move. William's attention returned to the walls, as Brody gave the order to blanket their front lines with flames.

“General, not one of those fatherless dogs sets foot on my walls, do you understand?” William yelled, rage filling his chest.

“Yes, sire, I will see to it personally,” Declan replied to the king. Turning to the soldiers on the walls he began yelling, “You heard him, you animals. Keep that bunch of rabble off of these walls or it’s your skins that will protect our siege towers when we return the favor!”

Suddenly, William heard a shout being relayed down the wall. Just as the words hit his ears and he could discern what they were, a volley of arrows darkened the sky above him. He grabbed Ashton and dove under the shelter of a stone over hang just as the clanking of arrows sounded all around them.

“You okay, Son?” William asked.

Too stunned to talk, Ashton just nodded.

“Ash, you get below and start doing your job, do you hear me?” William shouted above the noise, hoping that appealing to the boy’s sense of duty would help clear the youths head. Like a splash of cold water, the expression changed on Ashton’s face as he turned to his father.

“Yes, sire. I apologize for my behavior, Father,” his second son replied.

“It’s okay, Ashy. You are just feeling the same sense of overwhelming that I am right now. But we need you to do your job now. Look, here comes an opening. Run for the stairs and get to it without looking back!” William said trying to build his son’s courage up.

They watched through a small window in the wall at the commotion on the ground. William attempted to take in everything going on around him in the heat of battle. The walkway on the top of the wall had sheets of animal hides creating a temporary roof above them. The hides could then be pulled back quickly, allowing archers to return fire. But even this shelter didn't stop all the arrows and as the volleys plummeted, a constant clatter rang around them.

William and Ashton watched as row upon row of enemy troops bustled around on the battlefield below. Archers fired a constant stream of arrows into the sky, while swordsmen tried to gain the walls with ladders. Once a ladder would get too close, the men carrying it would be shot by the Andrayan archers manning the city walls. A few unlucky fools were ignited by flame throwers, spraying burning pitch onto anyone who got within their range.

Finally, when there was a lull in the hail of arrows, William pushed Ashton out. William breathed a sigh of relief as the door closed behind his son, as another volley rained down around him.

William followed the outcropping until he came to where Brody was bellowing orders.

"Fly the flags for archers at the ready. Any Elander that gets close, the order is shoot to kill. They are not to mount these walls!" Brody commanded his flag communications officer.

"What is the status of the long range attack to take care of those catapults and towers?" Declan asked a runner.

"Sir, they are opening the launch doors now, and are preparing to fire," the runner said. Declan waited for a moment for the hail of arrows to stop, and he started down the stairs with William at his heels.

They quickly rushed down into the city's walls, but instead of going all the way into the cavern, they stopped half way down. Stepping into a large open doorway, they entered the Defense Hall.

Here, contained in a long hallway measuring the length of the city wall, were housed ten giant ballistae. Eight of the ten machines were located near the center of the city allowing easier communication with the Gunner Sergeant. The other two were located at the far edges of the city to protect its corners. As far as William could see, the enemy's engines were within reach of the eight central defenses.

Each launcher was manned by its gunner, already, and although large missile like bolts were on the racks, the launching cables were just now being drawn into position.

Declan saw William paying close attention to the long range launch platforms in front of him. "Never seen them like this, huh?" he asked.

"No, I've never really paid that much attention before, to be honest," William replied.

"The Ballistae are really just large crossbows. The lathes are the large arms that place tension on the line. When the trigger is opened they cause the cable to snap forward launching the payload. Our Ballista use three lathes, an addition made by Brody and the Gnomes. He says they add more tension to the line, increasing the force and distance of our shots," Declan explained.

"How far can we shoot?" William asked.

"These are large bolts we are using. They are heavy and are meant for maximum damage. But they don't travel far. If we want maximum distance we load smaller bolts, and those can travel over a mile nearly reaching the forest," Declan beamed.

"I should have paid more attention to all this," William said, shaking his head.

“Don’t worry about it. That’s why you pay me in gold, so I’d pay attention to it all,” chuckled Declan.

Even though the cables were still being drawn into position, that didn’t stop the Gunnery Sergeant, James Blackwell, from bellowing orders.

“Get those defensive doors open; I want eyes on those catapults. We’ll deal with the towers later!” he yelled. A loud grating noise echoed in the room. Pairs of men pulled large stone doors lining the outer walls apart exposing the ballistae to the outside world. Nets dropped in their places, making it more difficult for arrows to bounce into the openings.

Gunners bellowed out commands to their targeting teams, as men rotated the large launching platforms, allowing the gunners to sight in on targets.

“Gun teams, status!” the Sergeant yelled. “This isn’t a drill people; let’s get this done right!”

“One on one, great.”

“Two on one, great.”

“Three on one, great. Three on two good.”

“Four on two great.”

“Five on three great.”

“Six on three good.”

“Seven on three great. Seven on four good.”

“Eight on four great.” The responses came down the line. William guessed that they were referring, left to right, to how they targeted the enemy’s catapults. “One on one” must have meant ballista one had a clear target on catapult one.

The sergeant looked outside one of the walls and noticed that the catapults were pulling into the desired range.

"Orders!" he shouted, "One on one. Two on one. Three on two. Four on two. Five on three. Six on three. Seven on four. Eight on four." Just as quick as he could bellow the orders the gunners began to fine tune their sights on their assigned targets.

A call of ready came from all eight gunners in sequence.

"Fire!" shouted the sergeant.

Quickly, men pulled on ropes, drawing the netting open. Loud twangs echoed through the hall as all eight ballista fired their huge tree trunk sized payloads. The sound of yells from the field below told William that their secret long range attack weapons caught most of the enemy soldiers by surprise.

Suddenly, a yell came from gunner six. "My launcher is damaged!" William grinned; this is what he was waiting for. Declan explained that he had ordered the gunnery sergeant to sabotage one of the ballista as a sign to Marcus that his men had indeed infiltrated the Czariana ranks.

Quickly, as the other machines were reloaded, and the sergeant began bellowing for confirmation, the gun crews checked the sabotaged launcher. It was confirmed sabotage, and as the men from that crew closed their launch doors, others moved in to try to repair it.

The strike results were loudly reported from the remaining gun crews. Number one Catapult was damaged but still mobile. Number two was no longer mobile but it was being prepared to fire anyway. Number three had minimal damage, but due to only one gunner making contact it was still moving and deadly. Four had appeared to be disabled but it wasn't clear.

When the crews looked outside to report the damage, they noticed that the large bolt from the sabotaged ballista had done something unexpected. Declan told William it would just drop out the gate and probably land nose down in the dirt.

Instead, the firing cables apparently didn't break as soon as expected, causing it to be launched more horizontal. Although it fell far from its mark, it had become a large sliding battering ram and slid through the ranks of the enemy's sword and shield division, who had been rushing towards the gates. It slid as far as to knock over several rows of archers that were right behind the sword and shield ranks on the field.

Back inside the Defense Hall, the gunner teams quickly moved to reload the ballistae. Large racks, filled with missiles, separated each ballista. Here, men were using ropes and cranes to move a new payload onto each active long range weapon. Again, like before, Sergeant James bellowed commands and once again ordered everything as before, except weapon seven was directed at target three rather than target four.

Before he could order them to fire, though, a loud cracking sound reached their ears as the distinctive noise of catapult launches filled the air outside. Wall watchers reported all four catapults had fired, and all but number four apparently cleared the wall. Instead, its boulder payload smashed into the Defensive Hall, breaking through the opening and destroying ballista eight. William and Declan ran to see what happened as James kept ordering.

Now that the catapults had already fired, they had time to properly line up their shots on the remaining threats. This had become more difficult, though, as enemy archers were now ordered to aim into the launch doors.

Just as the warning came from the wall watchers, another message came in. Volley after volley of arrows were reported originating from within the castle walls, being fired into the ranks outside.

Brody must have seen that a diversion was required and commanded the city archers to protect the soldiers in the Defense Hall.

William and Declan reached the far end of the hall and found one person badly wounded and three members of the gunner team dead. Grief overwhelmed the king, but it was quickly replaced by anger.

"Get this man to a medic, and treat these soldiers with full honors. They will be heralded as heroes for their sacrifice," William yelled.

Support teams quickly rushed in to carry out his orders as he turned to see what has happening behind him. The loud twang of the ballista filled the hallway again as the second volley was launched, followed by four successful confirmations.

"Sergeant!" Declan yelled.

"Yes sir!" the Gunnery Sergeant replied.

"I want those towers incapacitated. There are a lot of enemy troops on them that are only here because of that arrogant ass' vendetta. I don't want more lives lost than we absolutely must take!" Declan ordered.

"Yes, sir, you heard him. Crews prepare for the next volley!" the Sergeant yelled.

Declan followed William out of the hall door, who turned to his elfish cousin once they left the room, and said, "Thanks Dec."

"For what, milord?" Declan asked.

"When I saw that young woman, the gunner, dead with those men around her and the carnage caused by the catapult, I almost started calling for all hell to be let loose. If I had, I wouldn't have been able to live with myself once this thing was over," William explained.

"I know, sire. I felt the same way, but you made it clear to us before that those soldiers are just here because of a lie. We don't have to treat them with kid gloves, but we don't have to lose ourselves either. They have families to go home to as well. Marcus is whom we have to deal with. These other people are just pawns in his madness," the general replied, as they walked back up to the top of the wall.

Chapter 18

In the Age of King Corland the Fourth

The two weeks agreed upon by the five leaders went by quickly. William knew he was going to be in trouble for returning late. The problem was that when he finished freeing one village, another wanted to be recruited. So his people went further and further until he knew they would be late returning to the others. Now, three days past the deadline, they finally crested the valley edge to an amazing sight.

There were, as far as the eye could see, camps filling the valley floor. He was lost in the wonder of it, when a gasp at his side caught his attention. He felt a hand quickly grasp his tightly. He looked to his side to see Emma, obviously as lost in the spectacle of it all as he was. He squeezed her hand in return, leading his own new army of people into the valley.

That's when he noticed the tents in the middle of the valley. They were huge and brightly colored, and he wondered if they hadn't already met with the king.

As he and Emma slowly lead their group forward, they noticed movement near the tents. William signaled the column to come to a halt. There was no way they could navigate through the throng of tents below with the amount of people following him. He watched as a group of riders started to make their way towards them instead. *'That's new,'* William thought to himself; they had never used horses before. A sense of trepidation started to wash over him. *'What if,' he continued in his mind, 'the reason there are riders coming towards us and tents below is because the king has already attacked.'* The idea of his friends in chains started his heart to race.

The four riders drew up just in front of him, their faces aglow with excitement. He sighed in relief when he saw his four friends, "William, you're alright!" Chloe exclaimed jumping down and giving her brother warm a hug.

"Sure little sister, we're just late. I went a bit too far to get back in time. My leaders all tried to urge me to turn us around, but I just kept saying one more village. That is until I got a kick from Emma," he said nodding towards the young woman, "literally. Then we turned and headed back as quickly as we could. But I never imagined all of this!" he exclaimed, motioning towards the valley before them.

"Isn't it great? Word has been spreading like wildfire. Villages have been coming to us, instead of us having to go to them." Brody exclaimed. "I was the first one back. My group returned a couple of days early, and even as we waited for you all to return, more and more people kept coming to us. Most of Andraya is here!"

"Yes, and those who aren't here, we haven't made it out to yet. Either that or they are too far in the Capitol city region," Jacob said, shaking William's hand. "They have heard of the 'Freedom Fighters' and want to join. There have been other things that have changed as well." He grinned nodding at his horse.

"I see that, what's going on?" William asked.

"Why don't we settle the people you brought with you in and we can talk later. We have chosen to camp in the directions we travelled from. There is a large open space there on the Eastern side of the valley for your group to use," Declan explained.

"Great, I'll help them settle. Where should I meet you?" William asked.

"Down at the command tents," Declan declared, pointing down to the center of the valley.

"Command tents?" William breathed.

"Just hurry, we have a lot to talk about," his friend said grinning at him.

William didn't need any further urging. Being led by Declan and Brody, as Chloe and Jacob went back to the center of the valley, he quickly set out getting the new arrivals to their designated area.

Several hours passed, but when William was sure his charges were comfortable and fed, he left them with Emma and went down to the command tents. Declan and Brody had left long ago to take care of some business, but he knew they would be waiting for him. Most of the people he already knew welcomed him warmly when they saw him. Others, who were quickly learning who he was, became interested in seeing the young leader at long last.

Will wasn't sure what to make of it all, except that they now had a large enough group of people that they could easily defend themselves. He also knew that they stood out like a sore thumb. Fear rose within him when he realized they would now been seen as an open challenge to the king's rule.

But that thought barely registered in his mind as his gaze swept the people around him. Everywhere he looked he saw hope, energy, and excitement. It was the same environment his own travels had revealed to him, as they freed his countrymen. It was as if something big was about to happen, a shift in everyone's lives, and the entire kingdom knew it. That is, everyone but the Royals, William hoped.

All around him, people made their temporary homes. Tents, lean-to's, teepee's, all forms of makeshift shelters surrounded him. The colors were also very telling of the regions from which the people came. He saw tents of yellow, marking the grain growers of the central kingdom. There was the blue of the North West water tribes. Red, marking the region of Andraya where the vineyards grew and wine was made. Looking around he finally saw his beloved green, symbolizing the colors of growing and life from his region of the kingdom. All that was missing was the deep purple of the capitol region. The rainbow of colors was a visual representation of what he hoped. That the people of Andraya would unite, and freedom would once again come to their lives.

After the long walk to the valley center, he finally entered into the ring of tents that Declan had pointed out to him. It wasn't that they were that large, but they were designed unlike any tent he had ever seen before. They were almost like cloth huts, square with peaked roofs and they were all brightly colored.

Seeing his reaction, Declan came over and welcomed him into one of the structures. "Will, this one is yours," he said, watching his friend's face.

"Mine, Dec? What do you mean?" William asked.

"Yours, just like it sounds. You will sleep and work from here now; it's easier having all of us together to make decisions," Declan explained.

"Sure, but they're too fancy, we stand out like we think we're better than the others," William said, worried about how this would look.

"That's what we said, but the people demanded it. I don't understand a lot of this kind of stuff, but Brody and Chloe explained it to me. They said it's because even though we are trying to free everyone from the current government, people need a symbol to follow. We, or more specifically you, are becoming that symbol," Declan explained.

"Me? No, Dec, there is more to all of this than me," William said, suddenly uncomfortable.

"Yes you, William. Everyone knows it was your plan that freed our village. That same plan has been used several times since to free others. We found six more slave camps among the four of us, plus any you might have found," Brody explained coming up to his friends, having seen them from across the central camp. "You have become a legend to our people, and have been unofficially designated leader of the resistance."

Overwhelmed, William had to sit down. He nearly dropped to the ground as his legs became too weak to hold him up. But just as he was about to fall, Brody and Declan grabbed him and helped him to his tent. There they sat him down by a large wooden table with chairs all around it.

"The people have given the five of us a lot in gratitude for freeing them. That's above and beyond what they have done for each other as everyone is coming together as a community here. Our people are coalescing in a way we never dreamed, or heard of except for in stories," Declan explained.

"The Elders Council is a group of people from each village chosen by their people to represent them. We meet with them quite often as they help make decisions and have informed us of some changes the people wanted. Such as, the people want to be able to see structure in their lives. Even with the best intentions, we are turning everyone's lives into chaos.

"In an effort to reassure the people, they have asked that those of us who lead do so in an area that can be seen from anywhere in the valley. That way if they need assurance as to their safety they can just look down to the center of the valley to see us. Just seeing the command camp makes people feel safe. Knowing that their lives are being cared for helps make things easier on them. They are all afraid of the probable attack from King Corland when he hears about the revolution.

"They have also said that an image of their belief is important. It creates a rallying point for the ideals they are fighting for. The Command Council has decided that you should be that rallying point," Brody said, taking a seat next to William.

"Why me, though?" William asked, taking a drink of water offered to him by Chloe. She and Jacob had entered the tent shortly after the others.

"Because you made all of this happen." His younger sister explained. "Will, it was your leadership that took us from the cavern, to Layeni and back. It was your strategy that freed our villages.

"But there is more to it than that, Will. We are getting a lot of support from the elves in Parinth. Since you and I are half elves, the people see us as a bridge between the two races.

“I heard the others explain most of this to you already. How can you be smart enough to do all you’ve done for everyone and still be too thick to understand a simple principle like this?” she asked.

The verbal jibe seemed to wake William from his stupor and he grinned at his sister. “You’ve been waiting to knock some sense into me for a while haven’t you?” William said.

“Yeah, well I keep hearing people repeat themselves, and I decided you were being an idiot,” Chloe laughed.

“Alright then, everyone, sit down and tell me what you all know, and let’s plan our next move,” William said, taking the lead once again.

“Not yet, Will. You need to rest and delegates from the villages you just brought need to be chosen for the council. Then we will call a full meeting, and you can find out more then,” Declan suggested.

“Until then, there is a bath tent across the way. Bathe, eat and get some sleep. Word has reached us that King Corland might know about us, and so we have decisions to make,” Brody explained.

“Thanks guys, I’ll do what you suggested,” William smiled weakly. He was still having trouble assimilating everything he had been told.

The others got to their feet and were about to leave when Declan, who was in the lead, stopped, causing the others to halt as well. “One question though, Will,” he asked.

“Sure, Dec, what’s on your mind?” William asked, looking up at his friends.

“What was with Emma holding your hand when we found you?” he said trying to stop himself from laughing.

William instantly felt his face and neck flush, "Well, she was overwhelmed by all the people in the valley," William replied, "She just grabbed my hand for support, I guess," he said, trying to keep his demeanor calm while looking at the entire group.

"That's what I thought, too. Enjoy your rest, Captain," Declan said and turning, he and the others left the tent. When they were outside, William heard all of them burst out laughing.

He then heard his sister say, "You boys are so stupid." And as she continued to berate them for their jokes, their voices grew softer.

'T*he lot of them are a bunch of jokers,*' William thought, but he couldn't help but laugh as well.

Chapter 19

In the Age of King William the First

Nothing catastrophic had yet to occur from all the fighting. The four catapult boulders had done considerable damage to some homes and businesses but nothing that couldn't be rebuilt. The fact that most of the citizens were down below where it was safe was enough to write the damage off as negligible in William's mind.

The volleys and counter volleys between archer divisions was about as impressive. So far, twenty archers on Czariana's side of the wall were injured, none of which mortally. On the other side of the wall, it seemed to William that Marcus' men had taken more casualties. It appeared that they even had some dead due to their lack of cover, but still, their numbers were hardly affected.

The Elander troops had tried on several occasions to rush the walls. After the gun crews in the Defense Hall had destroyed the siege towers, the enemy attempted to climb over the walls with ladders. Since then, Marcus appeared to have given up such grand hopes of gaining the walls directly.

Declan had gone inside and opened the rear access from the cavern to do a survey of the damage in the city with the other ministers. In this battle, he really wasn't calling the shots, anyway, since it was Brody's role as Prime Minister and the Minister of Defense to see to the city's protection. William just stood and watched as the useless arrows flew through the air with no targets to impact within the walls.

He knew that Marcus would be getting impatient with the lack of progress from either side. This was the true goal William had in mind. By letting his opponent get angry and make stupid mistakes, things would only get worse for Marcus. The one thing William was sure of was that Marcus' inexperience could be capitalized upon. Since the youth most likely wouldn't take advice from anyone he saw as below his station, he would be on his own and would definitely screw up somewhere. With few people dying this was far from a regular battle. William was sure that his young opponent's battle lust would begin to get the better of him sooner or later, giving the people of Andraya a window to take advantage of.

Marcus' only options left to him were to breach the gate or wait until everyone starved. Not knowing the reserves in the city, that could take years and a young man wouldn't have the patience for that. He would lose too much face with his men in his mind. So it was, that William watched the forest in the distance and smiled when he saw a tree top start to rustle. They were building a battering ram.

Hours passed and as night began to fall he ordered the archers to stop firing. Instead, he decided to really get his opponent angry.

"Declan, Brody, call for Operation Fire Storm," William commanded. The two men nodded and, issuing orders to runners and banner communicators, they prepared for yet another sting to Marcus' battle plans.

As command flags were quickly raised, William's attention turned to a small figure shuffling towards him.

"Ambassador Shihome, it gladdens my heart to see you well in this troubling time," William said to the individual now standing before him.

The tiny Kingdom of Golameed, located to the East of Andraya, was the home of the Gnomish people. Small in stature and in strength they coped with adversity through what they called science. This, science, was the study of the world around them, how it worked and interacted. To the very studious people of Golameed, it was almost revered as a religion of sorts. While the other races excelled at magic, Gnomes looked at mysticism as illusion and parlor tricks. To them, real wonder came in the form of glass tubes and small explosions.

"As it does mine to see you in all your splendor, King William. I come to tell you that my people are ready for their part in the coming operation," the little man replied.

"Are you sure you want to involve your people in this mess, Ambassador?" William asked, genuinely concerned.

"The people of the Gnomish home land have never had such true friends as the people of Andraya. As our Empress' representative, I assure you we stand with you," the Gnomish Ambassador replied.

"Your friendship is enough for our people, Ambassador, but your science is welcome. Please prepare your people for their part," William said, placing his fist against his upright palm and bowing at the waist.

Ambassador Shihome returned the gesture and quickly moved to where his people were stationed.

William redirected his attention to the four catapults on the walls as they were angled towards the outside edges of the battle field. Huge barrels were loaded into their launchers as each device prepared to launch. The commanders waited until they received signals indicating everyone was ready, and then issued the command to fire.

All four catapults launched their payloads and were quickly reset and reloaded. As their projectiles hit the ground, they exploded in a haze of fluid, soaking everything in their path. William watched as understanding filled the men below, and they started running for cover. Volley after volley of barrels flew through the darkness, exploding as they impacted the ground outside the city walls. This time it was quickly followed by the sound of grinding stone as the launch doors below opened. As soon as they opened, the voice of the Sergeant was heard yelling fire and seven flaming bolts flew out of the city walls and landed where the barrels had targeted earlier. As quickly as the burning logs fell to the ground, the grass and anyone too close burst into flames as all of the barrels of spilled oil caught aflame.

The grinding sound of stone on stone echoed in the evening air, indicating that the Defensive Hall was closing their launch doors. Suddenly, a shrill whistle sounded inside the city walls adding to the noise of the commotion bellow. Next, a loud hiss filled the air as William turned to watch the Gnomish contribution to Czariana's defense.

He waited for several seconds and was about to write off Shihome's invention as yet another Gnomish failure, when the night sky filled with brilliant projectiles. The Gnomes had invented a secret concoction which they called Black Powder. Black Powder had the capability to burn rather violently and, after years of research, as well as countless scientists lost to the discovery, the Gnomes had perfected its use.

Now William watched as thousands of arrows propelled by Black Powder flew over the city walls increasing the chaos in the field below. William had asked that the arrows be aimed to avoid hitting anyone, a goal it appeared they had achieved as most of the bolts fell either to the sides of the enemy or behind them.

The screams from the field were horrible and William said a quiet prayer for the men who were burning or hit by a stray arrow. He hoped that they would die quickly or not be hurt too badly. This was the main part of the plan that bothered William, as much as anything. He desperately wanted to avoid anyone dying. The loss of the gun crew still troubled him, greatly. Regardless of Declan's comments on the value of life, inside he still felt for the men outside his gates and their families. Earlier in the day, when it was obvious that his presence on the walls wasn't required, he and Declan gave the news to the crew's parents.

He sat and grieved with them for over an hour. Declan had to leave to help Brody protect the city but William stayed as long as he could. He knew it wouldn't fill the void in their lives created by their loss, but he stayed until he could stay no longer. Emma came when she heard he was below and she stayed with them after he left.

'*If we had met them in the field,'* William thought, '*there would be a lot more people crying over the lost.*' He tried to convince himself this was the right idea, but a single death shook his decision to its core. It was because he realized that people had to die, since Marcus would not relent, that he came to peace with the Fire Storm.

The move had done what it was designed to; it created a bottle neck in the field outside the city gates. Now, like a funnel, all the soldiers were almost being herded toward the main gate. Looking at it now, William hoped it wasn't too obvious, but he didn't want to think about it yet.

He then confirmed that all the troops had been rotated and had eaten. Tonight was going to be a long one. All of the fighting was now done for the day. The oil in the field would burn for a long time yet, keeping the funnel and the chaos below going. The catapult gunners were instructed to keep it burning by firing more oil into the fire zone, if needed. "It appears to have worked," Declan said, looking down at the battlefield before the gates.

"Yes, and with minimal losses by the sounds of things," Brody replied, reading the grief on William's face.

"Will," Declan said softly. The king turned to his friends. "Will, death comes in a head to head conflict. We are trying our best, but that doesn't solve the problem some times. War is not as easy in practice as it is on paper."

"I know, Dec, but it doesn't get easier losing people to that inevitability," William replied, grief etched deep on his face.

"If all goes well, the killing will be done in a couple of hours," Brody said.

"Yeah, let's hope things go according to plan in the next phase. I'm alright guys; I just wanted the best case, no death. But I guess that's the way of things. Are the launch doors closed?" William asked.

"Yes, milord, the weapons are being checked and prepared for the night," replied Declan.

"Good. Well I'm going to get some rest. If you need me, send a runner, but hopefully they will be too busy with the fires to attack us for now," William replied and headed downstairs.

When he got down into the cavern, he was met with worried looks from a lot of the people as he passed them by. He tried to reassure everyone that things were going well, but he couldn't hide the fatigue on his face.

He kept walking towards the Royal Chamber, when suddenly he felt a hand grab his finger. He looked down to see a little boy, not much older than Czaria, looking up at him. He stopped and knelt down by the boy and lifted him into his arms. The little boy instantly wrapped his arms around the king's neck and gave him a big hug. William closed his eyes and hugged the boy back for all his worth. When he felt the little one pull away he looked up and saw a smiling face looking into his, causing him to smile back. They boy grabbed his nose and pretended to steal it and eat it.

The king began to laugh and soon he heard more laughter all around him. Taking in his surroundings, William saw he was encircled by people, all of whom were watching the two with great interest. Everyone was laughing with him and the little boy, who seemed to relish being the center of attention. The king saw a woman and man who looked like they were torn between laughter and mortification. Guessing that they were the boy's parents, he walked over to them and smiled.

"Is this young man yours?" he asked.

"Yes, milord. I'm dreadfully sorry," the woman said and curtsied on shaking legs.

"Don't be, madam, don't be. Your son made a hard day better." He smiled at the couple. "I want this boy's kindness to be remembered. When he saw something that needed fixing he fixed it. He saw I needed a hug and was happy to help. That is a true leader." He smiled at the boy in his mother's arms. "Young man, thank-you."

"You're welcome," the boy replied and the king smiled as the youngster sheepishly buried his face in his mother's neck.

With that he shook the man's hand, kissed the woman on the cheek, and kept making his way home to get some needed sleep.

Chapter 20

In the Age of King Corland the Fourth

William was woken from his sleep by someone shaking him. He looked up and saw Declan and Brody leaning over him. He quickly sat up, but Brody motioned for him to be quiet. Doing as he was instructed, he put on his clothes and followed them as they snuck out of the tent. Quietly, they moved from shadow to shadow until they were near the edge of the encampment. Finally, when they felt it was safe to speak, they turned to William with concerned looks.

"Will, we didn't want to tell you this in the camp," Brody explained, "but the scouts have reported that we are being watched."

"Watched by whom?" William asked.

"They appear to be scouts from the king's army," Declan explained. "Our people caught two and are holding them. We wanted to avoid panicking the people, so they are being held out there." He pointed towards a wooded bluff.

"Good idea; we will tell them in the morning," William replied.

"Do you think that is a good idea?" Declan asked.

"I am not keeping anything from those who put their trust in us. Timing is important, but not secrets. Take me to these men," William said. His friends nodded and led the way to the bluff. They were met by four scouts on the edge of the woods. The scouts then led them to the area the enemy scouts were being held by five more Elvin scouts.

Two men were bound and gagged by a tree, both of which looked a little roughed up. The trio walked over to the tied men and William ordered their gags removed. The guards did as they were told and soon both men were free to talk.

"So you're the head traitor," one of the two captives said. One of the Elvin guards moved in, but William stopped him.

"Yes, I am the appointed leader of these people. You are scouts for King Corland, then?" William asked.

"Well, we ain't here for tea are we?" the second man sneered.

"No, I doubt very much that you are. So anything here interest you?" William asked.

"Yes, how about how many traitors there are in this kingdom?" one of the men replied.

"Yes, well, one traitor is too many for any kingdom, don't you agree?" William asked.

Both men on the ground looked at each other confused.

"No answer? Well of course one traitor is enough. Any man who would have people move against the best interests of the kingdom should have to answer for his crimes, am I correct?" William said to the men.

"So, you admit to being a traitor to the crown?" one of the men asked.

"Not really. I am a traitor to the king, yes, but it would be more accurate to say the crown is a traitor to his people," William said calmly. "Our village was the first that the king turned into a slave camp. Innocent women raped and their men forced to watch, as families were torn apart.

"Then when he saw how much profit there was in a slave camp, he created excuses to make more. Like raising the tribute so high, villagers and townspeople wouldn't stand for it. He stole from the people he had sworn to protect and turned his back on us all.

"Now the king will answer for his crimes. He will repay for all the pain he caused, and if he won't, we won't put up with him and his kind any longer.

"Guards, free these men," he said calmly. His command catching everyone, including the captives, by surprise caused the guards to hesitate.

"You want them released?" Declan asked.

"Yes, men, set them free," he said again, and this time the guards quickly cut the bonds holding the captives. "Go back to the king and tell him what you have seen here. Tell him about the number of people, tell him why we are doing this, or tell him lies for all I care. But I want you to tell him one thing from the people and me. He doesn't have to send scouts to see us. He is welcome to come on his own and we will meet him face to face to discuss everything. Tell him we aren't afraid of him and will not cower in fear." With that, William turned and walked out of the bluff followed by Brody and Declan.

"Do you think that's a good idea?" Brody asked.

"I'm not sure, but we knew it would come to this sooner or later. I just prefer to make it happen sooner. If we act like we are doing something wrong then it gives him leverage against us. If we know what we are doing is right then he has none. Now he knows what we believe and will have to deal with it head on," William explained.

"And if he doesn't agree with us?" Declan asked.

"Oh that. He won't. We are going to have to face his people in battle," William replied nonchalantly.

"Battle!" Brody exclaimed.

"Our numbers are made up of woman and children as much as by battle aged men. How can we go to battle?" Declan added.

"What did you two think was going to happen?" William rounded on the two. "Did you think that enough people would side with us and he would just walk away? Did you think he would just give up his throne?"

"Well no, Will, but we hoped he would work with us instead," Brody replied quietly.

"My father went to the king and pleaded for reason, and since he was weak, Corland had him beaten until he was nearly dead. Then when he attacked the village our people asked him to reconsider and instead he killed your parents," he said pointing at Declan, "and allowed your mother to be raped!" he said even louder pointing the finger at Brody.

"He doesn't care about us; he doesn't care about the people. His family has ruled for so long they have forgotten that they are not entitled to their throne. They serve at the will of the people. They rule for the betterment of all of us, not just them. The government is broken, it is time to clear the slate and start anew," he said, turning around and hanging his head.

Tears began to roll down his cheeks, as he was no longer able to hold them back. Brody and Declan walked to him and placed hands on his shoulders. "The traitor killed our fathers and hurt our mothers," William sobbed, "he is going to pay. If there is no penalty for the guilty, there is no justice for the innocent."

Brody and Declan hugged him from both sides and all three of them cried together. All the emotions of the last month had finally come to a head and were now flowing free.

How long they stood there and cried, none of them knew, but when they stopped they realized they weren't alone. All around them were the elves who were no longer guarding the scouts. They stood and protected the three while they had their moment of weakness. Each of the elves silently stood and waited, until it appeared the trio no longer needed protection. As each one prepared to leave they stopped and nodded their understanding to William, and his decisions that evening.

"This news is going to be difficult for the people to hear," William said finally.

"You're right. They are going to question why the scouts were released," Declan replied.

"We will tell them just what you said to us, Will," Brody said, "That it is time for justice and time to move forward. If they don't understand they are free to leave. They knew this was coming; they just didn't know when."

"About what I said guys…" William tried to explain.

"No, Will, you were right about all of it," Brody said interrupting, "ALL of it." He stifled a sob. "I was just too afraid to deal with it alone. I guess in the end I didn't have to."

"I still shouldn't have been so hard about it," William explained.

"Perhaps more tact would have helped swallow the pill, but that doesn't matter. What does is that you are right and I appreciate that you have the heart to feel my pain, when you have your own to deal with," Brody explained, tears running down his face.

Declan couldn't say anything to his friends as the lump in his throat made it impossible. He had long ago accepted the death of his parents. After seeing their unmarked graves outside the village after they had freed it, their deaths finally became real to him. Will's words had hurt him too, but he was past the sharp pain their deaths caused him to feel. Now it was the dull ache that would never leave his heart.

Chapter 21

In the Age of King William the First

As night crept on, William, Declan, and Brody stood on the wall and watched the chaos below. The fires on the edges of the foothills were still burning in places, but most had long since burned low, having run out of grass to burn. Brody gave the command to stop firing barrels of oil into the fires, allowing them to burn out.

The decision was made about an hour ago to just let the fires die down, allowing some calm to settle over the men on the field below. William didn't want anyone else to get killed. They decided that after hours of fighting the fires, their enemies wouldn't have the energy to turn up as tantalizing an opportunity as the one they were now about to give them.

William nodded his consent to Brody who then issued commands to a pair of lantern communicators. One had his light turned inward toward the center of the city and the other had his out over the walls. Both flashed the messages to their receivers and once confirmation was flashed back, Brody then went into the gate house, located at the base of the turret above the main gate, and gave the order to open the gate.

The gears and pulleys groaned and clanked as the gate began to open. Then on cue, several guards upon the wall began to yell that someone was opening the gate. Others took up the shouts and soon the entire wall was a stir with people rushing to the gate house. The sounds of battle could be heard on the field below as sword met sword high above them on the castle walls. The three leaders stood and watched as their men sparred against each other, making it sound like a fierce battle was taking place for control of the gatehouse. They were careful to not have too many combatants. The Hawks hadn't seen anyone enter since the first group and there were only four of them.

William turned and looked over the wall from his place in the shadows and smiled as motion was stirring within the area of the enemy command tents. He suddenly saw a figure jump out of Marcus' tent and realized the enemy king was now aware of this latest development. Quickly, soldiers within the camp burst into action as orders were shouted and men started to form into battle groups.

Screams of pain joined into the unseen drama on the wall. It was so convincing that William was almost fooled into believing that a life or death battle for the gate was going on behind him. More men were called and shadows could be seen running from end to end of the wall to help "take back the gate" as the men shouted for support.

Suddenly, a loud battle cry came from the enemy troops as the men on the plain below surged towards the castle gate. Carrying on with the performance, yells of warning went out about the enemy attack. But it was too late now, as thousands of men surged into the city. Female soldiers started screaming as if they were being attacked, working the enemy troops into a frenzy of battle lust, causing many of them to surge even faster.

Minutes passed and the yelling hoard kept pushing into the city through the open gate. The sparring on the city walls started to quiet down a bit, giving the impression that the battle was coming to an end. This was enough to increase the urgency of the raging army, now flooding into the Kings Way.

William watched and listened as the din of surging soldier's shouts filled the night air. Calls of "Hurry before we lose the gate" and "I can hear it closing" echoed as the throng pushed forward. Even in the early morning darkness, William could see the excitement the prospects of malice brought to these men.

'*Declan was right*,' William thought to himself, '*these men aren't our equals. They have been reduced to animals in their lust.*'

Brody watched closely for the signal on the far side of the city. He knew the enemy's numbers would soon reach the maximum that the Kings Way could hold but the more that crammed in the better. He anxiously waited for the signal as the surging masses slowed to a pushing mob. When he was about to order the gate shut without the signal, it came. Flashing from the far end of the city, at the end of the Kings Way the warning was given.

"Close it!" Brody ordered. Suddenly, there was a loud clang and the wall began to vibrate. No one could see it from their vantage point but everyone knew what that shudder signified. The gate was falling back into place. But Brody was careful to let it drop at a gradual pace to allow people a chance to jump clear as it descended.

At one point, the groaning of the metal gears grew silent as the gate stopped descending. Concerned, William walked over to Brody to see what was wrong.

“They must have placed logs under the door to stop it from dropping.” Brody explained.

“What are we going to do now?” William asked worry edging his voice.

“Unless those logs are over a foot thick it won’t stop the gate for long.” His friend chuckled.

William watched as Brody nodded to the gate control officer. The man grabbed the door brake and completely disengaged it. The entire weight of the door was now being drawn down by gravity.

A loud groan echoed in the darkness, followed by a snap and the door quickly dropped. The familiar clang told everyone on the wall that the gate was now closed.

William looked down at the gate below to see almost all the cavalry still outside trying to get in to join their comrades. He searched the field and found Marcus and his general sitting on their horses at the rear trying to understand what had happened.

“Brody,” William turned to his old friend, “signal Logan to prepare himself,” he said as he turned and climbed to the command deck.

When he reached the top, he commanded the lamp communicator to signal what was happening to the Rangers. William knew they would be waiting in the forest for their part to come.

Watching the horizon he saw what he was waiting for. The long night was over, as the sun began climbing over the hills. He stood atop the city wall, a clear target for the men below, and waited. The yelling had long ago changed from one of a war frenzied army on the advance, to one of panic, as the men in the Kings Way finally realized that they had entered a trap.

While designing the city Declan suggested the construction of the Kings Way. Using the structure of a canyon, he decided that if the Czariana archers could hold high ground they would be able to open fire on an enemy from relative safety. This would allow their troops to kill anyone within the Kings Way with few of their own casualties.

The only problem with the idea was that a city cannot have its main road into it only branching off at its center. With that in mind Declan then designed each intersection along it with a large mobile wall. The walls could be moved into position and locked in place when the trap was needed. By sealing each side road and alley, they were able to create the ravine Declan envisioned. The mobile walls also had a large stairway to the top of each one, allowing soldiers to climb up and line the Kings Way quickly.

To keep enemy troops from getting out through broken windows or doors, each building that lined the Kings Way was designed with only walls backing out onto it. The problem was that when it was finished Brody commented that it looked like a death trap not a street. It was decided that fake windows and doors should be placed on the buildings to give the appearance of a regular central city street.

The final piece of the massive trap was added later in the city's design. To allow more people to be contained in the area, the end of the Kings Way that came right up next to the Central Court was opened into a large T shape. Now there was more room for enemy soldiers to fill before attackers would realize the trap they were entering.

Although the men who were packed tightly in the Kings Way had realized what had happened, the men out on the plain were still unaware what was occurring.

William nodded to the Lantern Communicator and waited for confirmation from the other positions on the wall. A few minutes later the communicator nodded back at the king, who then turned towards the remaining force outside the gates.

"To the advancing armies of Eland," he started. He heard other men along the Kings Way echoing his words. Along the entire length of the Kings Way, heralds were reading the exact same speech he was now about to make. Logan stood at the far end of the trap doing the same, rounding out the Royal announcement.

"To the advancing armies of Eland, this battle has come to an end. The soldiers within the city walls are trapped. Be warned that archers are prepared to fire at any act of aggression." William said, pausing to allow the information to set in to those who listened.

"Each of you now has a choice to make. You can either disarm and be taken peacefully or you can meet your end at the tip of a well placed arrow.

"Make no mistake, we have done our best in the last two days to kill as few of you as possible, but we will do so if we are forced. Barrels are now being lowered to you in the street, where you will deposit your weapons.

"To those of you outside the city walls," he carried on, knowing that the heralds behind him were still speaking for the benefit of those trapped in the street. "You too shall throw down your weapons or face an attack by a much larger force, both from the walls of this city and," he nodded to the Banner Communicator who raised a large green flag high above them, "from the forest behind you."

As he spoke people began to emerge from the shadows of the trees. First it was the support people and engineers from Marcus' army. But following close behind them was a large army of cavalry, archers and swordsmen. The new troops were all dressed in green and brown clothing to match their forest surroundings. William smiled to see his sister leading the Rangers forward.

This was the dangerous part. The men in the city had no chance. They were packed so tight that they couldn't fire a bow, and swords would do them no good against archers on the rooftops. But out in the field, if the soldiers weren't dissuaded by numbers alone, fighting would break out and the Rangers would be forced to fight for their lives.

Quickly William thought of something. "To you outside the gates thinking of fighting your way to freedom, if you commit any acts of aggression towards those on the field I will order your people in the city to be executed. If any blood spills this day it will be yours, make no mistake.

"King Marcus," William called out, "you have been bested. I command you to yield the field and accept our terms for your surrender."

Men inside the city walls and out on the plain began to lower their weapons not knowing what else to do. The general gave a command and more men began to do the same. Marcus started to angrily address the general but the stolid man only calmly explained their options. Turning from his king, he once again issued orders for his men to continue disarming.

"My coward of a general might have had the fight taken from him, but I'll do no such thing!" Marcus yelled. He suddenly spurred his horse forward and urged it right at the wall of Rangers behind him. William saw archers take aim but he held up his hand and no one fired; instead they allowed the shamed king to run for home.

"General!" William called. The man who had gotten down from his horse and was disarming with his men stopped. He listened closely as the king addressed him. "Your men will not be harmed if they cooperate. Can you guarantee that cooperation until we can speak?" he asked. Without hesitation the general bowed low to the king with his hand over his heart.

With that one act, it was done. The Siege of Czariana was over. William stepped down from the wall and sat on the floor of the command deck. He smiled to himself for the first time in days, knowing everything had gone alright.

Chapter 22

In the Age of King Corland the Fourth

The meeting with King Corland was set. The Freedom Fighters prepared the camp for the arrival of the king's delegation. It was decided that the camp needed to be arranged in such a way as to appear more as a city, rather than a large festival. They were arranged in four quadrants; by lining up the tents into straight lines they gave the camp a much more organized look. The valley was still filled with tents, but they were straight and precise in their alignment with each other. It was decided that the women and children would stay as hidden as possible in the tents, while large groups of men would line the road to the central command area. This would make it appear that where you saw some armed men, there were likely more.

All of the men who had armor were brought closest to the command tents, in an attempt to look like Knights protecting their commanders. Each piece of their façade was an attempt to look as imposing as possible. The cost of open conflict with the royal army would be too high, so great pains were taken to appear as strong as they could. They hoped all of the effort would cause the king to think twice about declaring war.

Unfortunately, though, one of the images being remade was quickly getting annoyed with the whole process. "Violet," William said with a moan, “these robes are hotter than the seventh circle,” he complained.

“Now listen here, General William,” the large woman said grabbing his leg and turning him straight for what seemed like the thousandth time, “you are meeting with a king and we want you to look as regal as he. So if we can do all this work to rearrange tents and lives you can stand the heat!” she scolded.

Violet was one of the people William’s group had freed when they all spilt up. She was a large woman, maybe ten years older than William, with an amazing spirit. When he found her village, she was being forced to mother the soldiers. She would spend the days feeding them all, and the nights in a less than complimentary role.

Yet after she was freed, she took to William almost instantly as his personal assistant. She fed him, fretted over him, and protected him with a single minded attention. It had come to Will’s attention that her own son had been killed when their village was captured, and it was to this that he attributed her attention. Long having lost his own mother, he couldn’t help but enjoy the kindness.

A giggle came from the tent opening. William quickly turned to see who it was and was abruptly turned straight again by his large seamstress. As he was spun forward again, William was overjoyed to see Emma at the opening of his tent. “Hi, Emma, am I needed for something? Should I come back to this later?” he asked almost pleading.

“No, *General*,” she giggled again, “nothing of the sort. I just came to see what all the commotion was about.” William’s attention shifted to the growing crowd outside his tent opening.

“Oh for the love of,” he exclaimed, “Emma can you disperse them please? It may sound like I’m fighting a pack of rabid dogs in here, but let them know it's not that bad. It's nearly, but not quite," he mumbled, which earned him a pin in the behind as a reward, causing him to shout in pain.

Emma walked out the tent and yelled out to the crowd that everything was alright and urged everyone to go about their business.

"There, you old goat, they are all gone," she laughed, walking back into the tent.

"I am not an old goat," William pouted, "and for pity's sake, I'm going to look a fool in all this purple," William complained again.

"Purple is the royal color, General," Violet said, putting another needle in the fabric as she tailored it to sit on his frame properly. "You know this would be easier if you squirmed less," she boomed, "and put some meat on your bones!" she mumbled.

"What was that Violet?" William asked with a grunt, and a scream as a needle found his rear end for a second time.

"If I wanted you to know what I said I would have spoken louder, wouldn't I? You need to learn of a woman's prerogative young man," she lectured sternly, but she hid a smile from the young leader as she said it.

"Emma, please get me out of this," William pleaded again.

"Look, Will, Violet is right. You need to appear as an equal to the king or we could lose a lot of face. Too many of our people will die if we have to go to war," Emma said in a matter of fact tone. "Besides," she said, her voice taking on a good natured tone, "you need to have your ego deflated a bit. Your head is beginning to swell like Declan's rear-end."

This caused all three of them to burst out laughing.

"Oh Emma, that's not funny," William said trying to control his laughter. "How is he by the way?" he asked.

"He'll be fine," she replied. "He screams like a girl when he has to go to the washroom, but the rash is starting to clear." She giggled at the thought.

"Oh I wouldn't want to be him in a million years right now," William said.

"Well that's what the fool gets for wiping his behind with poison ivy!" Violet exclaimed. This caused another round of laughing to erupt.

"Why, General William, you look a little uncomfortable. Are you hot?" Emma prodded him with another jibe.

"That's it. Violet I command this camp, yes?" William asked the woman working on his robes.

"Yes, General, in most things. But if you think you're going to command me to stop think…" she attempted to say, but was cut off.

"No, I know you are enjoying my suffering too much to give that up. But I was just thinking, isn't there a saying that says 'Misery loves company'?" William asked.

"William." A stern call came from behind him.

"Yes, General, I believe it goes something like that," Violet grinned, still working with the cloth.

"Violet!" Emma said louder.

"That's what I thought. Well then, I feel that it would appear more regal if, perhaps, I had a hand maiden for the meeting. What do you think Emma?" he asked.

"HAND MAIDEN!" Emma yelled.

The big woman held back her laughter with difficulty as she replied, "Yes, sir, an extra servant at your side would be a good idea. It would boost your image considerably."

"Good. Then could you please see to it that Emma is there to fill the role?" he asked.

"Why you pompous…" The strangled cry shouted from the tent entrance.

"Yes, General, I think I can arrange for her to be there with you," Violet replied, not looking up from her work.

"Excellent," William said. Then he thought to himself, '*You know, misery does love company!*' and he smiled. He really did feel better. Although he wasn't sure if it was because Emma was getting a bit of just desserts, or if it was because she would be there when he met with the king. The thought of meeting with the king suddenly renewed all of his fears. He had been studying as much as he could on the codes of war, but none of it belied his ever growing dread. Soon he would be face to face with the man who killed his father and destroyed their lives.

Two days later, the camp hummed in nervous excitement. The king was due to arrive at noon to meet over lunch with William and the other Commanders. Declan was given the role as second in command. The choice was easy. Since the second never sat during such meetings and, well, Declan still couldn't sit after his unfortunate choice of greenery, he was the obvious choice. Of course his study of warfare and his knowledge of weapons was the real reason. But his unfortunate circumstance made for a joke no one could turn down. Considering Declan's own penchant for friendly torment, everyone felt that turnaround was fair play.

When the herald was seen taking his place at the top of the valley, William, Declan, and six men in newly forged armor stood patiently waiting for the king's arrival. Then with all the fanfare one would expect from a sitting king, the herald proclaimed the approach of King Corland Lianthus, eighth ruler of the Lianthus dynasty. Following the loud proclamation, trumpets sounded and the King of Andraya rode into the valley, followed by a boy and six knights also on horseback.

But the king wasn't about to allow William and the people in the valley to be the only ones to be dramatic in this exchange. In a show of force, as soon as the king's delegation entered the valley, a trumpet sounded. It was quickly joined by others and soon it was clear that the entire valley was surrounded by troops.

The sight of the entire Royal Army surrounding them stole William's breath for a moment. But he had been warned to expect such a show of force. Taking a deep breath he quickly composed himself. He watched the king's delegation slowly make its way to where he stood.

William waited for the king to dismount, and Brody stepped forward bowing low to the king. "King Corland Lianthus, I present to you Lord William Duthain." Everyone had agreed that titles would be important so, once again, William received a promotion without asking for one. He was now Lord of the Free People of Andraya. They also gave him a last name. He never had one before, since the people of his village never kept to such a practice. But when everyone felt he needed one, he knew the name he would take immediately.

"If it wouldn't be improper, then I would choose Duthain." William had said at the meeting. Locking eyes with his foster father,

Bachand Duthain, he waited with bated breath for the response. The elf couldn't find his voice as his emotions overwhelmed him almost instantly. He nodded his agreement and hugged William hard against him. The memory brought a smile to William's face as he turned to the king.

"King Corland, I welcome you," William said bowing slightly.

"Thank you, Duthain," the king replied, being clear he would not speak the assumed title.

"Well, Lianthus," William replied. The disrespect he showed in return caused the king's face to turn bright red, "who is it you bring as your council?"

"This is my son, Marcus Lianthus, Prince and future King of Andraya," the king replied, introducing the boy, who never moved a muscle.

"I see, welcome, Prince Marcus. This is my second in command Captain Declan of the first regiment." William introduced his half elf cousin who stood silently behind him. Like Marcus, Declan didn't move, but the look on the king's face was one of unimpressed boredom.

William couldn't help but notice to what lengths the king was going to insult everyone around him. He wasn't sure how to read this, but his anxiety seemed to be calmed by it. Almost as if it was a character flaw William could use against the king.

"Well, King Lianthus, shall we dine?" William asked.

"That is why I am here, Duthain," the king replied. William couldn't help but see how Corland purposely ignored his attempt to show mutual respect. With that, Brody led them all to the tent where lunch was to be served.

King Lianthus sat with his son at his shoulder, and across the table sat William with Declan at his. William didn't know if the boy had eaten or not, but he made sure Dec had so he wouldn't be uncomfortable having to watch others eat. He wasn't used to having to pretend to be self absorbed. William was about to call for the servants to bring the meal, when a rustle at the tents entrance caught his attention. Whom he saw enter nearly caused him to spit his wine across the table at the king.

Emma entered the room, but instead of being clothed in the white outfit of a servant, she was instead dressed in a beautiful gown. The colors shimmered in the sunlight, as the air around her seemed to glow. William had never seen anyone so beautiful in his life, and realizing he was still sitting, quickly got to his feet, followed immediately by the king.

"My dear, I apologize for the delay," Emma said, gliding over to William's side and giving him a peck on the cheek. "I was detained, ensuring the meal was properly prepared," she said and turned to the king.

"King Corland," Brody announced from his place at the side of the table, "may I introduce Lady Emma Duthain, wife of the Lord Duthain."

The title caught William by surprise. By Brody's announcement everyone was in on this little joke except him. For a moment the room began to spin, but a sharp kick to his leg from Emma quickly brought him to his senses. Attempting to react appropriately, he pulled out his chair for her to sit.

Snapping his fingers angrily in Brody's face he ordered, "Another seat and be quick!"

His friend quickly brought another chair to the table allowing William to sit again. He was glad for the seat, since he wasn't sure if his legs would hold him up any longer.

Brody then clapped twice, giving the signal for lunch to be served. Once the table was laid and the royals were served, the servants left the room to allow the discussion to take place.

"Duthain, your presence here constitutes an act of war," King Corland said, starting the conversation as they ate.

"Yes, I'm aware of that, Lianthus, but I am hoping we can resolve our differences without having to come to that," William replied.

"I'm sure you do, since your camp is made up of as many women and children as men," Corland said, staring at the young man across the table from him.

"That it does, but each of them has a reason to fight. Although they don't have the strength of a standing army, they have the heart," William said, pretending not to notice the amount of knowledge that the king had obtained. It had been discussed that the details of their camp would already be known by the king. This piece of information was already assumed by everyone who prepared William for this meeting.

"Well be that as it may, the Andrayan army is seventy five thousand strong. We could walk over this camp without even slowing." Again Corland seemed to be testing William's reserve.

"Oh dear, you seem to have dribbled a little bit," William said, apparently not paying attention to the king. "Let me help you with that," he said, gently taking a napkin to the corner of Emma's mouth.

"Thank you, dear," she replied with what seemed to be a loving smile.

"You were saying, Lianthus? Ah yes, you're probably right there as well. And you're welcome to try. But you see, you won't do that," William said nodding at Brody to refill his plate.

"And why, dear Duthain, do you think that?" King Corland replied, giving up the premise of eating.

"Because the laws set down by the Rulers of Old declare that you can't," William replied. "No, since our forces are made up of women and children you cannot attack us."

"Your forces?" Lianthus said incredulously. "You call that rag tag collection of village scum a force?"

"My word, Lianthus, you should study the laws laid down by the First Kingdoms as well as the nature of your enemy better. Each of those people out there is responsible for a weapon. Each child has been assigned a knife, each woman a bow, or club, each man a sword or spear. We are, by the ancient definition, an army," William said, still eating nonchalantly. "But more important to our current conversation, you have declared we are an army," William added, stopping his eating and staring right into the eyes of the man across from him.

"I did no such thing, young upstart," the king shouted, jumping to his feet.

"Yes you did, you old tyrant!" William yelled back jumping to his. "When you claimed that our presence was an act of war. Our presence could only be an act of war if we were an openly armed, militant force! We ARE openly militant as evidenced by our actions. In freeing the slave villages you created and by capturing the soldiers that held those people, we have proven to be confrontational." William pounded the table in front of him making everyone in the room jump as plates and cutlery clattered.

"You came into this camp thinking you could scare us into submission with your fan fare and pomp. But you will never make us surrender. You killed innocent men, woman, and children. Your soldiers committed atrocities in your name, murdering, raping, and pillaging your own people for nothing more than greed! No, *King* Corland, we will not back down from our position and you cannot attack us because our women and children outnumber our men, and ancient law won't allow it. Instead, I issue the Challenge!" William yelled.

Years of pain, and weeks of battle had taken its toll, and the young man's composure gave way to rage. William had been running on instinct, making decisions at the spur of the moment. But the drama, the arrogance of the king, and the anger that filled the young man exploded from him.

A gasp filled the room from everyone including Marcus. "You would Challenge me for the throne!" Corland said in a shocked whisper. No one expected this turn, not even William, but it was the only way he could think of to save his people from going to war.

"I would, and do. King Corland Lianthus, I Lord William Duthain challenge you to hand to hand combat. If I should win, you will remove yourself from the throne. If you win, everyone in this camp shall submit to an order of execution," William declared.

"Young man, I am a seasoned veteran of multiple campaigns. I am master of several hand to hand weapons, some of which you have never even heard of. If you challenge me, I choose the weapon and you will have no choice but to use it. Do you realize that?" King Corland warned with a large smile on his face.

“I do. Choose your weapon and set a date and time,” William replied, leaning on the table staring down the man he hated so much.

“The date and time is in one week, at the Andrayan capitol city of Baruth, at noon. The weapon will be a Natal. I will see to it that one is made available to you. As required by the Ancient Laws, laid out by the kings of the Ten Kingdoms of antiquity, I give you my word,” the king grinned.

A Natal? William didn’t have a clue what the heck that was. As far as he knew, it could be a dinner fork. But that wasn’t going to stop him now that he made his move.

“I accept. We shall meet in one week from today, before your city gates and we shall decide this with Natal,” William accepted as scripted within ancient law.

“Excellent!” Corland boomed, and turning on his heel he headed for the opening of the tent. “I shall see you on the field of battle, Duthain. Madam Duthain,” Corland said bowing slightly to Emma. Then with a flourish he walked out of the tent.

When he had gone, everyone was silent. The air seemed to have been sucked out of the room. But William knew what they were thinking. What had he done, and did he go too far?

Chapter 23

In the Age of King William the First

The people began to move out of the underground fortress and into the moonlight for the first time in over a week. A day had passed since the people of Andraya captured the Eland army, but they were only now emerging from the cavern. William decided that night would be the best time since they wouldn't have to deal with the bright sun right away. While he left the movement of the people to his wife, he, Declan, and Brody all made their way out of the city to meet with the Eland general. Going down into the Hall of Defense, a launch bay was opened, and the three men climbed down to the field below using a ladder.

While they walked towards the location they knew the general was being held, a woman quickly rode up to them and jumped off her horse.

"Chloe!" William exclaimed rushing forward giving his sister a warm hug.

"Will, it's good to see you," she replied.

"It has been so long, little sister. You look well," William said.

"Living in the green does that to you brother. You look well, too, although with that much rock around you I can't see how," Chloe laughed, and punched her brother in the shoulder.

"Come with us Chloe, we have to meet with the enemy general now that Marcus has fled," William said. Chloe nodded to her brother.

"I sent two scouts to trail that coward. They will make sure he goes straight back to Eland without so much as splashing one of our people," she explained.

"Good thinking. I don't want him hurt though. All we need is for this blood feud with his family to spill over to the Eland Royalty," William warned.

"I'll send word as soon as we've finished here," she replied.

Brody and Declan also welcomed the young Ranger warmly. As they walked, they discussed the battle and all the other news that Chloe had learned in her travels. All of the conversation died down, though, as they drew close to the general, waiting for them at attention.

"I apologize for the wait, General," William said with question in his voice.

"High General Austin," the man replied.

"Thank-you, General Austin. Like I said, we apologize for the delay; we were seeing to the people in the city until now," the king explained. "We have brought healers with us, to tend to your wounded," William said.

"We have none that need healing my lord," the general replied.

"Excellent, so the fires didn't hurt anyone too badly?" William replied with relief.

"Not exactly my lord," the general said, "any man who was too injured to naturally heal, King Marcus ordered that they be killed."

Shock overtook William, causing him to go numb from head to foot. "He had them executed?" William said incredulously.

"Yes, my lord. He said we wouldn't waste valuable resources on them. In fact, when the men were dead he ordered them be thrown back in the flames to save having to carry them home." Again the cruelty of the act and the cold of the general's voice shook William to the core.

"General, may I ask you a question?" Declan asked coming forward.

"I am your captive, as are all my men. You can ask anything you wish, sir," he replied.

"You seem rather matter-of-fact about all this. Does it not bother you?" the Andraya General asked.

"Yes, to be honest, it bothers me greatly. Some of those men were people I served with for years. But you can understand that as a soldier I am to obey, not to question," General Austin replied.

"Not here, General. Never here," William replied in a whisper. Everyone was silent until William could digest this horrific news.

"General Austin, I have several judgments to lie at your feet, as the remaining commander of your army," William said.

"I accept full responsibility for the actions of my men, majesty," the general replied.

"Good, you are as I had hoped, a man of honor. Then I bind you with your honor, General, to the following terms. You and your men shall be prisoners of the people of Andraya for one year and one day. You shall swear on your honor to abide by that judgment and will be held to account for yourselves.

"I will not have you guarded, but instead, you shall be watched over, unseen by the Rangers," he said, motioning to Chloe.

"If anyone attempts to leave before the end of the term, they will have proven themselves dishonorable and shall be hunted down and executed. What say you?" William asked.

"That is most generous of you in your position, King William. I accept on behalf of my men," the general said, his stern face softening a bit.

"Good. The next term to be met by you and your men is the responsibility to help our countrymen and I rebuild. Everything that was destroyed on your path to Czariana is to be rebuilt and our people made whole again. What say you?" William asked again.

"Again my lord, your judgment is a just one and I accept on behalf of my men," the general said, already looking more relaxed.

"Excellent. The third term is that once all of the damage has been repaired, you and your men shall commit yourselves to helping construct a highway. It is being built between Czariana and the Gnomish capitol of Golameed. You will not have to finish the highway, should it not be complete before your term is completed. You are only required to work until the year and day have been completed. What say you?" William said, smiling slightly at the change that was coming over the man before him.

"King William, before I answer can I ask you a question?" the general asked.

"I would rather an answer first General, you are welcome to ask after that," William said, giving a clear indication of command.

"Yes, my lord. In response, I accept your term on behalf of my men," the general said, coming to attention.

"At ease, General. There is no need to get overly formal again, now please ask your question," William said, expecting the general to ask how many terms there were.

"Highness, why aren't you executing us?" the general asked.

The question caught William by surprise. "Why should we General?" he asked.

"We attacked your kingdom, we damaged the city, and we may have even killed your people. Why are we now given this chance to live?" the general asked, more to the point.

"General, we lost some of our sons and daughters when that catapult boulder smashed into our outer wall," William said, pointing at the damage to the wall. "Their parents are now grieving for their loss and all of Czariana grieves with them.

"We worked so diligently to keep you alive, despite your king's intentions. Why would we kill you now?" William said. A look of confusion followed by understanding came across the general's face.

"You understand now, don't you, General?" Brody asked, breaking his silence with a small smile.

"Yes sir, I think I do. Your ballista destroyed our catapults but attempted to miss our men, except for one apparent misfire caused by some of our saboteurs," the general openly admitted. William, Declan, and Brody knew differently but they never said anything. "The fire was also shot wide of most forces, but I thought you were doing that to make us a tighter target. But that wasn't your reason, was it?" he asked.

William shook his head no in response. "You were driving us to the gate then?" General Austin questioned.

William nodded in answer. "Why would you want us in your city, my lord? What has happened to my men?"

"I'll answer that in a moment, but I have one final judgment to hand down to you," William replied, and the general nodded his understanding. "General, the final judgment I place upon you and your men is that you shall govern yourselves. You shall provide for yourselves and you shall shelter yourselves. I will not force shackles on your men, but they must be responsible for their own lives. You can sell your weapons and armor; buy whatever you need from the merchants of Andraya. You may hunt and fish, but you will not have ground to seed and harvest. It's too late in the season for that this year anyway, and next year you would have planted a crop and would be free before it would be cut. What say you to my final judgment?" William asked.

"On behalf of my men, I accept. King William, you have honored me, my men and their families with your just judgment. I swear to you on my blood that my men shall either do as you command, or die in dishonor," the general held his hand over his heart and bowed low, as he did the first time William addressed him.

"Good. General, if you would command your men to take stock of your provisions and supplies. Inventory everything so we can help you manage the transition smoothly. General Declan," William said turning around.

"Yes, milord," the general replied.

"Can you and some men get priests from the city and tend to the dead please? They should be given proper rites of passage to the next world. General, if you have someone who can perform anything required for your dead, please have them join our people at the pyre," William commanded. Both generals quickly set out to do as they were ordered, leaving William alone with his sister and Brody.

"Do you think they will honor the terms you set out?" Chloe asked.

"You heard what I told him. For the next year, keep a large number of Rangers watching them at all times. We will probably divide them up for work projects, since there are so many. I also think we will give them the old quarry as a place to call home for the year. Odds are, we won't need all of them for any individual project, but seventy thousand laborers should help us accomplish a lot in the time I laid out." William replied.

"I plan on releasing most of them quickly, anyway. Once we have finished with Marcus and High King Porthanaclies, they can pretty much go home. I just don't want the Eland soldier numbers to be too high so we can continue keeping the death toll under control," William said as they returned to the city.

Chapter 24

In the Age of King Corland the Fourth

When the Natal was delivered, William wasn't sure what to make of it. It looked like a sickle, but instead of a rounded curve for a blade this one reached back in a shallow arc. The leather bound handle looked like the hilt of a sword. Extending from the handle, a two inch long shaft protruded until it turned forward at a ninety degree angle.

The Natal then had a four inch long extension that came to a sharp point. Drawing from the point, it curved backward on itself forming into a slender blade that was around six inches longer than Will's arm. The blade came to the end with another sharp point. At first he tried to swing it like a sword, but that felt wrong. Everyone who looked at it was confused as to the function of the strange weapon. But finally, after several minutes of confusion, Declan ran to ask Beorn to come and help.

The Elvin weapon smith had been travelling with them since they left Parinth. They all agreed he was the best person to advise William on this strange weapon.

Beorn picked up the Natal and studied it. He held it out like a sword, just as William had, but said that didn't feel right to him either. He turned it around and around until he held it as if the long blade were an extension of his arm and he grunted in understanding.

"Lord William," the large framed elf said, "this weapon isn't so difficult to understand now that I feel it like this. Hold it just as I am." He handed the weapon back to the young man. "You see if you hold it this way, the balance makes it feel negligible, almost as if it is a metal gauntlet along the entire length of your arm." William held it before him and raised it as if to block an attack.

"Yes, I see now, it would make for a great defensive weapon," William replied. "But I don't see how one would attack with it."

"Well," Brody interjected, "if it's meant to be an extension of your arm, perhaps it's also meant to attack as a part of your arm. Look at the pointed front and back tips of the blade. If you were to punch someone with that, it would do a lot of damage."

"Sure, Brode, that makes sense," Declan added. "By swinging your arm backwards you could use the pointed end of the Natal to deliver a stabbing elbow. But I think there is more to it than that," he said.

"I'm sure there is, but what stands out to make you think that?" Beorn asked his apprentice.

"Well, the blade is sharp. Come here to this tree, Will," Declan said. "Try to slice it with the blade."

William moved to the tree and swung at it. He allowed the arc of the blade to slice into the tree causing a long deep gash to be cut into the wood.

"My God, William, this thing is really dangerous!" Brody exclaimed.

"Did you expect him to send me a musical instrument? And worse yet, I need to learn how to fight with it, within five days," William said, fear edging into his voice.

"Easy, Will," Beorn replied, his normally gruff voice calm and gentle. "You will be prepared. Corland's choice of this weapon was made to get you to respond this way. Don't play into his hands. Now focus, as the High Elves and Bachand taught you. It is time to be the master of your emotions. Your life will depend on it." And with that, Beorn began explaining his thoughts to the attentive young man.

Two days passed quickly as William practiced night and day with the Natal. Beorn's idea was simple, use it like brass knuckles to fight a fist fight for attack, but focus on defense. All of his time using the weapon was to prepare for defending the different foreseeable attacks. Unforeseen combat traits of the weapon would have to be adapted to on the battle field.

Beorn also told him not to forget his other fist. Just because the blade was only on one arm, that didn't mean that the other one couldn't be used for punching, grabbing and anything else he needed during a fight. Will was instructed to run as often as he could to try increasing his stamina, another of the ideas added by Beorn. Corland was an older man, softened by years on his throne. William's best chance at beating the older man was to outlast him.

At the end of three days, as the camp prepared to begin the long walk to Baruth, William's mind was at ease. "Is everyone ready?" he asked his four leaders. "Yes, Lord William," replied Declan.

"Dec, do you have to do that, too?" William moaned. Everyone in the camp had taken to calling him Lord William. Of course they also started calling Emma, Lady Emma, which always made his heart leap. But his new title chaffed at him like a harness.

"Yes, milord, I do. You have earned the respect of our people, never mind those of us who would follow you into hell and back," his Elvin cousin replied, nodding his head towards Chloe, Jacob, and Brody. "No matter what happens in four days, you have earned the title king in my mind."

The others nodded their agreement and each one placed their hands over their hearts and bowed their heads.

"Now, it's time to go," Declan said, and giving a couple of quick reminders to his fellows, he turned and rode to the head of his command. They divided the people into four groups rather than five, allowing William's free time to be spent practicing, not setting up and arranging people.

Standing on top of a large stone, William watched the crowded valley. When he was sure everyone was ready, he waved his arm giving the order to move out.

After three days of travel, the camp finally saw the capital in the distance. Tomorrow would be the day of the challenge and they all wanted to get to their camp early, to allow William as much time to rest as possible. Finally, around supper they came to the clearing before the city gates and began to set up camp.

The four leaders set about their duties preparing the camp for their stay. William, as became the routine, went into the woods to practice with Beorn, who had become his unofficial instructor.

Finding a quiet spot where he could focus on instructions from Beorn, William worked on his technique. Swinging, kicking, punching and thrusting, the young man worked himself into a heavy sweat. He would focus on his imagined enemy and attack with the rage directed at the man who killed his father, and brought them all such pain. But when Beorn would detect that Will was getting too focused, he would lash out, causing Will to defend himself from the unexpected.

Working for hours, the two had stopped to discuss tactics when Brody came running up. “The king wants to meet with you, Lord William!” he said panting. Fear took Will’s heart for a moment but he calmed himself and spoke with as much confidence as he could.

“Where is he Brody?” William asked.

“He is at the main gate of the city,” Brody replied, and leading the way, he took William and Beorn to where the king stood waiting impatiently.

“Duthain, you kept me waiting!” the king boomed. William noticed that the boy was with the king again.

“Not my intention, Lianthus,” William replied. “I was detained.” The king looked and saw the Natal in his hands.

“Ah, practicing are we?” the king mocked.

“Oh, this? No, not at all,” William replied with a chuckle, which he hoped sounded genuine. “The Natal is a beautiful weapon. Any real warrior could figure it out quickly enough. No, I just enjoy the gift so much that I don’t let it leave my side.”

An irritated look flashed across the middle aged king’s face. “Well I’m glad you like it. But I didn’t call you here to discuss your love of the Natal. I want to know why all of these people are here?” he said indicating the large gathering outside his gate.

“There is nothing for you to be worried about, Lianthus. As the law of the challenge made and accepted decrees, they have the right to watch the battle being fought on their behalf. Their lives hang in the balance, as much as the two of ours do,” William explained.

"Well, I'll not have the lot of an advancing army within my city walls!" the king demanded.

"There is no reason for them to enter the city. I will announce that none of them should venture anywhere near the gates," William replied.

"Fine, but how are they to watch if they do not enter the city?" King Corland said, frustration painted across his face.

"What do you mean? We fight out here in the open," William replied.

"We were to fight in the city arena, before the people," Corland said, his anger clear. William knew the magnitude of the battle ahead was weighing as heavily on the king's mind as it was on his. That gave him a measure of confidence.

"You only have two options then, Lianthus," William explained. "Fight out here or allow my people in there!" he said pointing to the city.

"We will move the battle out of the city walls," Corland replied venomously. "Your people will never again set foot in my city, so long as I live!"

"Well that won't be much longer will it, King Corland, so they won't have to wait long," William replied casually as he turned and walked away from the king without allowing him to respond. William quietly hoped that the king's hatred towards him might grow. He wanted something that would cause the seasoned warrior to make a mistake. One, he hoped, that he might capitalize upon during tomorrow's battle. His feigned confidence was strangely calming. The nonchalance of his attitude almost made him feel invincible. He knew that this type of confidence was dangerous so he placed his emotions in check. But he still couldn't help but feel that things weren't as bad as he first thought.

When they had gotten far enough away from the gates and the raving king, Brody grabbed William by the shoulders and nearly exploded with excitement. "My God William, you treated him like a doddering old fool back there. What's come over you?" he said, nearly laughing.

"Well, to be honest, his problem only allowed two options according to ancient law. Either our people enter the city to watch the battle, or the battle was to be held outside the gates," William replied.

"Yeah sure, but you were so calm about it all. And the part about Lianthus' life nearly being over; since when did you become a seer?" he said, his laughter getting the best of him.

"Oh that, well, I'm not a seer but he got me angry," William replied, rather sheepishly now that what he said was being openly discussed. "He was trying to bully us around, and I got upset. I guess my troll got out." he chuckled.

"Got out and ran amuck I would say!" Brody replied laughing.

"I think you did very well, Lord William," the deep voice of Beorn spoke behind the two. William and Brody had almost forgotten he was there, he was so quiet. "You handled the man on equal terms, leader to leader, king to king," he said as he nodded respectfully at the young half elf, before walking away.

His words caught William by surprise and walking silently back to his tent with Brody at his side, he thought about tomorrow's fight. In one day, the futures of the people who put their faith in him would be placed in danger. Was he worthy of their trust? Beorn's words entered his mind and calmed his doubts almost instantly. Leader to leader, king to king.

Chapter 25

In the Age of King William the First

The next morning, General Austin finished documenting the inventory, as he had been asked by King William. He also finished tending to the remains of his fallen comrades and was finally able to meet with the king and his advisors at the city walls.

The animosity between the mountain dwelling dwarves and the elves of the forest was as ancient as the races themselves. The general had to admit his own father's prejudices colored his opinion of the half elf king. He was surprised to find, though, that his respect was growing each time they met.

Still, the stories his father told him as a child came to mind each time the general saw King William's pointed ears. Yet, the general's instincts told him he could trust the rulers of Czariana.

'He is only a half elf, after all,' the general told himself. *'Not that Dwarves liked humans any more than elves,'* he thought with a sigh.

What really solidified his growing trust for King William, was how King Marcus regarded the Andrayan ruler. It was no secret that King Marcus hated William and his friends. When Marcus had first become king, General Austin believed he would be a great ruler and followed when the decision to go to war was made.

It was only when the king started to go power mad, that the general began to question their new ruler. With every poor decision Marcus made, which went against Austin's own beliefs, he was beginning to believe that anyone his king hated might not be all that bad.

The rulers of the city led the general into the open blast doors and then up to the top of the walls. When he saw that the bulk of his army was penned like cattle, he was shocked. If it wasn't so serious he would have burst out laughing at the spectacle before him.

When he asked if the men were forced to sleep that way, it was explained to him that they didn't get much sleep.

"In their exhausted state," First Minister Brody explained, "they are less likely to do something foolish, forcing us to react."

The general couldn't help but agree with the idea behind the tactic. But even so, his men needed rest after a hard fought battle and a long night on their feet.

Now that he could account for the status of his men, Austin asked what was going to be done with them. King William explained that the general would be allowed to explain to them the terms that had been agreed to. At that point, if the general could confirm they would submit to those terms, they would be moved to the old quarry to setup their new camp.

The general then set out to communicate with his men. "Your Highness, may I extract my captains so I could explain your terms to them? I will need them to help relay the information to our troops," he explained.

"Yes, communicating with such a large group won't be easy. Logan, order a couple of squadrons forward. They are to help pull out anyone the general needs and to be guards as they move about the rooftops," William commanded.

"Yes, Father, right away," the young man replied. Soon fifteen captains were pulled from the street and had been instructed of the terms of their surrender. They then went out to explain to the trapped men what was to happen next, all under the watchful eye of Andrayan soldiers. Once William was satisfied that the information had been delivered, he began to issue his orders. "Gentlemen, I would like the bulk of our army to help in guiding these men to the quarry," he said to Brody and Declan. "General, you will pick several men who are still outside to prepare your wagons for relocation," the king said. "I also want your belongings inventory report delivered to me by noon." Everyone saluted the king, including General Austin.

"General," Logan said, "I think it would now be wise to separate the inventory for travel."

"What do you think would be best, Prince Logan?" asked the general, genuinely trying to help.

"Have your men put the food into one series of wagons, weapons in another, tents and supplies in another. That way when we come to the quarry we can have your men unload by phases, allowing us to clear unneeded wagons out of the way faster," the young man commanded. The general who had been thinking the same thing set about to do as instructed.

After hours of work, everything was moved around and ready to be transported. General Austin then met with General Declan and Minister Brody at the city gates.

"Is everything ready, General?" Declan asked Austin.

"Yes, General Declan. We have drivers on each of the wagons, and leaders for the cavalry horses," Austin replied.

"Good, and our men are also ready to escort you. Please be advised, General, we are not taking this move lightly. The king has seen fit to pardon your men, and I hope your soldiers don't take his kindness as a sign of weakness. My people have been given orders to kill if provoked. Please warn your people when they exit as it is imperative in keeping them all alive," General Declan explained.

"I would have expected no less. I will watch my men myself and have already informed the members of my command staff to keep them in line. Once we have reached the quarry and make camp, we will be able to explain the situation better to the men, decreasing the odds of violence breaking out," Austin replied. Declan nodded his agreement. General Declan didn't know how the next year would go. Sure it was great to have an indebted workforce to help finish some of the big jobs, but maintaining eighty thousand people was like watching over a city. He hoped William hadn't made a mistake.

Reading the look on Declan's face, General Austin cleared his throat to get attention. "Yes, General?" Declan asked.

"General Declan, you don't seem happy with your king's decision in sparing us all," General Austin questioned.

"Not at all. I know that if need be my troops can keep things under control," Declan said in all confidence, but seeing the look on the opposing general's face, he lowered his guard a bit. "But yes, to be honest, this feels to me like having a hornets' nest in the middle of my house. Leave it alone and everything is fine. Cause something to irritate the nest, and you will end up with stingers in your behind."

Austin chuckled. "General Declan, I give you my personal assurance, that I will not allow the nest to be irritated. King William has given us our lives, and as such, we owe them to him. Some of my men might not like having that hanging over their heads, but our honor requires that we do nothing to take that gift for granted. We will do as we are told, and when our sentence is up, we shall peacefully leave. You have my word, and my vow," the general replied.

This seemed to be enough for Declan, and he commanded the men to open the gate. The grinding of the gears in the gatehouse echoed loudly as the door began to lift. Soon it was high enough that the trapped solders were able to move out of its confines for the first time in more than twenty four hours. Led by Austin and the Czariana command team, and surrounded by Andrayan troops, they started to walk to the old quarry.

William had left the details of moving the enemy to their new camp up to his Commanders. He knew that they could handle things better than he could and he wouldn't be needed for any decisions. If need be his people would deal with the Elanders without him. Like Declan, though, he worried about maintaining a force this large, but he set that concern aside for now. The inventory indicated that their food stocks were large enough to last them a month. This would give them time to settle in. The middle aged king had returned to the Royal Court to begin getting the lives of his people back to normal.

His first order of business was a visit to the Gnomish Consulate Gardens in the delegation quarter of the city. Here, kingdoms surrounding Andraya were welcomed to keep delegations as an open channel between their rulers and the Andrayan Royalty.

Because of their tremendous support in the defense of the city, William made sure the Gnomes understood his people's gratitude. He ate lunch with Ambassador Shihome and spent no small effort explaining his wonder at the Gnomish weapon.

"Yes, Majesty, the Hwach'a is a fantastic defensive weapon," the Ambassador explained. "We have thousands of them defending our borders from attack. Because of their love of science, my people are looked down upon by most of the warring cultures of our neighbors. To be honest, we Gnomes have few such friends as the people of Andraya."

"My friend, it is we, people of Andraya, who can honestly say we don't have many friends such as the Gnomes. I must stress our sincerest thanks, as well as our oath to aide your people whenever you call. If ever you need us we will be there as quickly as we can, you can assure your Empress. May her sideburns grow long and golden," William replied, using the Gnomish blessing of long life.

The Ambassador smiled at this, stroking his own long golden sideburns. "On behalf of her Majesty, I thank you. But between you and me, her sideburns will most likely never grow any longer."

"Oh no Shihome, is she not well?" William asked, genuinely concerned about his Gnomish counterpart.

"Oh yes, she is quite well. It's because she had an unfortunate mishap with a flammable liquid she was testing several years ago. Let me just say that a loud bang and they literally went up in smoke. Because of that, they will never be the same," the Ambassador chuckled, causing William to laugh loudly, which prompted the Ambassador to follow suit.

After his meeting, he visited the damaged areas of the city with the ministers. Now they had to begin the reconstruction of Czariana and Andraya. Sitting at his desk, he listened to reports being delivered as a steady stream of young men and women ran to and from his open air office.

The Central Court of Czariana was designed to make it as open to the public as possible. The city was designed within a great semi circle, with the back of the city being nestled at the base of a huge cliff face. This made attacks from the rear nearly impossible.

Entering the city from the main gate led you down the usually very busy Kings Way. Following that to the very end of the street you would find yourself nearly at the Central Court itself. The Central Court was broken into three areas, the Open Court, the Ruling Court, and the Private Court.

The outer edge of the Central court was one long bazaar, which was located on the city side of the Czariana River. A market place filled with merchants of all of the trades. It was the central commerce area of the city. Shop owners paid a lot for a location in this prestigious part of town.

The first area of the Central court was the Open Court. Accessed only by crossing one of the many bridges that spanned the Czariana River, you easily forgot you were in the middle of a capitol city. The Open Court was a public park with fountains, clipped grass, and treed walkways. Like the name suggested, this area was open to everyone to enjoy. Like most parks, it was just a place to get away from the rush and shoulder to shoulder life of the city.

Across the Diameter of the Central Court, ran a small wall separating the Open Court from the Private Court. This area was created by the people of Czariana. It was a private retreat for the city's royalty to get away from the hustle and bustle of the city proper.

William was never comfortable with being forced apart from his people. With each successive title he achieved, he always felt he was pushed further and further from his roots. The decision not to have a castle was made because he didn't want to be different from them. But, the idea of an impressive ruling court was so ingrained in the minds of the people; they demanded something distinguish the royals from the common man. It was agreed by most of the people that in a negotiation with a foreign power, a strong presence must be projected. Otherwise, they would be seen from in a position of weakness, and that was something everyone could understand as undesirable.

In the middle of the Central Court was the Ruling Court. This large area, completely encircled by trees, was the location where Andrayan law was decided. Here, the three Ruling Court buildings were found.

First, in the middle of the Ruling Court was the aptly named Ruling Hall. It was from within this columned building that the Andrayan monarch ruled. To the left of the Ruling Hall was the Royal Household. This two story building had an open air lower level, and a closed upper level giving the royal family some privacy in their living quarters. It was a large building and was designed to house the household staff, as well as the Royals themselves.

To the right of the Ruling Hall was the Andrayan Central Hall, where visiting Royals could stay. This, like the Royal Household, was two stories with an open main floor. This was the building where celebrations and Royal Banquets were held. The upper floor was where the Royal Apartments were located to house visiting dignitaries.

It was from the Ruling Hall that William now attempted to set the city right, as well as the lands affected by the pillaging and destruction of Marcus' men. Chloe was with him, giving council as best she could.

"William, the villages that were destroyed will need to be rebuilt quickly. There are a lot of people without homes, and I'm afraid they're not happy with you right now," she explained.

"I knew they wouldn't be. Have you met with most of the people? What was lost?" He asked the one question that weighed heaviest on him.

"A couple of people lost items, but most of the damage was to buildings and furniture. Things we can rebuild." She replied.

"Good. Have your Rangers who aren't guarding the Elanders set out and take stock of what needs to be rebuilt. Tell the people that we will be heading out from the castle proper in one week. At that time we will go village by village, rebuilding all that was lost. We will also be taking steps to compensate them for their discomfort before all of this is done," he explained. "For now, have your people deliver strong tents to those without homes from the city's emergency supply stocks. There should be enough here and scattered through the lands to make them comfortable."

She nodded her agreement. "Yes, that will go far in lightening their loads. We will also tell them the story of the battle. Hearing victory against those that caused their current circumstances will give them hope and pride, helping them to rebuild. Anything else you need the Rangers to tell them, big brother?"

"Yes, tell them that I will be amongst the build crews, working to rebuild their homes," he said, focusing on some paperwork on his desk.

“You’ll be there as well?” she asked.

“Yes, I’ll be there as well. I will take part in the reconstruction of their homes. I will also be answerable directly to their criticism. Let them come to me to answer for their pain,” he replied, still working.

“Will, you’re the king. Working in the fields isn’t something that you should be doing,” Chloe replied.

“You’re a Princess, and you live in the fields,” he replied, finally looking up at her with a smile. “Chloe, we haven’t been a regular Monarchy here in Andraya since we ended the reign of Corland Lianthus. I’ll not start separating myself from the people now,” he replied. She nodded at him, and taking her leave she set out to issue her own orders.

“Oh, and, Chloe,” William said before she left, “stay with us for a couple of days, will you? I would like you to travel with us when we go,” he said. She smiled again and nodded her agreement. He missed her presence and now when times were hard he wanted it more than ever.

Chapter 26

In the Age of King Corland the Fourth

It was nearly noon and William, Declan, Brody, Jacob, Emma, and Chloe all sat in William's tent waiting for the announcement trumpets to sound. They were all quiet, focusing upon the battle to come.

"Will, if you need us we'll…" Declan started.

"No, if I fail in this you have to scatter the people. Abandon the tents and have everyone hurry to Parinth to get away from the madness of the king," William said.

"But you made an oath. If we leave, we break that oath. We would all rather die than suffer that dishonor," Emma explained. "I for one don't want to live if it's without you," she said, saying what she had wanted to tell him for so long.

William looked up into her eyes and reached for her. She came instantly to his outstretched arms and rested her head against his chest and began sobbing.

"Man, you guys are all acting like I'm already dead." William tried to laugh, but no one joined him. "Look everyone; this was the only way to avoid having everyone we love die at the hands of that tyrant. It was our only chance, and by the Laws of War I studied, he had to give us this chance."

"Yeah, but Will, you don't even know how to use the dang weapon," Jacob said.

"No, but if I die, even though your lives are his, historical precedent says that he should let everyone live. The decision is his, but all that blood on his hands would be more than anyone would want as their legacy. Besides that, who would bring in his precious crops? You may end up as slaves, but that isn't any worse than it was before," William tried to explain.

"I would prefer death than to suffer that, Will." Declan's anger edged his voice like a knife. "I will die at..." but he wasn't able to finish as the trumpet sounded. With that, Will motioned everyone to lead him out. They exited the tent in pairs. First Declan and Brody came, followed by Chloe and Jacob, and finally with Emma on his arm came William.

They marched through the rows of tents and people towards the area chosen for the battle. It was at the bottom of a small dip in the landscape, allowing for rows of people to watch the battle almost as if it were a natural coliseum. As they marched, William drank in everything around him. The freed people of Andraya were proud again. Banners, in regional colors denoting towns, flew everywhere in the gentle breeze. All of his people lined each side of his pathway. Some cried, some showed signs of fear, and some stood at attention and saluted their young champion.

Still marching onward, he began to recognize familiar faces. Some, like Bachand his adopted father, immediately fell in line behind him as he passed by. Soon his stepfather was joined by Beorn, Violet, Brody's parents, and many others, until his small procession became a parade. They wound their way through the camp until they reached the clearing.

William and his faithful followers approached from the East, as Corland's delegation led from the West until they stood eye to eye with one another.

"Ready to die, rebel?" Corland asked.

"Dying for my people would be worth it. Who do you die for?" William asked calmly.

"I'm not the one about to face a trained soldier," the king replied.

"You're right, which will make your eventual death all the more embarrassing for you," William smirked.

"Enough talk!" Corland shouted and slashed wildly at William with his Natal. The young man quickly jumped out of the way of the slash and, doing a back flip, landed away from his enemy. A startled scream burst from behind him as people scattered out of the way to watch the battle.

"You're an acrobat now?" the king laughed, his eyes wide in battle rage.

"I thought you were going to shut up and fight!" William said rushing forward with a leap directly at his opponent. He made a violent downward slash with his weapon, which landed with a loud clang against Corland's blade. Suddenly, the air was driven from Williams lungs as a punch landed in his midriff from Corland's weaponless hand. Black dots danced before his eyes as his chest muscles contracted.

Not even thinking about breathing, William followed the first rule Beorn taught him, when you're hurt roll away, which he quickly did. Corland's Natal sliced past him and only grazed his shoulder instead of impaling him in the neck. But the shoulder wound hurt enough to drive William's body into action, and he quickly drew another breath. Getting to his feet, the young half elf anchored himself and took the next flurry of attacks from Corland in stride, defending each slash and dodging each stab attempt. He suddenly sensed a shift in direction from the king. Moving quickly, William slipped back to back with the battle hardened ruler causing the momentum of the man to spin him off his feet as he attempted a backward elbow slash.

The two men sliced and dodged each other as they attacked over and over again. William was amazed at the ferocity of the attacks from the king. Using years of experience, the king began to swing wildly at his young opponent. Then with a flourish, he spun his blade about, using the momentum gained to launch a vicious attack that nearly impaled William.

But Beorn's training didn't leave William unprepared. Instead, when William began to sense an attack was coming he began to look for openings in his rival's stance. Several times William saw the same opening and finally he decided to take it. Ducking under the king's backswing; the young half elf dove into his opponent. Driving his shoulder into Corland's exposed armpit, he slammed the king backwards causing him to cry out in anguish.

During another back and forth sequence, as Will was on the attack he noticed what appeared to be looks of fatigue cross his enemy's face. Thinking another chance had come, he shifted his feet, opening his defenses slightly to allow him to launch a stronger attack. He threw his weight behind his weapon in a gamble and almost lost.

Just as he drew his blade downward, the king rolled forward with shocking agility. He slashed wildly at his over eager opponent aiming a killing blow to Will's chest. If it wasn't for the youth's sure feet, a long scratch could have sliced him wide open. It was a mistake Will wasn't about to make a second time, as he slowed his own tempo down to control his raging adrenaline.

Both men had red stains on their clothing, as small and medium sized wounds were opened on each of them from the intensity of battle. Fear was replaced by venomous anger and William let it course through him, setting his nerves on fire.

But remembering his earlier mistake, he cleared his mind and attempted to control the tempest that his rage-filled adrenaline created within him. Keeping a clear head, he focused on the stance his opponent had taken.

Now it was William's turn to be on the offensive again. Instead of using his Natal, he shifted to kicks and punches. Corland defended the onslaught and with a determination driven only from experience, the king fired back. Kicking the legs out from under his youthful opponent, Will quickly caught himself only to return the kick and roll back to his feet. Using his bunched knees, he sprung forward, driving his shoulder into Corland's gut, pushing him backward.

William rolled around and swung his Natal. But the force of his spring attack had given the king enough momentum that his slash only cut open Corland's leg. The king let out a yell of shock and pain as he rolled onto his back and grabbed at his wound. William composed himself and took a moment to rest as the king's glare cut into him from across the battleground.

"I am going to make you regret this, boy!" the king said through gritted teeth.

"You have already made all of us regret our lives under your hateful yoke. You killed my father, enslaved my people, and drove a band of children into the wilderness. You shall burn for eternity for all you have done in the quest for gold," William said, his anger seething through him.

He was about to launch again when he saw Corland's body set itself, and the words from Beorn echoed in his head. '*Anger is as much a weapon against you as it is for you.*' The weapon smith constantly warned. Quickly calming himself, William changed tactics. He launched himself at Corland, as he was sure the man expected, but at the last moment spun on his heel.

The surprise counter attack Corland planned missed William completely causing him to fall to the ground. Quickly, the half elf rolled behind the king and fell to his knees. Grabbing the older ruler around his neck he drove the point of his Natal up against the winded mans chin. William stopped short of killing him, but instead held him firmly in place.

The crowd who just moments before were screaming for their champions, now quieted as William held the king's life in the balance.

"Yield, King Corland Lianthus. This battle is over, yield and let it be done!" William yelled loud enough for everyone to hear.

The king mumbled something, but William pressed the blade harder into the man's throat drawing some blood. "Yield Lianthus. I have bested you and am offering you your life. Don't force me to take it." William said quieter but still loud enough that everyone around could hear him.

"I," King Corland started. William could feel the man shaking in his grip and knew his opponent was livid. "I...I yield!" He shouted. The silence erupted in a massive cheer as the Freedom Fighters surrounding them heard the tyrant's surrender.

With the fight over, the young half elf was able to pay attention to everything around him for the first time. Looking up at the city walls, he saw people watching from any vantage point they could find. Every window that could see over the city walls was filled with a face. Some were watching the fight from towers and balconies, high above the city. He guessed that the entire royal court and much of the wealthy merchants from the city saw everything. But more importantly, he made eye contact with a man in full armor near the city gates, surrounded by soldiers. By the insignia on his armor, William knew the man to be very high ranking in the king's army.

The man looked at William for a moment, as if considering his options. Making his decision quickly, he bowed to William, and signaling the troops around him, dropped his sword to the ground. All the surrounding troops did the same thing, signaling their acceptance of William as the victor.

William quickly pulled his blade back and got up from behind the king. He stumbled exhausted towards his friends, a smile upon his face. He didn't care what the consequence of his victory meant, he just wanted to rest. Suddenly, a scream emanated from the crowd. William turned and saw Corland, dagger in hand prepare to throw. The small blade left the king's hand and William felt a thud in his chest as he fell to the ground, a great weight on him.

He heard a twang that seemed almost surreal in the dull pain that filled his head. It hit against a rock and darkness overcame him.

William woke slowly and as his senses returned he realized that he must have been out for a long time. It was dark all around him, except for a small brazier that burned in the middle of the room.

He tried to get up but felt a hand hold him down. He looked, trying to recognize who it was, but it was too dark.

"Be calm, William, it's all over," Emma's voice said softly.

"Am I dead?" he asked hoarsely.

There was a soft chuckle and sob as she replied, "No silly, you're alive. You're just hurt and probably fairly weak. You've been asleep for three days," she explained.

Three days! The number echoed in his aching head making him queasy. "What happened?" he said, feeling his chest for a wound. Not finding one confused him.

"You forced Lianthus to yield, which was clear to everyone nearby. Not just to us but the people of his own Delegation as well. As you walked away from him, he drew a dagger he had hidden in his boot and threw it at you. Jacob jumped and pushed you out of the way, but he landed on you and your head hit a rock," Emma explained.

"He saved me?" William croaked.

"Yes," she replied softly.

"I'd like to see him, to thank him," William said taking a sip of water from the cup she handed him.

"You can't," she said and her body shook with grief. "When he pushed you out of the way, the dagger hit him instead of you. We couldn't save him; he died before you both hit the ground," she whispered.

Again the ringing in his ears got louder and the shock ran through his body. "He died saving me?" William echoed, tears running down his cheeks.

Emma lay down next to him and hugged him close as he began to cry. His fatigue and grief was too much, and any control he would normally have was gone. Now he cried into her bodice. Letting out a loud and tortured shout, he felt the darkness creep over him again.

When he next awoke, it was light out. He was hoping that it was all a horrible dream, but there was Emma still holding him in her arms. He recognized the moisture on his face as his tears, as he tried to recognize his surroundings. He looked around the room, careful not to wake her, and saw Declan, Brody, and Chloe sitting at his table.

He caught their attention and quickly all three rushed to his bed side. Declan carefully helped William out of the grip of Emma's arms and then guided him to his feet. They all protested, but William insisted, using sign language that they move to allow Emma to sleep.

"She hasn't slept in days," Chloe told him in a whisper when he was seated at the table.

"She wouldn't leave your side, she tended you constantly," Brody added.

William looked lovingly at the young woman sleeping in his bed. He motioned for them to sit next to him so they could talk quietly.

"She told me," William said softly, the emotions still raw in his chest.

"We know, milord, we heard the cry and came running. She explained it all to us," Declan explained. "We haven't left since."

"Where's Lianthus?" William asked, hate filling the void created by pain.

"Dead," Brody said.

William looked over at his old friend, a look of shock on his face.

"I did it, brother," Chloe said softly. William turned his attention to his sister, who looked tortured with the memory of killing a person. "When he threw the dagger, I pulled my bow from my back and let an arrow fly. It took him through the throat," she explained.

"And what of his family then?" William asked.

"They are in the city under guard, until you could decide what you wanted done," Declan replied.

"What I want done? Guys what is there to be done? Corland is gone, we are free," he said, trying to sound more energetic than he really felt. That's when his empty stomach growled, reminding him it had been three days since he ate. Chloe quickly got up and left the tent to get him some food.

"You don't understand do you, Majesty?" Brody asked.

"Understand what? And what's with the Majesty business?" William asked, his emotions running high, as he attempted to keep his voice down.

"Milord, you are now king," Declan replied. "You won the title, fairly, when Lianthus yielded. You are now the ruler of the lands of Andraya."

The shock drove into him as if he received another punch to his midriff like the one Corland landed during their fight. He was a king? How could that be? He didn't want to be king; he wasn't fit to be king. None of this made sense.

At that moment, Chloe returned and before any more talking could go on she forced him to eat. The warm food seemed to help him digest the news easier.

"So what do I do now?" William asked.

"You do what you have been doing for months," Chloe replied. "You lead. Create a new government, and make the lives of the people of Andraya better. Remember all the things you wished could come true for the people? Well, now we can make it happen under your leadership."

"But I can't do it alone," William whispered.

"You're not alone, Will," Declan replied, getting to his feet. William's Elvin cousin walked over to him and knelt before him with his old sword in his hands. "I will never leave your side, and I pledge my sword to you," he said.

Following his lead Brody did the same with his blades, and Chloe did the same with her bow. William felt a soft hand on his cheek and he looked up to see Emma standing at his side, and she too fell to her knees and bowed before him.

"None of us will ever leave your side, my king," she said.

"Get up, all of you," William said not knowing what was expected of him. "I would rather you stand at my side than kneel at my feet." He stood before each of them. "Declan, you and Brody are my oldest friends. We will need a Commander of the Army and I will need an advisor," he said, hugging them both. "Will you help me by filling those rolls?" he asked.

"I would be honored," Declan replied.

"As would I, my king," Brody added

William smiled and nodded to both and then moved before his sister.

"Will, before you say any more could I ask one thing of you? Don't keep me chained within the city walls. I need the forest," she said, her pain still clear in her voice.

"Chloe, my sister," he said and paused, "Princess Chloe, I have always had an idea about an alternative army to the main one. I place you in command of the alternative army. We will discuss how it will function, but I vow to you that it will not be bound by the walls of any city."

Finally, he moved so he stood in front of Emma. "Lady Emma," he started and gazing deeply into her eyes time, seemed to stop. Pulling himself away he smiled at her and lowered himself unsteadily to one knee, "I would be honored if you would rule at my side as Queen of Andraya," he said.

Emma seemed strangely distant for a moment but when her gaze met his she pulled him to his feet and kissed him deeply. "I would rather die than ever leave your side, my king." She smiled at him and took his hand gently. "I accept."

Everyone in the room burst into laughter and hugged each other in joy. They had defeated a tyrant and working together they knew they could build a better Andraya for everyone.

"But for now the joy must be held off for a more appropriate time," William said, as grief took his heart again. "I need to find Jacob's parents. I need to be with them and to help prepare for his burial." He tried to walk to the door but stumbled. Declan grabbed him before he could fall. Being helped by his best friends, William walked out of his tent and into the camp outside. As he did, cheers rose as people saw him out for the first time in days. The cheers grew and grew until the ground seemed to shake from the roar.

Through pain came joy. And through death came the promise of new life for the people of Andraya.

Chapter 27

In the Age of King William the First

The week was full of planning for the march towards Eland as Declan prepared the army to roll out. Brody, Minister Reese, Dominique, and Tobias worked on a plan for repairing the damage to the outer wall, and the damage within the city proper.

William sent out an advanced work force to the damaged villages and had them prepare lumber for the rebuild effort. This was to reduce the actual time they would have to spend working in each village to repair the damage. He had asked Emma to rule in his place after he left. She was always his closest advisor anyway, and the people greatly respected her, making his wife the most logical choice.

Chloe had her Rangers prepare to move out with the main force. They were to monitor and police General Austin's men that were coming along to help with the rebuild efforts. The remaining captives were sent to work on other projects around the kingdom. They too had Rangers watching them, even though they would never know where they were being watched from.

William sat upon his war horse, Midnight, and watched the culmination of all of their preparations. From his hilltop vantage, he could see the rank and file of troops, followed by the army corps of engineers and other support people. Behind them came the captives, surrounded by the green and brown clad Rangers.

Once all the division leaders signaled their troop status, the king signaled the trumpeters to sound the advance. The massive force didn't have to go far, though, to reach their first stop. The Village of Haroth was half a day's march from Czariana. When they arrived they found most of the village was in a state of good repair. Apparently, Marcus was going to use it as a base of operations if William led his forces to confront them in the field.

But there was still work to be done here, and leading a team of carpenters, the king threw off his heavy riding clothes and began helping. Villagers, who had returned upon hearing that their village would be soon repaired, worked diligently at his side. Soon many of the people, who said they wanted to meet with him at day's end, seemed to be genuinely touched by his efforts.

Several times his generals had to tell him to slow down though. "Milord, you have to pace yourself," Declan warned. "There is no need to run yourself ragged."

"I have to work harder than everyone else," William replied. "I have to prove myself to these people. I have to prove I am worthy to bear the trust they have placed in me."

"Sure, and we understand that, your Majesty," Brody injected, "but this is the first village of many, and I assure you, the others will be worse. What good are your efforts today if tomorrow you're too tired to give it your all? Remember, William, none of us have done this kind of stuff in a long time."

"You're right guys, I know. Thank you both for your council. I'll manage myself better so as to not let any of our people down," William said, swallowing his pride. He knew they gave their advice in his best interests, but he so desperately wanted to prove himself to his people, he found it hard to follow.

Once the long day was over, William was invited to hold court at the village's repaired tavern. It was there that anyone with problems, grievances or complaints could see him personally. The line to see him was short and he was able to retire at a reasonable time, confident everyone left satisfied.

After everyone had been seen to, the proprietor of the tavern approached William. "Your Majesty, it would do me great honor if you would stay in a room here in my humble establishment," he said with a bow.

"Master Inn Keeper, your invitation is quite gracious, but I am afraid I must decline. You see, your Inn doesn't have enough beds for all my troops, and since they sleep on cots, so too shall I.

"But it would please me greatly to be able to dine with you and your family if I could. And perhaps you wouldn't mind if I set my tent beside your tavern so I could visit with the people before I retire?" he asked his host.

The smile on the Inn Keeper's face radiated as he accepted and rushed to tell his wife and children of their dinner guest that evening.

The next day they moved on and carried out the same routine. It seemed that the further from the capitol that they went though, the longer the lines of complaints grew. It began to seem to the middle aged king that they might spend a week rebuilding homes, followed by another spent counseling angry citizens. Many people used the opportunity to argue local level problems and politics. William hoped he could deal with more issues pertaining to the destruction of their homes. But once their homes were rebuilt, most people used the opportunity to argue their other issues. The nature of people guaranteed that if you gave some of them a forum to complain, then most would find a reason to take advantage of it.

The final village, before reaching the Andrayan-Eland border, was Xanthor. The devastation here was incredible. It appeared as though Marcus let his men completely loose, as nothing was left of the settlement. Burned husks of buildings scattered about the churned up ground, with nothing resembling even a wall remaining. William, Declan, and Brody spent several days working with village elders to plan the completely new settlement. They were amazed at how much had been destroyed there. Teams of people were setup to help offer what talents they could to the rebuilding of the community.

"Anyone who has talents in furniture building will fall under Shade's command," William instructed the assembled command team in his tent. "Framers will answer to Logan, and landscapers to Declan. Brody, you are in charge of roads and drainage."

"Father," Logan interrupted, "the village elders are upset by the presence of the enemy troops. They are angry that this misfortune even took place and are saying they want no part in anything that the enemy soldiers touch in the reconstruction efforts."

"Well unfortunately, this is one time they are going to have to be disappointed," William replied, a frown forming on his face. "I have tried to be understanding. I have tried to be sympathetic. But at some point the people will have to recognize our own limitations.

"We didn't ask for this. We also didn't want anyone to suffer because of Marcus and his vendetta. But all of us are doing our best as a kingdom to make things right, and I think we are doing a good job of it.

"Brody, we will attempt to get as many of the captives to work with you. That way they avoid directly working on people's homes. Chloe, I want you to take a large group as well for logging. We are going to need more lumber to complete this project, and they can help mill it. If anyone in this village has any issue with that," William said looking at everyone in turn, "send them to me. I'll deal with it directly." Everyone nodded their understanding and left him to himself.

William sat down at his small travel desk with a sigh. It was true, that the further from the capitol, the less forgiving the people were. Xanthor was one of the few villages left untouched by Corland during his reign of terror. They were also some of the former king's most steadfast supporters and never really accepted William's position as king. William had no doubt that some of the elders still resented his position, and that this request was tainted by that history. Granted, the request wasn't without validity, but he was too tired after nearly three weeks of travel and hard work to care.

Nearly two more weeks passed when they finally completed Xanthor. He was forced to face the elders about the enemy work force, which he handled as adeptly as possible. But it made no difference, and he knew he left with fewer supporters in Xanthor than when he arrived.

At this point, the workers and soldiers went in different directions. The Eland soldiers, who had become a more than willing work crew, moved out and helped craftsman create new living items. Tables, chairs and other such furniture were still required for the citizens of the other villages. It was decided during the earlier builds that moving the army forward was important, and such luxuries would have to be dealt with at a later time. The captive Eland soldiers were going to move back towards Czariana, helping build the items the people would need in their day to day lives.

William, Declan, Brody, and Chloe moved the army forward and by mid day had left the Kingdom of Andraya and had entered the Kingdom of Eland.

Now it was time for the soldiers to heal from their hard work in the villages and prepare for the upcoming battle. It was also the time that William decided to make his first move. He sent a runner to find his commanders and his son and called them all to meet with him.

"We need more information on the city of Lytton before we attack it," William said.

"I agree. We also need to know more about the surrounding terrain," Declan added.

"Logan, are the Night Hawks travelling with us?" William asked.

"Yes, Father, they are positioned in different squadrons around the camp," Logan replied casually.

"Good. How many are with us?" William questioned.

"Six four-man attack teams," Logan explained.

"Alright, I want two teams to scout ahead with reports on the Lytton city defenses. Send your best team available to scout sensitive areas of the city. They must never be caught, do I make myself clear?" William emphasized to his son, drawing a nod in reply. "I want two more teams to scout the terrain, and the final two will travel ahead of the camp and keep watch for spies from Lytton. I don't want anyone we come across killed. Instead, our people are to capture them and to wait for us to join them. I want to know everything we should, two days before we reach the capitol city. At this pace, that should mean report back in twenty days," William commanded.

"Brody, start preparing defensive plans for our men. Do you have the new battering ram prepared?" William asked.

"No, Majesty. We will build it when we are closer. It was too heavy to travel with us and would have added another week to the march. I'm not worried about its construction though; we have the launcher with us, so all we need is the frame and we're ready," the minister of defense replied.

"Excellent. Dec, do you have anything to add?" he asked.

"No, but I would suggest a change in Logan's orders if I may sir?" the general asked.

"Sure, what do you think?" William said.

"Have Chloe send out a couple of teams of Rangers to spy on the terrain ahead. Their skills in the wild would make their judgment better for such a task. Also, send the two teams of Night Hawk Rangers to spy ahead of us," he explained.

"But my people don't need the Rangers, Uncle Declan," Logan replied, "with all due respect, Aunt Chloe." He blushed.

"I think what General Declan is trying to say is your people are best at using the shadows of the city to do their work. In contrast, my Rangers are better suited to being stealthy in the wilderness,." Chloe explained to her nephew. "Between the two groups, we could be able to run information back and forth between the army and the scouts faster than if your people were alone," she explained.

"You want my men to be runners then?" Logan said sounding offended.

"After a fashion, yes, that is what I want from them," she replied. "The Rangers would be best for hunting down spies trying to elude capture. But your people are soldiers, first and foremost, and would do well at keeping anyone we capture under lock and key."

"You're right. My people do work best in the city. They are also the best swordsmen I could find," Logan replied.

"I would have perhaps left out one or two of your choices. But you are correct, when it comes to swords, you picked our best," Chloe said with a smile.

"What do you mean?" Logan asked perplexed. "How can you know which soldiers are mine? Not even Father knows that."

"Logan, there is very little your Aunt and her people don't know," William chuckled. "Do you really think all they are paid for is to backup the army and protect the wilds of Andraya?"

Everyone watching the young Prince started to grin as understanding crossed his face.

"Spies?" he said, more for clarification than in question.

His tone caused everyone to burst out laughing.

"Father, what do you think?" Logan turned to William for his opinion.

"I agree. Logan and Chloe, make it happen. I want to know as much as we can as soon as possible, understand? Use the Rangers to scout the wilds ahead, and get teams of Night Hawk into Lytton. I want to know everything about the land and the capitol." Both of them nodded and left the tent.

"We'll be ready, Will." Brody said with confidence.

“Yes, I agree” William replied. “I just want to make sure we are completely ready. We can’t keep our soldiers as safe as when they were in Czariana’s walls. Now that we are the aggressors, we will have a more intimate dance with death, I fear.”

Chapter 28

A Time between Ages

William spoke to the crowd at Jacob's funeral. He never sugar coated anything, but instead, laid out their history, only omitting the story about the fight with Declan. He told of their growing friendship and finally of Jacob's loyalty, that grew to the point that he traded his life for Will's. It wasn't a long service, and only William spoke, but it deeply affected them all. What was supposed to be a time of joy was tainted by loss of one of their own. Yet as William spoke, he noticed something that caused his heart to stay strong. Flapping in the wind, the colored flags he was often moved by were all there as before. But now, added to the rainbow that was his kingdom in waiting was the purple that was previously missing. The kingdom was once again unified as a single people and even in the sadness, his heart began to soar.

Everyone mourned for two days after the funeral, but on the third day they began preparing for the coronation.

Violet took complete control of the Royal kitchens. She seemed to have appointed herself head chef when no one was looking. This happened much to the chagrin of the current Royal Head Chef. He whined that he was going to complain to Emma, who had taken over the household duties of the queen. This, of course, landed him with a black eye from the large woman, quickly bringing the issue to a close. Emma, on the other hand, began working with all of the Royal Maids to prepare the castle for William's arrival. He made it clear that he would only take up residence in the castle once he became king.

The other problem was that the former queen and her son, Marcus, refused to vacate the castle. Instead, they were locked inside the inner fortress that was the Royal Chambers, with the dead king's body. Emma allowed some of the staff, still loyal to the Lianthus family, to remain behind to care for them as per instructions from William. The rest were sent from the castle when different rooms were found to be sabotaged with traps set for the new king.

From time to time you would hear the former queen wailing out her balcony window. Her sobbing cries saddened William deeply, but any attempts to help were angrily turned away. So it was that the old Royals were left to their own devices.

All the while the new king in waiting was panicking in his tent. He was desperately trying to find a way out of the predicament he currently found himself in.

"Brody come on, I can't do this," William said for the tenth time that day alone. "I'm not a king."

"Look, Will, we've gone over this again, and again…and again. You are our leader, you've done a great job and you will continue to do a great job. Second, you challenged Corland for the throne, you won, and it's yours. I didn't shock the heck out of you and challenge him did I?" Brody asked.

"Well no but…" William tried, but his heart was gone from the argument already.

"But nothing. You saw what needed to be done, you placed your life on the line to save us all, and you came through. There is nothing more to say," Brody explained.

"Have you seen Emma lately?" William asked, changing gears so quickly Brody almost choked on his ale.

"No, she's been too busy with getting the coronation ready. Are you sure about getting married?" Brody asked, typical of the young bachelor.

"Yeah I am and someday soon, too," William said. "When I awoke and she was there, I knew she was all I needed in life."

"Oh geez, you're going to make me puke!" Brody complained. "Alright, if you love her so much why don't you just marry her now?"

"Right now?" William said. He was suddenly overcome with a numbing sensation at the idea.

"Sure, why not. Heck, why not turn the coronation into a Royal Wedding while you're at it," Brody said, grinning at his friend's response. But his taunting quickly came to an end when he saw the expression on William's face shift. "I was just kidding, Will," he said, starting to panic. "Will, what are you doing?" he asked as William got to his feet with a grin.

"I need to speak to Violet. I'm going to find a runner to get her for me," William said, bolting out the door.

"Will! Now, William, calm down. Don't do anything hasty here!" Brody called running after him.

"What's going on?" Declan asked catching up to them keeping pace with Brody.

"I made a joke that he should make the coronation a wedding, and he started grinning like an idiot. Now he's going to send for Violet!" Brody explained in a panic.

"You darn fool," Declan nearly shouted. "You know he's a romantic! This is just what he needed so he wouldn't have to admit he was becoming king!" Declan said.

Finally they found a young runner, marked by the symbol of a falcon they now wore on their chests. William dispatched the youth to the castle kitchen to bring him Violet. He then sat down and waited. As Brody and Declan argued with each other over who was to blame for what he was about to do, a plan began to form in his mind.

Sure, marrying Emma on the day of the coronation would be perfect. What woman wouldn't love to be married on such an important day? He just needed to find a way to surprise her with the idea.

He didn't have to wait long as the young runner returned with Violet in tow, a half hour later.

"Lord William, this young man said you sent for me?" she said, huffing and puffing as she came before him.

"Yes, Violet. Brody had an excellent idea." A loud moan came from behind him. "That's what I want to discuss with you." They quickly moved to the privacy of his tent, talking about the possibilities. The look on Violet's face was one of pure joy as he explained everything he had in mind.

They talked the whole night, and the more they planned the drunker Declan and Brody got. They were passed out like puppies, curled in a ball on the floor, long before the pair finished talking. William and Violet had it all decided as dawn began to spread across the land.

"Okay, so can you make her a wedding dress without her realizing it?" William asked.

"I surely can. I still have the dress I made for her for the meeting with Corland," she replied.

"White and pretty, right?" William asked.

"Lord William, I'll make that woman the prettiest Andrayan to ever grace Creation," the heavy woman laughed. "Now I best get, and you best sleep." Looking at his friends on the ground she chuckled, "They aren't as excited as we, are they?" she asked.

"They just think they've lost a hunting buddy," William laughed. Violet laughed too and, agreeing with him, walked out the opening of his tent.

Three days passed and the day of the coronation finally arrived. Will didn't have a hard time keeping the secret from Emma, since he only saw her twice over that time. Picking the wedding party was easy. Declan and Brody obviously filled the role of best men, while Emma's sister Elaina was asked to be maid of honor. Chloe was, of course, her second Bridesmaid and all the people involved were happily prepared when the anticipated hour arrived.

Finally, the time for the joint wedding and coronation had come. The trumpets played triumphantly along the city walls, and when the signal was given, William, followed by Declan and Brody, marched to the city gates in full regalia. Declan, who was now the commander of the armies of Andraya, was in a full custom made suit of armor, made by Beorn himself. Brody, as First Minister of Andraya, was clothed in the robes of a scholar, while William, who was both defender and ruler, was in a suit of armor with a cape flying behind him, his long black hair open to the afternoon breeze.

Everyone lined the path to the city gates where the ceremony was to be held. When William stood before the High Priest of

Andraya, he nodded and another symphony of instruments rung out. At this time, the bridal procession began first with Chloe walking down the aisle, followed by Elaina. Finally Emma came, being led down the aisle by her father and mother.

William couldn't believe how radiant she looked. Somehow Violet had not only made a beautiful gown for her, but her hair was tied in a summer braid around the crest of her head. He then noticed that a crown would fit nicely inside the ring.

As she finally realized what was happening she froze, but when her eyes met William's her fear melted away. She held tightly to her father's arm and when she looked up at him, saw him crying. She stopped and gave him a warm hug, and turning, she kissed her mother.

She then took William's outstretched hand and took her place at his side. He smiled at her and she at him. As the Priest began both the ceremony of their wedding and the coronation of the new king, William finally felt at home.

Chapter 29

In the Age of King William the First

The army moved slowly, heading towards the Eland capitol of Lytton. So far they were in the wilderness, but even now the paths became roads, and the wild was looking more and more tame. William was worried about this eventuality. It was a problem he had no simple solution for. Soon they would begin passing villages, and they couldn't risk leaving people behind to attack them from the rear.

Declan had suggested that they take this route. William had been to Lytton several times, but always by the main highway. Where they travelled now was not so much a path, but more of a cart trail it appeared to William. Declan said it was less likely that they would meet as much resistance, and King Porthanaclies likely wouldn't expect them to travel this way. By going this way they would encounter fewer villages, saving them from having to deal with that threat.

With that being said, though, he was also not going to command his troops to kill innocent people. Just because they were loyal to their king or high king, as the case may be, was no reason to kill innocents.

High King Porthanaclies came to Andraya once, during the blessing of the new capitol city. He was a good man, who meant well, but he was a classic example of a king. He was the sixth generation ruler in his family line and believed he was born to it. When he spoke, he attempted to speak above you and it made him sound a bit foolish, but he wasn't all that bad. He really seemed like a good fellow. That is if you could get around his annoying tendency to use the wrong words while trying to impress those around him.

William hated the thought of forcing his way into the city and taking a share of the treasury from Eland. That money was paid in taxes by hard working citizens. Once again, the people would suffer. But William had long ago stopped trying to save everyone in the world. He knew his limitations, and the people of Andraya were his to protect. Regardless of how he felt towards the high king, Porthanaclies granted Marcus the use of the royal armies. From what little he could gather from General Austin, Porthanaclies did nothing to dissuade his son-in-law's desire for war. Because of that, he would have to be held accountable for his part in the advance on Czariana by his troops.

William's attention was suddenly caught by a carrier pigeon flying overhead, as he came out of his thoughts. He watched as it headed towards the communications commander, lazily floated on the currents, and landed on the man's shoulder. William spurred his horse forward and pulled up next to him.

"Word from home?" William asked, startling the man.

"My king! Yes, it appears to be a message from your wife. I would have brought it to you, Sire; you didn't have to come to me." The man smiled.

"I saw it landing and thought it might be something important. I didn't think I needed to bother you with finding me." William smiled back and took the note.

It was longer than most, and that worried William. Most messages by pigeon were kept short so as to not wear out the bird on its flight. He quickly straightened the paper and began to read.

"William," the letter began. The king didn't have to check the signature on the bottom; the familiar hand writing was Emma's. "*I hope this message finds you well in the field. Everything is alright here in Czariana. The Kings Way has been returned to normal and the city crews are quickly rebuilding the damaged streets and buildings from the catapult attacks."*

'*Good*' William thought to himself, '*I knew she wouldn't let me down.*' He smiled and continued reading.

"The launch bay that was destroyed has already been fixed and Chief Engineer Owen has started work on reinforcing them so the same thing will not happen again. The people are settling back into their lives and everything seems to be going well," she wrote. He almost started laughing as he pictured Owen running back and forth down the defense hall.

"But I write with distressing news. Several men from General Austin's army have escaped. I fear that they are heading straight for Eland and Marcus to warn them of your advance. Chloe's Rangers are on the move tracking them, but they slipped away without the general's people realizing it until it was too late. They have already been gone for two days, and I'm afraid even the greatest hunter would find their trail hard to follow now." The news created a knot in William's stomach. This wasn't good. He wanted their approach to be a surprise, allowing them to throw the defenses into chaos until he could parlay with Marcus and Porthanaclies. He didn't want them prepared.

"General Austin has submitted himself for punishment for his men breaking their oaths. The man is taking this very seriously and has even stated if we set him loose he would find the men and kill them himself. I don't know what to do, William. I fear for you and our people. Please be safe, and don't take unnecessary risks."

'*I don't take unnecessary risks.*' William said aloud but he continued to read.

"And yes you do take unnecessary risks. Shall I remind you of how you earned your crown?" William rolled his eyes but was forced to agree. That was risky.

"Let me know as soon as you receive this. I want to know you are in full knowledge of what you face. Until then, I will not be able to sleep for worry. I love you as always, my heart. Come home to me." And on the bottom of the letter was Emma's signature.

So some men escaped and the general wants to be punished and loosed upon them. William quickly decided that neither would be prudent. He decided that by not allowing General Austin to be able to restore his honor for the year would make him more diligent in maintaining the rest of his men. But men who knew what William was doing and were heading to Lytton were a problem.

Declan rode up and William handed him the letter. "What do you think?" the king asked his general.

"I think what's done is done. It is just now more important that we move faster. We are still five days away," the general replied. "We should be receiving word any time now from the scouts you sent ahead. Sir, I would say that we no longer set camp, but have the men sleep on the open ground. This will speed up movement and would allow us to travel farther each day.

"By sending people to meet spies head on, we have the edge. But people who would approach us from behind, where we can't see them, will put us at a disadvantage. I suggest that we press on," Declan explained.

"I agree. Tell the commanders that we are travelling farther and not setting up camp. How are the field machines coming?" William asked.

"I just came from Brody. His men are working as quickly as possible. He is running two crews, a day crew and a night crew. His day crew cuts wood and builds, and the night crew drives the wagons with the pieces, as well as the day crew on them allowing the others to sleep. It's a good plan, it allows them to build and not be too far behind the main force," Declan replied.

"Excellent, he is doing an efficient job as usual," William said. "Alright, we continue moving. Spread the word of what has happened so the troops know why they are being pushed harder. Other than that, when we stop tonight I'll reply to Emma and tell her what we know."

Declan nodded his agreement and rode towards the communications wagon to call his men to discuss the issue.

But the king didn't have long to ponder this new problem. His attention was caught by one of his personal guards, who pointed at a small cabin hidden in the forest. William signaled towards the clearing, and ten of his armored Knights broke away from the column and made for the house behind him. He was surprised to see an elderly couple waiting for him on their front porch when he approached.

“Good day to you, Master, and you as well, Madam,” William said tilting his head in respect.

“Good day to you, kind sir,” the man replied. “That is a large group of people you lead.”

“Yes it is sir, I apologize if the noise is causing you distress,” William replied.

“Noise no. But seeing an armed force heading into the center of our kingdom, so quickly after we heard word that one headed out, causes its own form of distress,” the woman added.

William laughed. “Yes, madam, I can see how it would do that. You know who I am then?” he asked.

Both people shook their heads no, which again caused the king to laugh. “I am King William Duthain, ruler of Andraya,” William introduced himself. The woman seemed to grow faint and the man grabbed her to stop her from falling.

William quickly jumped down from his horse to help the man. “Milord, I deeply apologize for not showing proper courtesy to you,” the man said, leading his wife with the help of William into their cottage.

“No harm done, father,” William replied, helping to seat the woman.

“The stories are true!” the woman breathed, looking at her husband, who handed her a cup of water.

“Stories? What stories?” William asked, concerned that news of their approach had already slipped through his net.

“The stories we have heard about you, milord,” the man replied. “They say that you weren’t born a king, but rather were a peasant.”

“Is it that obvious?” William laughed.

"No other king would show respect to an elder and call him father, King William," the woman said with a shy smile.

This again caused William to laugh. "Ah, good mother, but respect is something we must earn, not be born with. But I admit, you are the first of a problem I foresee in our course towards Lytton."

"Problem, King William?" the man asked, sounding fearful.

"Yes, father. I fear that I cannot allow Elander's to form up behind us as we travel, pinching us between Lytton's walls and them," William said.

The man and woman instantly looked like a pair of startled deer. "Oh good people, I refuse to hurt anyone who is not an aggressor. That is my problem. If I were ruthless like King Marcus, I would kill you and burn your home to the ground. But I'm not Marcus." William sighed. "May I sit?" He asked, pointing at a chair. The two older people nodded quickly. "No, instead I must protect my back while protecting you people as well. You see, we are only advancing on Lytton because of the destruction caused by King Marcus' troops in Andraya. We are coming to High King Porthanaclies to demand payment for the hurt of our people. What right would I have to make such a demand if I hurt you along the way?"

"So you're not going to kill us, milord?" the man asked.

"Or harm our home?" the woman added.

"No, I will not allow that to happen. But I'm afraid that I can't take chances with people at my back, either. Instead, what would you do in my place?" he asked the couple.

This caught them completely by surprise. Not only were they being asked for advice from a king, but a foreign one and it would pertain to them directly.

"Well, sir," the man said slowly, "I guess if I were you, I would take any of us people you come across with you as prisoners, until you could keep a large group of us together. It would mean fewer troops would be needed to watch your back."

"Hmmm, yes that would work. Is there such a place nearby so as to not take people, such as you, too far from home?" William asked.

"Not for us, I'm afraid. The next town you will come across is still a ways away. You will probably reach it tomorrow afternoon. It's one of the closest towns to Lytton," the woman explained.

"You're actually very lucky, King William," the man continued, "The southern portion of Eland really doesn't have a lot of communities, and the road you are on has fewer yet. You see, all the good growing is north of Lytton. You will come across the town of Tyrene, that I mentioned, and some scattered farms all around. From there, it's pretty much open road to Lytton."

"So if I take you from your home, you would have to travel an entire day to get back, on top of the time you would be held while we dealt with King Marcus," William said. "That is a long time to leave it unprotected."

"You really do care don't you, King William?" the woman asked, obviously touched.

"Ma'am, when I was a child the former ruler of Andraya, King Corland Lianthus, captured our village. He wanted fifty percent of our crops that year and the people didn't feel he deserved it. The children of that village were hiding when the king and his men came, and we were able to escape.

"When we returned many years later, we freed our people and I won the throne in open combat. That is how I earned my crown," William explained. He quickly thought of the letter from Emma in his shirt.

"I know how hard the people work for what they have," he continued. "I would hate to have that damaged in any way," he explained.

"Milord," the woman said, reaching across the table and placing a hand upon his, "my heart weeps that we don't have a king such as you. My husband and I are old, way past years of battle. But we will go to Tyrene to help give you some comfort in your efforts," she said.

"I thank you, mother, but an idea has just struck me. I have some people in my employ who prefer to avoid cities. I believe several are young, and although they are battle ready, I would like them to see more years before facing one," William said in response. "How would it be if I leave one or two of those people here to watch you, for my comfort and yours? They would then leave when we returned?"

"Oh, milord, it would gladden our hearts not to leave our home," the old man said in reply.

"Then it will be done. In fact, you helped me remedy two problems on my mind. Well, I must quickly catch up with my men. I will leave a man here until he can be relieved by your guard," William said, standing quickly and taking the man by the hand, and shaking it, he smiled. "It is because of people like you, that I lead. If not for this, I would be a carpenter," he smiled at them, and accepting a kiss on the cheek from the old woman, he left the hut and rode off.

Chapter 30

Beginning of the Age of King William the First

The day was done. The feasting was long over, and the only people left in the great hall were a couple of guys with their heads on the table, snoring loudly. The newly married couple was in their temporary chambers, since the old Royals had yet to leave the tower, cuddling each other.

"That was quite a surprise my dear," Emma said.

"Yeah, it was mostly Brody's idea," William, picturing Brody groaning in his current drunken stupor, chuckled.

"What if I wasn't ready?" Emma asked, giving him a critical eye.

"Then I would have married Declan, I guess.," William laughed, which caused Emma to giggle with him.

"Did you doubt I would go up?" Emma asked him seriously.

"For three days, once Violet and I put the plan into action, I worried that you truly didn't want me," William replied, gently stroking her cheek.

"How could I not? I loved you long before you became our leader, even before you knew I existed. You always seemed so happy, confident, and loyal. I knew I would be your wife someday, I just thought it would be more at my choosing," she sighed.

"Did I wrong you by doing this?" William asked, suddenly worried.

"No, my love, you made this already wonderful day perfect," she replied. "You and Violet did everything I could ask for."

"Well that was easy; your mother helped us with most of it. Of course I asked your father for his blessing first, which he gave after we had a long talk. Oh, don't worry about that. It was a good talk, one I'll hopefully have with our daughter's suitor in the future," he said quickly.

The mention of a daughter caught Emma by surprise, "You want a daughter?" she asked.

"I want children," he replied. "Daughters, sons, I don't care. I want little ones filling our lives with laughter."

"I want that too, Will," Emma replied. "So, Majesty," she grinned laying on top him and looking down into his eyes, "What is your next move?"

"I need to discuss it with Declan and Brody. But yeah, I think I have an idea where to go from here," William replied seriously.

Emma quickly grew serious as well, "You do? Want to talk about it?" she asked.

"Sure, I plan on tearing down the castle," William said, which caused Emma to laugh, but his serious look quieted her.

"You're serious?" she said.

"Yes, very. I intend on moving the capitol city back to our old Village and creating a new one," William said.

"That's great, but why tear down the castle?" she asked.

"I plan on leaving the tower here. I will see to it that the former Royals who remain have the ability to come and go as they please. But they aren't the Royals any longer and so a castle isn't required for them to govern from. Instead, we will move the blocks to the new site and build a new city with them," William said.

"Start the new Royal blood line in a new location?" she asked.

"There will be no Royal blood line any longer, my love," he replied.

"Another change?" she asked

"Yes, the people shall vote for their king. Every two years or more, whatever the people decide is best. I plan on building a council of elders that will rule the kingdom with me. Then when my time is up, the people can elect a new king," he explained.

"Can you do that?" she asked. "I mean, would the Laws of the Ten Kings allow that?"

"The Laws of the Ten Kings applied to warfare, mostly. There are some keys to diplomacy and commerce, but by and large they deal with the rules of engagement and the codes of war," William explained. "Actually, they don't even have to pertain to civil war either, to be honest. But I wagered Corland hadn't really studied them and all I needed was for him to accept. Once he did, he was then bound by the laws.

"But those laws don't guide individual kingdom's governance. That is still the final say of the kingdom's rulers. Although one thing is clear, for our people to remain protected by the Laws of the Ten Kings, our ruler must remain a king. We can't change that title," He explained.

"Do you think the people will accept such a change to how they are ruled?" Emma asked.

"Hopefully. I never asked to be king; I was just made one by necessity. I don't want to force myself on any of them," he replied.

Emma stroked his hair and smiled at him, "Oh my king, I think we are in for a very interesting life," she said. He grinned back at her and blowing out the candle by their bed moved forward and kissed her.

The next couple of days were filled with meetings. First, William and Emma met with Declan and Brody. Then, Emma had to start organizing the Royal Household since that was historically the duty of the queen. There were meetings with the council of elders, the leaders of Baruth, and the former members of the Lianthus court.

Knowing the people of Baruth wouldn't approve of moving the capitol to another city, Will had to think of a way to do it with as little fallout as he could. He was beginning to see a side of political manipulation that he didn't like. The problem was how to make such sweeping political changes, without making too many enemies in the process. The answer to his problem was given by an unlikely source, the former queen herself.

When Emma attempted to check over the Royal Suites she was physically thrown from the tower by the former Prince, Marcus. Now this, of course, infuriated William, but it gave him the power and resolve to make his move.

Followed by the entire Council of Elders, leading members of Baruth, Declan, Brody, Emma, and Chloe, William demanded that the queen open the door to the Royal Tower. She refused, but instead talked through the door.

"Madam, your reign in Andraya is over. You must leave the castle. It is the ruling center of the kingdom and it is from here that we shall have to do it," William called through the door.

"You are not the rightful ruler of Andraya," the reply came through the door. "My son is now ruler of Andraya, since you murdered my husband."

"We didn't murder Corland, madam. He made his own decision that cost him his life. If you do not leave this tower we will be forced to move you," William said.

"If you attempt to force my family from this tower, the people of Baruth will rebel!" the voice of a young man, most likely Marcus, boomed.

"He's right, my lord," replied a very jovial merchant named Akond. "Although the people support you, since we all know you won the throne legally, they still have the utmost respect for the Lianthus family. As such, the population would look unkindly at removing them from their home."

"I see," William replied. "Fine, as my first decree this Royal Tower is now to be called the Tower of Lianthus. Here shall be the home of the Lianthus family until they choose to leave it. Also, I now decree that by the choice of the people of Baruth, in their support of the Lianthus family, I cannot in good conscience allow my family to live here as well. The treatment of Queen Emma by the former prince is example enough. I will not allow my people to be threatened," William replied. Everyone, including the members from Baruth seemed to agree that he was without many options.

"Instead, we shall take apart the entire castle around the tower, brick by brick and move it to a new location. This new location shall be the new capitol city of Andraya. I shall make the choice for that new location within a day. To you members of the Baruth ruling class," he said turning his attention to their delegation, "pay heed to how my hand was forced in this. You gave me no choice." He yelled loud enough for all around him to hear.

Leading the way, he and his friends left the castle and officially moved out of the city. This caused quite a stir, and the people of Baruth didn't know what to say. They had been the capitol city for so long, yet they couldn't fault the new king for his decision. If the Lianthus family didn't want to vacate the seat of power, it would have to be moved.

Several groups of people from the city came to the king with different ideas to avoid moving the capitol. Such ideas as just build another castle or tear down the old one and move it across the city were brought forward. There was a suggestion to build another castle in clear view of the tower, one that would be the envy of the Lianthus family. But William replied that none of these would be practical.

"The affront of being forced to live next to a group of people who would not accept the legal and lawful rule of the citizens of Andraya would be too much," William told them all, and they all admitted he was right. So in the second week of his Royal ascension, William Duthain, King of Andraya, moved the capitol city from Baruth to a new location. Nestled in the shadows of the great Rothar Mountain range, the new city, Czariana, was born on the former site of their village. True to his word, each brick from the castle of Baruth was removed and transported to the new location. They were used to create the first outer wall of the city. It was later added to and made into the massive structure that now defended the city from intruders.

Emma was right; they were in for a very interesting life.

Chapter 31

In the Age of King William the First

The troops had been marching for a day since passing the town of Tyrene. When they arrived at the small town, they met with stiff resistance from the townsfolk. William wouldn't allow any innocents to be hurt or killed so it took longer than it normally would have to take the town. He was beginning to see how much time the added care was taking him, and he didn't think they had the luxury any more.

Scouts had reported signs of burned out camp fires to the east of the army, indicating that either someone was shadowing them or trying to get by them. The fires were very small and were probably used by someone moving with little or no equipment. No other person would light such a small fire unless they needed one for cooking hunting kills without being seen.

This information bothered William the most. Since the letter from Emma he knew their chances of surprising the men of Lytton would be nearly zero. But he wasn't going to let that stop his advance. Turn back now and the people of Andraya would be targets for a more vicious attack. No, this stopped here and now, even if he had to personally see Marcus executed and had to take over Eland itself.

Through his whole life, William had more and more responsibility forced on him. Some days he wished he could just live the life of a village carpenter. Working hard, but only taking care of his family and not an entire kingdom. He smiled to himself thinking of coming home to Emma after working a long hard day.

He was lost in his thought when a rider galloped up to him. "You're Majesty!" the rider called out when he was close enough. The man quickly brought his ride to a halt before the king.

"Yes rider, what is it?" William asked.

"Sir, I come with the report from Commander Charlie who is leading the recon in the city," he said, handing the document over. "But that isn't all, Sire. She is trapped behind enemy lines. Somehow word of our movements has reached the royalty in Lytton and they have dispatched an armed force to meet us on the field," the man said.

William was disappointed, to say the least. But setting that aside, he thanked the messenger and sent him to rest.

He quickly read the report from Charlie but decided to study it at a more appropriate time. It was not important yet. "What do you think, General?" William asked, looking over at Declan.

"Well, milord, there isn't much else to do but prepare the army for battle," Declan said.

"I agree, Majesty," Brody added. "I say leave the support crews here to setup camp. This will give us a defensive fall back point if we need one. I'll prepare the area for just such a contingency."

"Yes, that makes sense. Brody see to it please. Declan call the commanders and let's prepare for a head to head attack. Tell the troops to prepare for battle," William said quietly. Declan saluted with his hand over his heart and rode quickly away to begin preparations.

Hours of consultations and flurry passed as Brody prepared the camp, using every person at his disposal. While he did that, Declan had the Cavalry, Archers, and spearmen prepare to march in battle formations. A battle plan was quickly drawn up using the field reports gathered by the Rangers. Just ahead was a large open field where Declan was sure they would meet the enemy. Based on this information, they figured they would have to march a half hour before coming upon them.

Soon William and Declan were at the head of the army, who was once again moving forward. Chloe and the other Rangers were sent to attack from behind the opposition from the cover of the forest.

The forest began to thin on their side of the clearing, and although all was silent, William saw a glimmer of something metallic shining in the sun light. As they broke through the forest edge, they saw a large force of archers and cavalry across the clearing, waiting for them. William and his army rode forward, his men moving out on either side of their king and general, like the wings of a giant bird.

They continued to fill the clearing, using their numbers to intimidate the opposition. William watched all the faces he could see for a reaction, and the one he received the most gave him heart.

"Sire, these men are greatly outnumbered," Declan said to William.

"Yes, it looks that way," William agreed. "Let's hope we can keep this confrontation to a minimum." They rode onward until they reached the middle of the clearing, at which point, Declan gave the order to halt and they waited.

Soon, a small group rode towards them from the enemy army. William and Declan let them ride forward, making them come right up to the wall of Andrayan forces. The riders slowed to a walk and stopped in front of King William and General Declan.

"King William, of Andraya?" one of the four men spoke.

"Yes," William replied.

"I am here on behalf of the people of Eland to ask that you turn back your act of aggression and leave these lands in peace," the man said, almost as if he memorized the words only hours ago.

'So this wasn't a regular herald or general,' William thought to himself. This realization made sense. Commander Charlie's report said that the city was guarded by a skeleton crew of soldiers. Of them, most were newly conscripted from the citizenry, others were retired soldiers and still others were children.

"Where is your commanding officer, soldier?" Declan asked suddenly, his deep voice filling the clearing.

"Sir, I am the commanding officer of this force," the man replied.

"I see. What is your rank soldier?" Again Declan's voice boomed. William had heard this tone and intensity before from Dec when he was training soldiers. His authority was rarely challenged when he took this posture.

"My rank, sir?" the man asked.

"Son, you're obviously not a stupid man, the question was simple enough!" Declan boomed even louder.

"I am First Captain of the field defenses!" the young man quickly replied. William wasn't sure what Declan was doing but he decided to leave his cousin do his job.

"Listen to me, Captain," Declan boomed, "you have been sent here to gauge the depth of our convictions. You and your men are all green recruits, if I read faces correctly. Only yesterday you were nothing more than a soldier yourself I would wager!" Again William wasn't sure what was going on, but the tone of Declan's voice was quickly getting angry.

"I was a Sergeant, Sir!" the man replied, attempting to maintain his dignity but failing miserably.

"A Sergeant to a Captain? That doesn't strike you as odd, soldier?" Declan boomed. William had seen Dec get this angry before and for his own safety, kept his mouth shut. What had angered his general so much and so quickly?

"Sir, do you intend to turn or face my men?" the Captain asked, sitting straight and raising his voice. Declan had baited the man into anger, this was going to be dangerous. Well, dangerous for the Captain if William knew anything about the general.

"Son, I intend to release these soldiers to tear your troops to ribbons!" yelled General Declan. "I intend to walk over you as casually as I would saunter across this clearing. I would do so without second thought or bother, because my real goal is your commanders who sent you here today. Those are the same commanders who are now cowering within your capitol city walls, while you are sent to die. Now young Captain," he said the word with loathing, "I have to ask you, what do you intend to do? Archers!" he yelled as he drew his sword and held it above his head.

William didn't have to turn around to know that every archer instantly grabbed an arrow and drew their bows aiming high at the ranks across the clearing.

"Now, I am going to count to three before I signal my troops to open fire," Declan warned. "I will not spare you or your men either," he said nodding, and quickly four archers stepped forward and took close aim at the men on horseback. "Your generals have sent you to be fodder, thinking we were weak and didn't have a stomach for battle. Well they were wrong, and now you poor, arrogant children are going to die. Why? I'll tell you why; it's because Marcus is an arrogant son of a dog. And it's because he holds your life as precious as a pile of pig dung. So I ask you again, what are you going to do?"

The young man was caught completely off guard, and William was sure he was going to order an instant surrender. But instead, he and the three others accompanying him quickly turned their horses and bolted back towards their troops.

"One!" Declan yelled, his face red with rage.

"Two!" he yelled, watching for any change from across the field. Instead, it appeared hurried orders were being given by the young Captain.

"Three! Fire at will!" Declan commanded. Tens of thousands of twangs echoed in the clearing as the air darkened with arrows. Screams of pain quickly followed as volley after volley of arrows flew across the clearing. There were replies of cries as enemy archers got some shots off, but those soon ended and as quickly as it started, it was over.

"Halt fire!" Declan ordered raising his sword above his head again. An eerie silence filled the air where arrows once flew. Lowering his sword first to his shoulder and then re-sheathing it Declan signaled for a legion to come forward. The swordsmen moved ahead and their commander walked over to the Andrayan General.

"Captain, I want you and your men to go over there and dispatch the wounded," Declan ordered. The man saluted and commanded his men to follow. Declan then called forward another command group and started giving orders to take the wounded Andrayan troops back to the base camp and have them tended. Those who couldn't be moved were to be helped right there on the field.

He then gave commands to the ranger, who had warned them of the attack, to find Chloe. She was to get word to Commander Charlie to get back to the main camp as soon as she could. He also commanded that all scouting parties should return immediately. The man nodded his understanding. Quickly riding across the clearing and into the forest, he began searching for his commander.

"Dec?" William said, watching as the legion searched for wounded to put out of their misery.

"Not now, my king, I know you prefer it otherwise, but this must be done," Declan said, his voice was quiet but the rage was still seething.

When the legion of men returned they reported their findings to Declan who thanked them and told them to return to their positions. He then ordered the archers to move forward and recover any arrows that were reusable.

The cold callous way in which Declan was issuing commands reminded William of the past. Declan had acted the same way after he found out his parents were dead. He explained it once that he found it easier to step away from himself when the darkest situations had to be faced. It helped him make difficult decisions quickly.

Finally everything was done, and they were about to turn and ride away when Declan stopped and turned to William.

“My lord, I request permission to have the enemy buried,” Declan asked.

“Granted, General,” William replied, not having said anything to his cousin and friend for nearly an hour.

“Then sir, I’ll lead the burial myself. I would ask you lead the rest of the troops back to camp,” Declan requested.

“I agree, General. I’ll see you back at camp,” William said, and was saluted by Declan who started issuing orders to troops. William rode through the troops to the forest edge, and giving the order to move out, he led the men back to camp.

Chapter 32

In the Age of King William the First

That evening Declan returned quietly and went to his tent. William had asked Brody to keep an eye out for Dec's return, and the first minister soon let him know.

"Come on, Brody, he may need us," William said.

"Yeah, I think this one's going to be hard for him to handle," Brody replied as the two walked over to Declan's tent.

They stopped at the opening and waited a moment, then William called out to his general. "Dec, can we come in?" he asked.

"Yes, milord, come in," Declan's tired voice replied.

William and Brody walked into the tent to see Declan stripped down to his waist, washing himself in a basin of water. They looked into the basin and saw a mixture of reds and browns staining the water.

"You okay, Dec?" Brody asked.

"Yeah guys, I'm alright. We just finished praying for the dead and marking their stones. We had to use boulders that we could move by hand, and the carving isn't great, but we marked the site for them," Declan sighed.

"What happened out there, Declan?" William asked.

Declan sighed again and leaned forward on his knuckles, his hands submerged in water. "I sent a message to Marcus," Declan replied.

"You did?" William asked.

"Yeah I did. I'm sorry I didn't clear it by you first, Will," Declan replied.

"That's your job, Declan," William said. "When we are on the field of battle, you call the shots. I'm not going to second guess my top Command Staff."

"I appreciated that, after it was all over, and I began digging that hole," Declan said.

"You dug the hole yourself?" Brody asked.

"Most of the ground breaking, yeah. But the men helped me dig it deep. There are a couple of hundred men buried there. I only hope the same amount got away," he said.

"Have you heard from Chloe?" William asked.

"Yeah, I saw her after you all left. She had men following those who got away, not sure what we wanted done with them. I told her to let them go, and she recalled her men. They helped with the burial," Declan replied.

"So you let them go?" Brody asked.

"Like I said, I wanted to send a message to Marcus. Now he knows that blood will flow if he is a fool. Marcus thinks we're weak, cowardly, and unable to bring this battle to its most gruesome conclusion. Well today I showed him he's wrong," Declan explained.

"I didn't know this was in your nature, Dec," William replied.

"It has been for a long time, ever since I saw my father and mother's graves. I have hated the Lianthus family so much I can't wait to see that lick spittle dead. But these kids," he sighed, "these kids were wasted lives. After we beat him, without taking so few lives at Czariana, he thought we weren't a real threat.

"Now that he has seen that I am merciless, and you are giving me free rein, he has no choice but to take us seriously," he said, once again cleaning his hands. A hand maid entered the tent but stopped when she saw the trio before her.

"Young lady, could you arrange for a bath for me, please?" Declan asked. She curtsied and hurried out of the tent.

"Marcus won't care. Porthanaclies won't either, if I know him well enough. But they will prepare a strong defense of their perimeter," William said thinking aloud.

"Yes, well, all of the scouts should be back in camp tomorrow morning. I would recommend we stay for one more day, give our people a chance to unwind after today and then move on. We should be half a day's march from Lytton," Brody said.

"I agree. Have the hunters and cooks prepare a large feast for tomorrow night. We will eat well, and prepare for battle in two days," William commanded. Brody bowed and hurried from the tent.

"Dec," William said when they were alone, "why did you lose it?"

"Marcus made that fool Captain a patsy. That coward hides behind people. He speaks of leading and being a warrior while he hides behind women's skirts. Even his new kingdom is a farce. He married that poor girl for power, not for love," Declan replied. "I would think the majority of their forces are our prisoners. This handful of men that are now in the ground and whatever they have left, will be no match for us when we get there. That is, unless he can get support from another kingdom to him within two days."

"I don't think so. Eland is at least a two day march from most other capitols, and Lytton is nearly a week from most borders. If we move fast enough, and dispatch diplomats to the other kingdoms explaining our situation we shouldn't meet with any other resistance," William explained.

"So we don't have a lot of choice. We are going to have to make High King Porthanaclies regret ever approving Marcus' plans to attack Andraya. We are going to have to take a high toll on his people," Declan said.

"Why, Dec? Why do we need to force the king to pay with more blood?" William asked.

"Because if we don't then he will retaliate, and harder than the first attack by Marcus. Porthanaclies may be old, but he isn't stupid. He's fought in wars before. In the battle of Yelioth, I fought at his side to learn from a seasoned Commander, remember? Do you remember how long that war went?" Declan asked. "He fought night and day, he was vicious and aggressive. He told me that we had to force the barbarians to yield to our strength at that time or they never would. Majesty, we have to make him do the same. We must become a threat too dangerous to warrant another attack."

"You decided this today?" William asked.

"No not really. He is feeling the call of battle, and his new son-in-law is rekindling it. His battle lust is driving him now, but he needs to be slapped back to his senses. He must remember to never pick a fight with a bigger dog, it just gets you bit," Declan said.

William understood what his general said and agreed. When the hand maiden returned, William took leave and let Declan deal with his day as he knew he needed to.

Two days later William, Declan, and Brody stood at the edge of the clearing before the castle fortress of Lytton, Capitol city of Eland. The outer walls stood like a row of teeth, protecting the jewel of the kingdom, Lytton Castle. There, like a spear aimed at heaven, the castle rose above the city, an awesome sight to behold.

Although William still thought it was a waste, he fully understood that this was the image his own people wanted to impress upon visiting Royalty with Czariana's royal court. The city of Lytton was built upon a hill with the castle at its top. There it rose like a monument, high above the city walls. On each of the four corners stood a tall tower, their pennants flapping in the high breeze. Large walls connected the towers, making an imposing fortress that could be used as a final fall back point if needed.

Then within the fortress walls towered the box like central palace, its huge central spire jutting into the sky. Each window opened to a balcony, and each balcony was lined with people. The entire structure was built with white rock, an image of tranquility, with war at its door. Nonetheless, it was time for action. Brody and Declan quickly moved among the soldiers giving orders to man and woman alike. Ranks of archers took their place, creating imposing battle formations far from the castle walls, well outside the reach of bowshot. Of course, the walls were also out of their reach but they would move forward when the time was right.

They also dispatched a small battalion to setup the Parlay tent, and when it was ready they raised the flag of Parlay. This would not be carried out as Marcus had done, they wouldn't delay this discussion. Instead, William and his friends wanted the battle over quickly.

Chloe and her Rangers were sent back to Tyrene to support the troops maintaining the people there. Once everyone was accounted for from the recon teams, the role of the Rangers became one of support, not attack.

William, Declan, and Brody had spent hours discussing the tactical information gathered from Commander Charlie's mission into the city. Their plan of attack was clear.

Declan was right, the city was only being defended by a skeleton defense force made up mostly by generals, who stayed behind, and a few hundred troops. The majority of their archers were captives in Andraya, since Marcus thought he would need them more during his siege of Czariana.

Several battalions were then dispatched around the city to watch for any messengers and anyone attempting to escape. But typical of Castle construction, Lytton had very few gates around the city to allow a more focused defense.

William was focused on ensuring that everything was going as planned, when he was warned that he would be needed at the Parlay tent shortly. He and Declan rode down to the tent with the standard number of Knights at their back, as required by ancient law. William thought about it and wondered why any Knights were required at all. It was a piece of information that intrigued him. They arrived at the tent, just in time, as the Lytton city gate opened and the delegation from within rode towards them.

William and Declan watched as nine people rode across the clearing. By the laws of Parlay, six of them should be protection. That meant that three of them were royalty or commanders.

The delegation from Lytton came to a halt near the tent, and all of them got down from their mounts. William was surprised that the three commanders were, in fact, the three royals, Marcus, High King Porthanaclies, and his daughter, Marcus' wife, Jasmine.

William's gaze passed over all three, but he was startled at how average Jasmine looked. With all of Declan's jokes about her being a horse face, she wasn't all that bad looking. A little pug nosed I guess, but she was nowhere near a horse face. William glanced at his general with a look of confusion on his face.

As if he could read his cousin's mind, Declan quietly whispered, "Just wait for it. You'll see."

"King William, we come to Parlay," High King Porthanaclies said.

"High King Porthanaclies, we welcome you, too, as brothers in arms," William replied, showing respect to the High King by using the phrase taken from ancient law. "I know your son-in-law, King Marcus, but I have never met this beautiful woman," William said politely smiling at the woman at the high king's side.

"This, King William, is my daughter, Queen Jasmine," Porthanaclies introduced. The woman smiled and held out her hand. Instantly, William knew what Declan was talking about. The woman's mouth was horrible! Her smile would have scared young children, but without skipping a beat the king took her hand and kissed it.

"I am honored to meet you, madam," William said, "Now if you would, please come in and sit for a spell, we can discuss this meeting of our kingdoms."

Following him, everyone entered the tent and took their positions. As high king, Porthanaclies would lead the discussion from the Eland position. His daughter would stand at Marcus' side, since they were considered equals during the Parlay. Declan took his regular position at William's back.

"King William, you are the aggressor here, so the opening parlay goes to you," King Porthanaclies said calmly as his tea was poured by a servant.

"I am honored at your show of respect. High King, the people of Andraya are here for repayment. Damages caused by your troops under the direction of King Marcus during his attack on Czariana were considerable. During his march upon our capitol city, he and your men destroyed every village in their path. Some were worse than others, but all of them were uninhabitable," William replied.

"That is the nature of war, King William," King Porthanaclies replied. "You do not allow an enemy at your back. It is my understanding that the villages were empty and no one was hurt?"

"Very true, High King. Our people were warned and moved out before any damage to their persons could be done. But with that being said, since they had evacuated before your men arrived, there was no enemy behind your troops to force such destruction," William replied. He could see that his repeated reference to the troops belonging to King Porthanaclies was starting to get to Marcus.

"Indeed. I can see your point. Marcus what say you about this?" the high king said over his shoulder.

"Majesty," again his reaction was interesting. The word Majesty rolled out of the youth's mouth like it left a bad taste behind. "General Austin let the men release some pent up aggression on the villages. It was not of my doing," he replied.

"I see, so instead of this being your doing, it was mine?" the high king replied. This was better than William had hoped for. The obvious loss of his troops, opening the kingdom to attack had angered the high king. "Well I won't be making that mistake any time soon. What is it you demand, King William?" Porthanaclies asked.

"Fifty thousand bars of gold as repayment for the destruction committed in this act of war. It will also act as compensation for allowing this act of unprovoked aggression to take place," King William said taking a sip of his tea. King Porthanaclies visibly shook for a moment but his outward composure didn't change. "We have always been friends, High King; our people have traded since before my reign began. There has never been an angry word between us, and yet this attack upon our people has taken place."

The high king gently cleared his throat. "The villages and damages to your city would not cost half as much as you are asking, King William. We are indeed friends of old, and a war between us would do neither of us any good. But when my family welcomed young Marcus into it, we took on his grievances as well. That included his right to the throne of Andraya," he explained, "It has come to our attention that our soldiers are not dead in your lands, but are held by their honor to be your captives for one year. When they are free, the balance that is currently in your favor changes."

"I see, and so you are saying that if I take what is rightfully due the people of Andraya, I would be opening further aggression between us?" William replied.

"Indeed," agreed the high king.

"So I should take my men home, with some paltry sum you deem worthy and sit upon my unjustly obtained throne and be happy?" William asked.

"Well I would suggest my counter offer wouldn't be paltry, but it will be much less than fifty thousand bars," the high king replied, sounding very happy with himself.

'*The arrogant fool has bought all of Marcus' lies, including the ones about being divined to be king!*' William thought to himself.

"I see, and when your men return, and King Marcus wants another go at attacking us to free the throne of the usurper, you will back him?" William replied.

"The future is unclear, young King William, but I must stand behind my family," Porthanaclies said. William saw a self-satisfied grin appear upon Marcus' face.

"I see, well I agree we won't be taking fifty thousand from the treasury," William replied, sounding a little down trodden.

"I'm glad to see you're coming to your senses, King William," Porthanaclies replied.

"Instead, I am going to take all of it!" William exploded. The violence of his voice shattered the calm within the tent. "You send your new puppy to try to regain some of your lost victories of old, and then insult my people and me? Marcus comes to our gates, threatens my people, my wife, my children because his father yielded a fair fight? Yes, Corland was killed, after he attempted to kill me with a dagger to my back! Instead he killed a friend of mine and lost his own life in the process." The high king was about to interrupt.

"Oh, I'm sure Marcus told you everything. Everything he wanted you to know. Did he also tell you that I challenged Corland, to a fight of honor as dictated by the Ten Kings? Did he tell you that after a fierce battle, Corland yielded, and that I offered him his life instead of death? I'm sure you know just as much as that idiot wanted you to know.

"Yet I know that you knew all that before Marcus darkened your doorway. You knew, High King, because we've always gotten along, and I've never made secret how I earned my throne. You've heard the stories with your own ears, from many of my people. Yet you still allowed this fool's vendetta to blind you. Know this, High

King Porthanaclies, I will take from this city and your people to pay for the hurt caused to mine. I will also take to show you what your pride has cost you, and I will also warn you of this."

William leaned across the table until he was nose to nose with the old startled king. "If you or anyone who comes after you, ever comes into Andraya bearing arms again, I will come back to Lytton. And when I return, not only will I take everything in the Royal Treasury I will take the entire blasted kingdom!"

Then, as suddenly as William exploded, he calmed and retook his seat. He took a deep calming breath and a sip of tea. He stared across the table at the shocked expression looking back at him.

"You've gone mad!" Porthanaclies said finally.

"No, but I am angry, High King. When you treated me with respect, I thought we could at least discuss this like equals. I thought we could act as the Rulers of our kingdoms and come to an understanding. But when you showed me that you no more respected me than your sorry excuse of a son-in-law does, I had enough.

"We do not want to spill blood, King Porthanaclies. Why do you think your men are still alive in Andraya? I came here hoping that even if you disagreed with my demand for fifty thousand gold bars, you would offer something definitive and clear. But your offer of a threat was enough. By the rules of War set out by the ancients I will not attack until tomorrow morning," William said, lowering his tea cup and getting to his feet. "After that, only surrender will save you." He finished, and followed by Declan he walked out and back to his troops.

"That went well," a sarcastic voice said behind him.

“Yeah, it went great,” William replied with a sigh. “Can you do what I just warned him that we will do?” he asked.

“Attack? Take the city and not stop unless they surrender? Consider it done, milord,” Declan replied.

“Good. Let’s do this and get away from these lunatics,” William said as they continued walking to the forest edge.

Chapter 33

In the Age of King William the First

The next morning dawned cold and dark, as if nature herself knew that battle was about to commence. William sat upon his charger next to Declan, watching the shadowed walls of the city before them. Brody was preparing the war machines that were hidden in the trees behind them, waiting his role in the coming battle. When the first rays of sunlight fell upon the top of Lytton's city walls, William nodded to Declan. The general called the advance and the troops began to march forward.

Four long rows of men moved towards the city walls. Lead by an archer with a crossbow, followed behind by a swordsman with a large shield on his back, they moved forward. William knew now that Lytton's defenses were indeed minimal as they had yet to be fired upon.

When the archers were well within longbow range of the city walls, they laid down bales of long grass that they carried and perched themselves behind them, taking sight on the soldiers defending the top of the city walls. None of the shadows, hidden between the parapets, moved to William's amazement. He was beginning to question what was going on. What was Marcus waiting for?

As the Andrayan archers took their positions, the sword and shield troops who had followed them, took up positions behind the archers and laid their shields against their backs.

William and Declan were behind the troops, outside of a standard archery attack but still at risk of ballista and catapult volleys, watching everything with interest. Declan, as curious as the king, watched the men upon the wall, studying them in the dim morning light.

"It's almost as if they aren't men at all?" he said in a whisper.

"What do you mean?" William asked.

"Well milord, either those men are seasoned veterans or they're not men. Any rookie would have flinched by now, someone would have moved. The morning is crisp enough you can hear our troop's armor clearly, yet you hear nothing from the wall. I don't think those are real men," the general replied.

Declan rode forward a bit and getting down from his horse he knelt next to a front row archer. "Soldier, have you targeted a man on that wall?" he asked.

"Yes, General, directly in front of me." The soldier replied quietly.

"Good, take him down." Declan ordered and instantly the soldier held his breath, gently squeezed the trigger on his crossbow and sent the bolt flying through the air. The only sound was the whistle the bolt made as it flew straight and true landing in the chest of the target. To everyone's surprise the defenders on the wall didn't do anything! No one, not even the victim moved.

Suddenly, there was a loud whistling noise and in a long high arch above the castle walls a volley of arrows headed in their direction.

"Defense!" Declan yelled and quickly the Sword and Shield men, standing behind each archer, moved forward. Slinging their shields over themselves and the archer they prepared for the volley to fall. Declan quickly slapped the rump of his charger which ran off towards the forest and dove under a shield as the arrows landed around them. The noise of arrows bouncing off of the shields and thudding into the ground surrounded them, shattered the quiet of a moment before.

An occasional cry rang out from the soldiers on the field before the gates, as several unprotected appendages were pierced by the falling arrows. William watched as the arrows thudded into the ground just feet from where he sat upon his mount. He was glad for Declan's accurate knowledge of the enemies range. Even though he had to fight to keep his charger in check, he remained untouched as volley, upon volley rained down from the sky.

Seeing that Declan was in no position to give orders, William wheeled his horse around and rode back to the troops.

He rode to Brody quickly and yelled, "First Minister, move the catapults forward and attack the enemy archers behind that wall!"

"You heard the king, put your backs into it!" Brody called. The joints in the large war machines creaked as the men began pushing them forward. The catapults had been designed to defend against such an attack. The men who were pushing the war machines forward were inside the frame, hidden behind sheets of leather, protecting them from the falling arrows.

Slowly the two large catapults moved forward until they were behind the rows of archers and within the range of the city walls. They were then anchored in place by spikes behind the wheels, and as soon as they were ready, William bellowed the order, "Fire!"

Both machines snapped as their payloads flung through the air and smashed into the city walls. Briefly, in the locations around the impact, the arrows stopped firing. But they were once again filled when whoever stood behind the walls became confident in their protection.

"Reload and prepare to fire!" William commanded, and Brody began issuing orders to the field teams to prepare the large war machines for their next volley. When they were ready they were once again fired. This time with a slight trajectory change, their payloads soared over the walls and into the city proper.

This time the tactic had the desired effect and the rain of arrows slowed to a trickle. Seeing his chance, Declan ordered a withdrawal of the troops who quickly stood up, and with the shield men behind creating a wall of steel they hurried back out of the range of the arrows before they started to fly again.

During this time, Brody had the men reload the catapults and was preparing to fire again. A quick nod from William was all he needed as he gave the order to fire. William watched as two more boulders flew over the city walls. An unexpected crash echoed through the morning air as a large building seemed to drop down on itself. One of the Catapult boulders must have struck it, causing it to drop like a house of cards.

'That is what would have happened to Czariana if we hadn't taken those catapults out.' the king thought to himself.

As Declan ran up to the king, his squire led his horse back to him. He remounted and took stock of the situation before them. "Crossbows will be no good with that kind of arc," he said calmly. "They put up dummies on the walls to hide their numbers in the streets. Nice move. I see the high king hasn't lost his touch." A small grin flashed in the corner of his mouth.

Declan turned to a trumpeter. "Sound the longbow advance!" he called and the trumpeter blew the notes calling forth the longbow men. The archers moved forward with the shield men, this time the shields were in front, deflecting the hail of arrows from the city. "Fire when ready!" Declan called and soon the arrows from the Andraya archers joined the hail from the city. Back and forth the arrows flew, bouncing off shield and stone, wounding some, killing others.

William watched as the battle went nowhere. He looked over at Brody who was once again calling for another couple of boulders to be loaded. William called him over, and as soon as he was in earshot he commanded, "First Minister, break down that door!"

Chapter 34

In the Age of King William the First

Brody saluted William and rode off calling out orders to his work crews. On the field it was Declan's job to command the troops and it was Brody's to command the support teams and engineers corps. As he quickly rode to the tree line, a large cube rolled out from the underbrush. While the archers had been engaging the cities defenses, Brody's engineers had completed assembly of their secret weapon.

This large armored vehicle contained a Ballista somewhat like the ones located in the Defensive Hall back in Czariana. It too had three lathes, increasing the velocity and impact of the bolt inside. But the difference with this was it was designed to act as a battering ram to destroy the city gates.

Four teams of Oxen, hidden inside the protective shell of hides and copper shields, pushed the battering ram into place. Once there, Brody once again started yelling commands and the sounds of struggling men told William that the crews were placing tension on the large draw cable. The king moved behind the battering ram to see what was happening inside the open backed vehicle. There, teams of men turned a large pivot, winding the draw cable back into position. The battering ram bolt was already loaded on the rack and once the cable was pulled back into place, the Ballista was aimed at the middle of the large gates. When the gunner was satisfied with the aim of her weapon, she gave Brody the thumbs up who yelled for all clear. The teams inside the mobile battering ram quickly moved away from all the moving parts and when he was sure of everyone's safety Brody yelled, "Fire!"

The loud distinctive plunk of the converted long range weapon echoed through the air as the huge bolt flew from the small opening in the front of the wagon. The projectile soared through the air. Its long chain noisily uncoiled with each foot that it flew towards its objective.

The impact of the battering ram slamming against the huge city gates resonated in the air around them. Everyone watched with bated breath as the pointed head of the ram caused it to lodge deeply in the door. Then as its immense weight drew it downward, the bolt fell to the ground, taking with it a large piece of wood gouged from its target. Once again Brody began issuing orders as his men ran back into place and began pulling the bolt back towards the ram rack to reload. William watched with pride as his countrymen worked together like a well-oiled machine, preparing the next launch of the battering ram.

His interest was quickly interrupted, though, as Chloe rode up to him coming to a skidding halt. "William!" she called as he turned to see her.

"Chloe, what is it?" the king asked his panting sister.

"My Rangers and I were on our way to support the soldiers in Tyrene, like you ordered, when I received a message from Emma!" she said.

"What's wrong?" the king asked, fear rising in the pit of his stomach.

"There are rumors that some of the captives are making plans to attack the city while we are away!" she exclaimed.

"What!" William roared. "Austin is using this as his time to attack!"

"I don't think so. The report said he was trying to keep a lid on things, but he was having difficulty. He seems to have lost a lot of face with the surrender," she explained.

"Alright, you and every ranger and soldier guarding Tyrene get back to Czariana now! Take the entire cavalry as well. Brody!" William yelled, looking for his old friend.

"What, milord? We are preparing the weapon for the second launch," he yelled back.

"Hold for a moment, if it is safe," William called. Brody quickly rode up to where they all sat upon their horses to listen to his orders. Just as he arrived, Logan pulled up to see what was happening. "Get the gun crew ready for the next launch, and then join Chloe. Logan prepare the Night Hawk to return to Czariana. The Eland captives may attack the city while we're away," he said, trying to remain calm. Brody and Logan's expressions instantly turned to shock and anger. Turning, they both galloped back to their commands to prepare for their departure.

"Lord, should we send back any other troops?" Declan asked looking over the ranks of those remaining.

"No, Chloe will already have nearly 15 thousand troops to work with. Between them, the Rangers left behind, and the Czariana defensive troops, she should be able to defend the city until we return. We need the rest of the troops here to finish this infernal siege of Lytton," he said, anger flashing across his face.

"William?" Chloe questioned.

"I was a fool! I trusted that honor and dignity would prevail in those soldiers. Now I know they are just cut throats. Go quickly little sister; use what secrets you have to move our troops home and protect the city, our people, and my family," William said, as fear tinged his voice.

"I'm not going back to protect Emma from the Elanders, big brother," Chloe said with a smile. "I'm going back to protect them from her," she said, and turning, she galloped quickly towards the cavalry. William smiled as she rode away, but the anger he felt still filled him.

He watched as Brody gave the orders to a commander. The king recognized Shade, Brody's son, who had recently been promoted to Commander of the archers. He looked over at Declan who was also watching what was going on.

"The young man is getting another promotion?" William asked.

"It appears as such. That boy is nearing your record for the most promotions in a year. I fear our titles may be next, milord," Declan chuckled. William laughed too, regardless of his anger. Both men were proud of their best friend's only son.

"He's a good choice though. Shade has always had his father's love for invention," William added, to which Declan chuckled in agreement.

Finally, when Brody was apparently satisfied, he turned and saluted both of his friends. Using the sign language they created as children, they both wished him God Speed and good luck. Winking, he turned his horse and galloped to the trees.

"It'll be alright Will. They will take care of everything," Declan said, watching the soldiers move quickly back towards home. "They will get there faster, too, since they aren't trying to go unnoticed."

"I'm a fool, Dec. I shouldn't have let this happen," William said, the pain filling his chest.

"No, milord, we are fools. I believed Austin as well when he said we could trust the caliber of his men. But no matter now, Czariana can be defended by an infant, never mind a woman as extraordinary as Emma. She's had to deal with you all these years, I'm sure she could handle an army in shambles," Declan said turning back towards the Eland capitol's city walls.

William did the same just in time to see the battering ram launch a second time. This time when it hit the wall it smashed into the opening and had to be pulled back as its tip got stuck in the much larger hole.

While all of this went on at the battering ram, the Andraya archers shot a continuous stream of arrows over the walls. They were attempting to draw the defensive fire from the city away from the battering ram launcher any way possible.

The launch and reloading of the battering ram continued for the next couple of hours. The door was being hit, but after the first couple of successful impacts, the ram did less and less damage. The king watched as a second gun crew was called in to take over for the first crew. He was amazed when the people that were manning the weapon were literally carried out of the siege device. That's when he realized that with the mid-day sun, the oxen, and the effort of pulling that log back, it would have been exhausting for the crew inside. Seeing the soldiers laying on the ground behind the vehicle, William started shouting orders. Quickly, several support teams rushed forward and carried the men back to the shade of the forest behind them.

The ground around them had gone from green to black, as the ground was literally covered in arrows. The seemingly tireless archers just kept firing, trying to divert attention from the battering ram. So many arrows had been fired, that William noticed some of the archers were using arrows that had landed around them. He too was beginning to recognize the red and blue fletching of Andrayan arrows sticking in the ground amongst the black Eland arrows.

"Well, it looks like Brody's ingenuity is about to pay off," Declan said, pointing to the huge hole in the center of the city gates.

Chapter 35

In the Age of King William the First

Declan and William watched as the battering ram was launched again. This time it didn't just slam into the door, it slammed through the weakened wood and nearly went all the way into the opening it created! They continued to watch as a small rope that was tied to the log was pulled, causing a loud clang, as well as a cry of warning from within the city. The log had now turned from a battering ram, into a large three prong grapple!

A band of metal held down three long fingers reaching from the arrow head, down along the length of the ram. By pulling on the rope the spring loaded fingers reached out and gripped the door around the inside of the hole. The men within the protective cube were heard grunting again as the slack was picked up on the chain, dragging the grapple firmly into place.

More orders were issued, and quickly, the oxen were replaced by horses that were backed up to the armored vehicle. They were then hooked up to the large chain on the ram as they attempted to pull the doors down. William watched with wonder as his friends invention was put into action.

The teams of horses were urged forward, and as the slack in the chain was quickly picked up, the handlers pushed their steeds on. The force the horses were putting on the chain was incredible, as you could see their hooves tearing the ground beneath them. But it was good solid clay below the grass, and finally, when deep enough gouges were dug, they began to pull the huge grapple.

It wasn't long after they started that the sounds of creaking from the giant doors began. Suddenly with an explosion of wood and twisted metal, the door flew open. The horses tripped forward with loud shrieks of surprise as they collided into one another. William then turned turn his attention away from them as Declan bellowed for the Andrayan troops to retreat. The ranks of archers and shield men quickly responded by pulling back from their positions. "We're going to see what they do next," Declan explained as the men took their places on either side of them, watching and waiting for his command.

At first, nothing moved within the gaping opening in the castle walls. Slowly at first, then more rapidly, men, women, and children started to walk out of the gate. It appeared that the residents of the city began to empty onto the plain before the walls.

King William watched in disbelief as a human shield was erected before the destroyed city entrance. Children whimpered in fear, as they stared at the Andrayan army watching them incredulously. William couldn't believe his eyes; the cowardice of what he was seeing completely overwhelmed him.

Declan turned to the king, apparently awaiting the command. "We can't harm those people," William said, staring Declan in the eyes.

"No, sire, I didn't think we could," he said with a sigh, and his shoulders relaxed as if all the tension escaped out his mouth. "What do we do now, then?"

"We talk to them," William said. He spurred his horse forward, but before he got close, he felt an arrow glance off his chest. He quickly pulled his horse to heel, and turning, they retreated.

"Those cowards!" William said, rage filling the void of emotions rather than fear. "What do you think, General?" he asked, nearly spitting with rage.

"They have the disadvantage, and as such must request parlay at this time. They could challenge you to one on one, as you did to Corland, but they would have to put Eland on the line. I don't think Porthanaclies is willing to go that far," Declan explained.

Spurring his horse forward, Declan stopped outside the safe zone of the city's archers. "People of Lytton," he shouted, "we offer you safety within our ranks if you choose!"

"And anyone who tries to leave," he heard Marcus' voice shout, "will be shot for treason!"

Declan stared at the scared faces before him and sadly shook his head. Turning, he began to ride back to King William's side. As he rode, he caught Captain Shade's attention. Signaling the young man, the general called Shade who quickly joined his two commanders.

"Captain, your father left you in charge of the war machines?" the general asked.

"Yes, sir," replied the youth.

"Fine, retarget the catapults at the city. Launch your payloads into the walls, and avoid hitting the people. I want them to be showered by rubble, not stones," Declan commanded.

"I'll do my best, sir; we're throwing boulders not rocks," the Captain said, and saluted them both. He then ran and began shouting orders.

Declan then began calling up his sword and shield, and ordered all archers to change weapons to add to the force. He then moved them forward, creating a wall of shields before them.

"What are you planning, Dec?" William asked.

"Some crowd control, milord," the general replied with a grin. He then signaled to Shade who yelled the command to fire.

Screams burst from the people by the gates as the boulders flew through the air. The stone payloads impacted the top of the walls causing rubble to fall on the people. Declan nodded his approval to the young Captain, who ordered a reload. As the people crowded forward, they looked behind in horror. Declan turned to his trumpeter and ordered the advance.

The Andrayan soldiers moved forward, stomping the ground, creating an ominous sound as they moved forward as one. Their shields shone in the dull sunlight as they moved. Suddenly, a hail of arrows flew at them. Declan then issued a command and the entire force shifted into defensive mode. Creating a massive wall of moving steel above and all around the advancing Andrayans, the Lytton arrows simply bounced off of them, not able to get through.

Still the army moved forward, crowding the people who were being pinched between the oncoming soldiers and the city walls crumbling behind them. The women and children at the front of the group cringed as the first of the soldiers came upon them. But to their surprise they were merely walked past. The Andrayan troops pushed to the rear of the frightened civilians where they stopped. Now the shields of the Andrayan soldiers were protecting Lytonian's from their own army!

William smiled at his old friend and slapped him on the shoulder. A defensive wall was created above, between and most importantly behind the people. The catapults had stopped firing to avoid causing more chaos, when Shade saw the Andrayans were in place. Because people had moved away from the city to avoid the debris, there was a gap between them and the walls. The opening that was created was now filled by Andrayan soldiers.

Declan nodded to a trumpeter who sounded a blast from his trumpet and the forces once again began marching. This time they started moving back towards the general and the king outside of the Lytonian archers range. When the soldiers started marching away from the city, they urged the frightened people to move with them. The soldiers met with resistance at first, but when the people realized what was happening, they began to move as well. Slowly, marching along with the step by step cadence established by the Andrayan troops, the people moved to safety.

The hail of arrows increased from the city walls, now clearly manned by archers emboldened by the lack of return fire from the Andrayan troops. But the cocoon of shields kept the massive, slow moving group protected. Once in a while an arrow would get through and a cry would ring out but the soldiers and civilians never stopped moving.

"Any one that is wounded is being helped along by soldiers and hopefully fellow townspeople around them," Declan explained. Finally, the entire host of troops and civilians were out of bow shot and only stopped moving when they reached the safety of the forest edge.

Declan issued another order and soon the entire population, now safe from harm, was surrounded and guarded by the soldiers of Andraya. Then with another command, support people from the forest rushed forward to help the wounded.

"Now let's see what those desperate fools do!" Declan chuckled, watching the city. When nothing happened, Declan ordered a guard rotation established to watch the people and called for the soldiers to stand down. The men stayed in armor but were able to rest after a long day of battle. The archers were so exhausted that they were given the first opportunity to sleep, and most slept where they fell.

William, Declan, and Shade talked, leaving guards to watch the castle gate. "The day was a good one," Declan said, stretching his legs out under the table as they ate.

"What are the casualty numbers like, Captain?" William asked.

Speaking casually in the privacy of the king's tent, the young man replied, "Seven hundred men were wounded during the initial attack from the city. Then throughout the day another hundred and thirty eight were hurt during both the counter attacks and the civilian extraction."

"How many died, Shade," the king asked.

"Ninety two, Uncle," Shade said quietly, "And we may lose three or four civilians wounded during the extraction."

William shook his head. Ninety two people are dead, because of a vendetta. He sighed deeply.

"The numbers could have been a lot worse, Will," Declan said, calmly eating another helping.

"I know gentlemen, I know. I just hate losing anyone because I ordered a war," the king sighed again.

"Uncle William," Shade said, "If it helps, the soldiers, men and women alike, have pretty much all agreed that what we are doing here for the people, who lost their homes, is worth it. A couple wishes they were on their way home to help defend Czariana, but for the most part, they are behind you. When we moved forward to protect the innocent people of this city from their own rulers, they were given a reason other than gold for being here."

"Hmm, yes, I heard that as well when I was checking on the prisoners," Declan explained. "The futility of this afternoon's archery display was weighing heavy on the troops. They haven't seen a lot of battle, so they aren't used to such mundane tactics. Doing something for the good of another seemed to fill them with purpose."

"Really?" William asked surprised. "They needed that feat that much?"

"It's really not a surprise, my king," Declan replied. "They're Andrayan citizens, how else would they react?" He grinned and punched his old friend in the shoulder and took a long pull of his ale. William chuckled at his friend and was about to turn back to his meal, when Ashton burst in the tent opening.

"Father, there is a sign from the city!" he said panting.

Chapter 36

In the Age of King William the First

"Child, we REALLY do need to do something about your entrances," William smiled and patted his son on the back as they all headed out of the tent and back onto the field. They turned toward the castle and there, flying above the castle walls, was the sign of Parlay.

"How long has it been there, Ash?" William asked.

"Fifteen minutes, you're Highness," Ashton replied. The king looked at his son out of the corner of his eye. Seeing only a look of duty in the boy's face, he accepted the official title from his son for what it was.

"Alright, so we will head down in a half hour," William replied, looking up at the setting sun. "Chloe should be at Tyrene tomorrow morning," he said.

"Don't worry about that now, Majesty," Declan replied. "One war at a time. Besides, she will be back at Czariana in two or three weeks by my calculations if they don't get held up."

"Dad may have some ideas on how to get them home faster. And no one knows the forest like Aunt Chloe," Shade added.

"Yeah, you're both right, I better focus on the task at hand. Ash, get the royal guard prepared. Captain, you will join us at this meeting," he said, his words more a command than a request.

"Of course, your majesty," the young Captain replied. They went and checked on the wounded and made sure preparations for the dead were being handled. The sight of a dead child being prepared for burial nearly overwhelmed William.

He didn't care how much time was left; he headed towards the prisoners instantly and easily found the grieving mother of the dead child. Her painful wails met them much sooner than the sight of her. Being escorted by guards, the king moved through the sea of people until he stood before the young woman, lost in her grief.

Without saying a word, he walked up to her, sensed the apprehension around him and quickly pulled her into his arms. Her wails grew louder at his embrace as all he could do was hold her and stroke her hair as she cried into his chest. Other people began to cry, as if his strength allowed them to give into their fatigue fueled grief.

He lost all track of time, but she finally cried herself to sleep. Lifting her into his arms he took her to where the Andrayan support people had made her a bed under a tree. He laid her down and walked silently away.

He rejoined the Lytton people, and finding a man who had stood close to them the entire time he held the woman asked, "Where is her husband, father?"

"We don't know. He was one of the men who didn't return from Andraya," he replied.

"Most of those men are still alive, for now," William replied, torn between relief, anger, and sadness.

"Sire, did you say they were still alive?" another man asked.

"Yes, most of them. Some of them were wounded and King Marcus ordered them killed instead of being tended to," William replied curtly, letting the shock settle upon the people. "More of them are likely to die before the end of the week," he added again, pausing to let it sink in.

"You are having them executed?" a voice called from the throng.

"No!" William boomed, his temper on the verge of exploding. "When we were successful in capturing most of your troops alive, General Austin surrendered. He gave his word that your countrymen would be honorable and serve a term, working in Andraya. This was to pay for their crimes against the Andrayan people. Many in their path were driven from their homes before the Eland army burned their villages to the ground!" The crowd didn't seem surprised to hear of such nobility from the general, but reeled at the brutality of the pillaging.

"Then why execute them, sire?" another voice called, apparently crying.

"They are turning against General Austin, that is why. We just received word that they are perhaps going to break their word and attack the city while we are gone!" William shouted back. A cry of surprise shot through the crowd.

Calls of; 'Our men wouldn't do that.', 'I can't believe that.' and more echoed through the assembled people.

"I don't care what you believe. I have the word of my wife, the Queen of Andraya, that information has reached her of such a possibility. I have sent people to deal with it. I pray for their lives that they hold to their honor, or fewer of them shall return at the end of the year," he said and turning away he left the crowd to discuss what they had learned.

"Do you think it was a good idea to tell them?" Declan asked, walking at his side as they finally moved towards the castle.

"Maybe not. If they want to go back to the city, to be used as human shields again, let them. I for one will not threaten my men's lives a second time for their hides," William replied.

They continued forward until they came across the Lytton Delegation waiting impatiently just outside the mess of broken arrows on the ground.

"We have been waiting for nearly an hour!" the visibly angry high king nearly shouted as the Andrayan delegation drew near.

"Follow me!" William commanded and turning around he started walking back towards the camp. He didn't look back, at this point he didn't care if they listened or not. Either they did as he said or they left, either way, he wasn't going to fight much longer.

When he finally reached the edge of the guarded townspeople, he turned and saw that he was indeed followed. Close at his heels High King Porthanaclies, his daughter, and the cause of all their misery, Marcus, kept pace.

"You were upset that we made you wait an hour!" William yelled, loud enough for most of the crowd to hear and quiet down. "The reason I was late to our Parlay was because I just spent an hour consoling the grieving mother of a dead child."

"Your men are so low that they would kill a child?" Queen Jasmine exclaimed pretending to grow faint.

"No!" William shouted, shocking the queen out of her theatrics. "Your men are so low they would kill a child!" The instant silence was so thick it seemed to freeze everyone in place.

"Now wait a moment, King William, my men would do no such thing!" the high king exclaimed.

"Really?" William shot back. He turned and saw Shade. "Captain, bring me that man we spoke to earlier." The Captain saluted, and as quickly as he left, he returned with the old man in tow. "Father, when did that young child die and by whom?"

The old man hesitated to answer. Then a sudden scream of pain echoed through the silence, as the young woman re-awoke to the nightmare she was now living. Her pain seemed to free the man's tongue and he turned back to the royals before him, tears running down his face.

"He died when an arrow broke through the shields and hit him, sire," he said shakily.

"Where was the arrow fired from, and what shields protected you?" William asked again, the force of his voice carrying over the crowd.

"The arrows being fired at us were from the walls of the city. The shields were carried by your men, Majesty," he said quickly.

"Your men killed a child from your own city!" William boomed storming towards the high king and pointing a finger in his face. "You attacked our home, and then when we came for payment, you decided you preferred war. When we had overcome your defenses you used your own people to protect your gold," William boomed.

"We lost men while they went out to protect your people!" William continued. "Andrayan soldiers shed their blood, their lives for Elanders. Why? Because they were innocent, that is why!"

"You were being unreasonable!" Porthanaclies attempted to say, but William just turned and walked away.

He turned briefly, and pointing an accusatory finger at the old man he said, "Your pride and the gold you coveted was unreasonable. We used to be friends, High King Porthanaclies.

When the other rulers would laugh at you, I would stand at your side. When you made a fool of yourself, I alone stood by you. What did you do? You sent your soldiers under the care of that jackass," he yelled pointing at Marcus, "and lost everything! Your friend, your gold and," he paused this time speaking quieter, "your people." And with that he turned and walked away.

"Declan, tell our people the Lytonian's are free to leave if they choose," William commanded. Declan saluted his king and turned to give the orders. William just went to his tent and prayed his wife and countrymen would be safe.

Chapter 37

In the Age of King William the First

The next morning started much different than the day before. Where it was dark and cold yesterday the day started bright and sunny this morning. William dressed in his armor again and walked out of his tent to a surprise. He was surrounded by civilians. He saw Declan and quickly walked over to him.

"What's going on, General?" William asked his weary eyed friend.

"We released the people last night, after High King Porthanaclies returned to the castle. The young woman wanted to see the man who consoled her last night. When she found out it was you, she refused to leave the area," Declan replied, pointing out the woman who was being pestered by others trying to get her to eat.

"Okay fine, but the rest?" William asked.

"They wouldn't leave her," Declan finished for him.

"Oh my," William said. "Where is this going?"

"I don't know, milord, but I think we're about to find out," Declan said, as he stepped back to make room for the woman. Seeing the king, she quickly walked towards him followed by the other women tending to her.

"Sire," she said and curtsied as best she could in her state of fatigue, "may I speak with you please?" she asked.

"Certainly sister, come and sit. Please ladies, I assure you she is safe with me," he said, motioning for the others to stop. "General, could you arrange for some breakfast for us please?" he asked.

"Aye, sir, right away," the general replied, moving off for him.

William motioned for the young woman to enter his tent. "Would you please sit down?" William asked, pointing at a chair.

"Thank you, sire," she said, taking a seat.

"Did you sleep at all?" he asked, and she simply shook her head no. She looked like she was about to cry and he grabbed for something to offer her but she held up her hand.

"Don't worry, sire," she said. "I have no more tears today," she whimpered softly.

"I'm sorry this befell your family, madam," William replied, grief filling his voice.

His genuine response seemed to help the woman find more tears as several fell down her cheeks. "I know none of this is your fault, sire," she replied. "Your men tried to save us; you yourself tried to speak with us but were driven away."

"I still wish I could have done more," William replied.

"We both do, sire, we both do," she said sadly.

"Madam, what can I do for you?" he asked.

"I wanted to thank you for coming to me in my grief. I'm afraid my sadness seemed to steal the pain from the others with lost ones yesterday," she explained, "but when you left, I spoke a little to my father, the older man you spoke too. He said that my husband may not be dead," she said.

"No, he may not be. But did he tell you of our other problem?" he asked.

"Yes, but if my husband survived the initial conflict, I am sure he is still safe," she replied.

"Why is that, sister?" William asked.

"Because he was loyal to General Austin and if the general says not to fight he won't take up arms against your people," she said. The confidence with which she spoke filled William with hope.

"Oh I hope so, little sister; I hope so for both our families," he said softly. His fear must have entered his voice as the young woman quickly got up and hugged his head to her chest.

"He is all I have left, now that our son is dead," she said holding him. "He must be alive."

William slowly got up to his feet and held the woman before him. "When this is over, I will take you to Andraya if you wish. I will reunite you, and you will be welcome to stay with him in our lands for as long as you both wish," he said.

She smiled at him and nodded not being able to speak. She turned and walked from the tent just as Declan entered with the two plates of hot breakfast.

"Madam, please wait a moment," William called. She stopped and looked at him. "Take the plate and eat. We both must be strong for our families and our people," he said. She looked down at the plate of warm stew and took it with thanks to Declan.

The general entered the tent and set the food down on the table and took a seat.

"We're going to try to reunite them then?" He asked.

"Yeah, with God's help he will still be alive when we get back," William replied. He sat down in his chair and began eating, thanking Declan for bringing it to him. "So what have we heard?" William asked.

"Nothing new, milord," Declan replied. "The walls are still guarded by archers, real ones this time and the parlay flag has been lowered. Now we are just waiting."

"Alright, so we wait. Any news from Chloe yet?" he asked.

"Yes, they stopped for two hours last night and moved on to the village. She sent a pigeon from there. She expects to be back in Andraya in six and a half days. She then expects to be back in Czariana in about ten or eleven days after that," he reported.

"Good, that's the best news so far. I hope she gets there in time," William sighed.

"If not, the queen is smart. I'm sure that she placed the city in lock down when she first heard that trouble was brewing," Declan explained. "The people can hold out for a long time, and even though most of the archers are gone, the city defense teams are still there. So she has some seasoned soldiers to advise her. That, and how many of our people don't know how to handle a bow?" he chuckled.

His reassurances helped ease William's mind a bit. At the very least, the idea of the city already being in lock down was probably right. His wife was a smart, strong woman, he reminded himself. William continued to eat in silence and noticed Declan's facial expression.

"Is there a problem, General?" William asked.

"No, no problem. I was up most of the night making sure our guests out there didn't try anything. They just wouldn't listen and I thought they had been through enough, so I didn't threaten them with soldiers. Instead, I had the protection tripled around your tent last night and I stayed watch for most of it," Declan explained.

William stopped eating and smiled across the table. “Dec, you and Brody are my best friends,” William replied, “You are both more than that, you’re brothers to me. Why is it that you both bow to me instead of acting as my equals?”

Declan chuckled. “To be honest with you, Will,” he replied, “when I was younger it was because you were a great leader. You still are, but back then I convinced myself that was the only reason.”

“And now?” William asked.

“And now, I can honestly admit I would hate to rule,” he said laughing.

“I knew it all along, you pain in the neck!” William said, pointing his fork at his friend causing him to laugh again.

“We’ve come a long way from a couple of kids in a hole in the ground,” Declan chuckled.

“Yeah. I hope history looks back at us and smiles,” William replied, to which Declan only nodded. The room was silent again for a couple of minutes until it was filled with the sound of snoring.

William looked up and saw Declan sleeping in his chair. The king smiled at his friend, got a pillow and blanket from his bed and tried to make the general more comfortable. He then got up, taking his plate with him and eating on his feet; he walked out of the tent.

The day went slowly with nothing new occurring. The people of Lytton stayed together but wouldn’t leave the king’s camp. He found out that Marcus had ordered them to be used as the shield. He said that William was a coward and wouldn’t harm innocents. There were more people still in the city as Marcus only ordered the poor out onto the field.

William helped with the digging of the graves. Then, when it was time, the people of Lytton joined the soldiers of Andraya in commiserating the remains of the dead to the ground.

Everyone cried, including most of the soldiers, when the body of the baby boy was lowered into his place. When it was done, everyone present took a shovel or worked with their hands, and the graves were quickly filled. Small grave markers were positioned, and one of the people, who was a carver, promised William he would create proper markings for all of them.

William was tired and hungry, when Declan tapped his shoulder and pointed towards the castle. There upon the wall flew the white flag of surrender, and riding towards them were three people, alone. Setting aside his fatigue, William walked slowly to meet the figures riding towards them. Being careful to stay outside the still clearly defined range of archers, they waited until Porthanaclies, Marcus, and Jasmine sat before them.

The high king saw the dirt on William's hands, clothes, and face and looked over him to the graves near the trees.

"You buried the child then?" the high king asked.

William just nodded too tired to trade words with a man he now considered a fool.

"I see. King William Duthain of Andraya, I surrender the city of Lytton to you. Do with it what you will," the high king said.

William nodded, expecting as much and turning, he and Declan began to walk away.

"Still playing in the dirt like a peasant I see," Marcus' voice rang out behind him. William didn't stop walking, didn't even care what was said.

The sound of a sword being drawn and a loud cry and a scream shot through the evening air, as a thud brought William to a halt. He cautiously turned around and saw Declan looking at the ground behind them. William's eyes followed his friends gaze to the body of King Marcus on the ground with a sword in his chest.

William looked up at the high king, his sword scabbard empty and a scowl upon his face. The king simply nodded to William, and grabbing the reins of his stunned daughters mount, he led her back to the castle. The Corland family line was finally ended, and so too was the Vendetta.

Chapter 38

In the Age of King William the First

The next day William, the townspeople, Declan, and a large guard entered the city of Lytton. They were led to the castle by generals of the Eland army and shown to the vault. William was amazed by how much money was before him. Andrayan taxes brought in a lot of money, at ten percent of each village's crop. It was usually enough to balance the accounts for the kingdom with enough to spare to build roads or special features for villages.

But he had never even seen this much money, and neither had anyone who stood with him watching it gleam in the torch light. William sent in accountants who sorted, counted, and recorded every piece. They then reported to William what they found. The jewels alone were enough to pay for all the trouble they had experienced, and although he felt gold fever, he decided to change his decision to take all of it.

He toured the city with its planners, and after getting an approximate value, he gave that much gold to the generals and told them to rebuild what was destroyed during the conflict. He made sure enough people heard him so they couldn't steal the money for themselves. Eland was about to see a major upheaval with the end of the Porthanaclies line, as his daughter had no husband and the high king had no sons of his own. William wasn't about to make it worse.

He then took one half of the entire treasury and left the rest to the citizens to do with as they saw fit. William was tired, home sick and didn't really care what came of it when he left. Let their greed overwhelm them if need be, they would decide. Fifty thousand was all he asked for and so half of the total treasury was considerably more than he originally demanded. The treasure was then loaded onto closed wagons and was surrounded by guards as the Andrayan soldiers packed up camp and headed for home. Unfortunately though, they moved even slower than before, because the added weight of the treasure made the wagons harder to pull.

The evening of the first day quickly descended upon the marching army. They set up camp and William quickly wrote a message to Emma. He told her of the victory, and the loss of the child. He told her he loved her and to send word as soon as she could.

He sent the pigeon that night wanting it to reach her as quickly as possible. He kept to himself that night and went to bed early, wanting the day to end quickly.

The next day they continued on and so the routine began and continued on for the next three weeks. Finally, nearly seventeen days after sending his message they entered the Kingdom of Andraya. It was strange how good being on home soil made everyone feel, and new life was breathed into the troops.

William rode daily with the young woman, Lyra, at his side. They talked about families as she told him her story, and he told her his. She was amazed that a peasant boy had become king by his own hand. She had heard much of his story before, making it all the more believable hearing it again from the man himself.

It wasn't until they were only a couple of days from home that a reply came from Emma. The message on the pigeon told him briefly that the insurrection had been put down and everything was okay. She then informed him that it was General Austin that commanded Elander and Andrayan soldiers alike to accomplish it.

Apparently, the problem was caused by Mercenaries who just wanted to leave. When it was all done, nearly two thirds of the Elanders had revolted.

William replied that they were only a couple of days away and he was eager to hear the rest of the story in greater detail. He didn't have to wait long though, as the next day they were met on the road by a delegation of smiling friends.

William was overjoyed to see Brody, Chloe, Logan, General Austin, and a man William didn't recognize. When the riders pulled up, Lyra let out a cry of relief, and jumping down from her horse she ran into the waiting arms of her husband. They both instantly started crying as she led him away to tell him the details of what had happened.

William watched them go to find privacy for their pain. Turning his attention to his friends, whom he welcomed warmly, nearly brought tears to his eyes in relief.

"I am so happy to see you all," William said hugging each of them in turn. "General, it's good to see you, too," he said shaking the man's hand.

"We're glad you're home," Brody said grinning at his two friends and his son, "well almost home. Emma would love to be here, but she felt it was important to maintain the kingdom until she could hand it back to you properly."

"As much as I want to see her right now, that is probably the best. Dec, we won't make it home tonight anyway. Let's set camp so we can talk," he commanded.

Declan nodded, and he left with Brody at his side to see to the preparations for the camp.

An hour later, everyone was comfortable in William's tent telling stories.

"So the high king killed Marcus, himself?" Logan asked incredulously.

"Yes. He had enough of the coward, it seems," Declan replied.

Everyone absorbed the news in silence until William spoke up.

"Okay, that's our story, how about yours?" he asked.

"General, I suggest that you start telling the story, since we weren't there until later?" Brody said.

The large framed Half Dwarf cleared his throat and began. "Everything was going well after you left. Your people treated us with dignity and respect, we were creating a structured tent city, and when the work crews came home, each man had a bed and food available. To be honest, I thought it was refreshing, almost relaxing. The trouble started when some Mercs, who don't owe me their allegiance outside of a paycheck, wanted to leave.

"I met with a couple of them and they made it known that they didn't think they should be bound by your terms and wanted out. I told them that their services were paid for until the end of the campaign and that wouldn't be for another year.

"They of course disagreed, and when threatening me didn't work, they started causing trouble with my men. The first couple of days they wouldn't work. Then rumor had it that some of the men were talking about taking their chances with the Rangers. Finally, when word reached me that there was talk about storming the city, I sent word to the queen.

"By this time, you had just entered Eland, and the queen sent word to you. The pigeon must have gotten lost since it took so long to find you," he explained. "In fact, I believe you got our second warning first, about the men who had escaped?"

"You mean most of this happened more than three weeks before you received support from our people?" William asked amazed.

"Yes, well, it was closer to four weeks, to be honest," the general replied. "But I sent word to the Rangers via the queen and asked that the Merc's be eliminated. My hope was that they were all that was holding the revolt together. The queen agreed, and we staged their escape, only to execute them when it was safe to do so. We tried to make it look like they were cowards to discredit them."

"Did it work?" Declan asked.

"Sure, for a week or so. But the problem is that too many people had already taken a liking to the idea, so new leaders stepped up to take their places.

"For nearly two whole weeks we waited for support. Fewer and fewer of us went to work. I had the weapons sent back to Czariana, and it was a good thing because shortly after, they acted.

“I have been an Elander my entire life. My father, a dwarf from the Golden Kingdoms, was banished early in his life. He moved to Eland where he met my mother, and I was born. So you can believe me when I say I was surprised and ashamed at my people’s choice to turn their backs on their honor.

“The numbers against us were great. Over half the men sided with the renegades, while a large number refused to take a side. All work stopped as those loyal to me, like Artole here,” he said pointing at Lyra’s husband who was holding his wife quietly listening, “worked with the Rangers to keep things under control.

“I’ve lost count of those who attempted to escape and were dealt with by the Rangers, but many tried their hand at running off. If any were successful, I suppose we will never know. Anyway, the rebels created weapons from rocks in the quarry. Luckily, the queen had thought this might happen and sent us our armor and weapons of steel back to allow us to hold them off.

“At first, this was all we needed. The queen couldn’t send us what defenses she had left, but the few archers I had on my side kept them at bay. Unfortunately though, our arrows wouldn’t last forever, and their leaders knew it. During this time, a few well placed arrows would steal some of their spirit, but even then their battle lust had been reawakened.

“For over a week we held them, hoping they were all talk, or would come to their senses. Unfortunately for us though, they weren’t and didn’t. Their attack surprised us. They came at night and rushed our camp at the mouth of the quarry. They charged in such a rage that several of my men fell by simply being overwhelmed.

“We then began to fight back. It was our steel against their sticks and rocks. We fought all night, our blades giving us the edge, but numbers and time were against us. By end of the day my men were about to falter.

"It was then that we were saved," he said to the captive audience.

"What the general means," added Chloe, "is that is when we arrived. When we got to Czariana, we spoke to Emma," Chloe explained, picking up the story from the general. "We made sure everything was alright, but when she explained what was happening, we rushed to the quarry."

"We could hear the sounds of battle in the distance," Brody said breaking in, "so Chloe commanded her Rangers to head to high ground around the quarry as I led our people in head on.

"Our cavalry changed from sword to bow, and as we charged into the throng, we did so as a driving wedge," Brody explained.

"Sure, but you didn't come in as a single wedge!" Chloe exclaimed. "He had our troops attack in three wedges. William it was brilliant!"

"Well not brilliant, but yes we did separate into three wedges," Brody blushed as Shade beamed with pride next to him. "This allowed us to split the enemy into five manageable groups."

"Seeing the newly arrived forces join the fray gave us new life," General Austin added, the excitement of the story drawing him back in. "Most of those under my command were on either side of the central wedge. I hoped that Minister Brody's men would know us from the others."

"We did," Brody said. "When we spoke to Emma, she informed us that the Loyalists, as the general has taken to calling his people, had armor," Brody continued. "So we targeted everyone without any."

“It was here,” Chloe tagged in, “that my Rangers and I reached the rim of the quarry. From our vantage point, we began firing arrows at the enemy on the outside edges. The addition of our attacks created chaos in the enemy’s ranks…”

“…Allowing those of us on the ground to capitalize upon it and change the tides again,” General Austin jumped back in. “Cavalry, sword, and pike all advanced, eventually drawing the wedges forward into a solid line. Elander and Andrayan alike stood shoulder to shoulder and faced down those who stood before us.”

“But it wasn’t long after that the enemy surrendered,” Brody said, calming the story down a bit. “Surrounded by archers on high ground, a wall of steel in front of them, and most of their leaders dead, they laid down their weapons. We shackled the survivors, administered aid to all the wounded, and have been treating the prisoners as prisoners ever since.”

“Well, it seems to me that all of Andraya owes all of you a great debt of gratitude,.” William said, amazed at what had transpired. “But it is late now, and after such an amazing story I find I’m exhausted. Why don’t all of you retire for the night, and we can carry on the discussions in the morning.” Everyone agreed and quickly retired to their tents until the morning.

Chapter 39

In the Age of King William the First

The next day everyone packed up camp and started travelling again. This time the same group that met the night before, rode together in a carriage brought from a nearby village.

"So the Porthanaclies Royal Line has come to an end?" General Austin asked.

"It appears so," William replied. "With the death of Marcus, it would limit Porthanaclies' options. Even with Marcus, it would just be an extension of the Lianthus line."

"True, but now with no clear heir to the throne the nobles will begin fighting over the right of succession. My country is about to face a dark time," the general said sadly.

"Yes it certainly is, but from the darkness light will shine," Declan replied.

"What do you mean General Declan?" Austin asked.

"What I mean is we suffered great darkness as children and we made Andraya a better place," Declan explained.

"We can only hope to find a leader like you all have," General Austin replied with a smile.

"Oh, I don't know," said William, "I think the Elanders already have a great leader at their disposal."

"Who? Me? No, King William, I am just a soldier. I have no place ruling a nation," the general laughed.

"I am just the son of a farmer," William replied. "Two of them, come to think of it. I lead because my people needed a leader. It's not birth that makes a king, General, but heart."

Everyone agreed and as the conversation changed direction, the general quietly digested the king's words.

The city of Czariana loomed before them as the king, now mounted on his charger once again, fought the urge to gallop to it like a homesick pup.

Finally, the long column of soldiers came to a stop before the gates. William held up his hand to signal everyone to stop as Emma, who had been standing there waiting for them, walked forward.

William jumped down from his horse and walked up to her. "My king, I deliver your capitol, better than you left it," the queen said with a smile.

Without saying a word, William grabbed her and drew her to him. He then lowered his face to her and gave her a long passionate kiss hello.

When they finally pulled apart William smiled, "The very fact that you are in it and safe, makes it the most wonderful place in the world."

Emma caught her breath and smiled at her husband, gently stroking his cheek. "I've missed you, too, my king."

Holding her against his side he turned and caught Brody's attention. "Brody, could you and Declan please take the cargo to the city vaults?"

"Yes, sire, we will see to it at once," Brody said with a salute. The two leaders, followed by the wagons and their security details, moved forward into the city as instructed.

"Emma, I would like to discuss what happened while we were away, from your perspective," William said to his wife. Then turning to the others he continued, "Logan, lead a group of men to relieve the guards at the quarry and prepare our troops for guard detail, please."

"Yes, Father, I'll get right to it," Logan replied.

"Chloe, why don't you and the general relax for a while? I would like to dine with you tonight, if you would join us? Also, see to it that all the command staff from General Austin's people, the Andrayan soldiers and the Rangers, joins us. I want to celebrate both victories with as many of our people as possible. I would also like to discuss our options at supper," he said to his little sister.

Chloe nodded her understanding as Emma gave William a smile. Taking him by the hand she led him into the city, back to the Royal Manner.

Everyone was seated in the Central Hall when William and Emma joined them. Soon all in attendance was eating and laughing, all the while exchanging stories of their adventures. Then, when the meal was over and the tables were cleared William turned to all those assembled and spoke loudly so everyone could hear.

"Emma and I have talked at length this afternoon about what has happened over the last couple of months," William said.

"I didn't realize that ten minutes before supper constituted 'at length'," Brody said nonchalantly which earned him a kick from Chloe.

"Anyway, carrying on," William said rolling his eyes at his grinning friends, "Emma has made it very clear, General Austin, that we are in your and your men's debt," he said, standing and bowing low to the general.

"There is no debt, Majesty," the general replied, touched by the honor of the king's words. "I was not going to break my word or allow innocents to be harmed by cowards."

"Indeed. It is because of your honor, that should you wish to free your people from the tyranny of your nobles, you shall have the full support of the Andrayan people," the king declared to the cheering assembly.

The general was speechless. Since his earlier conversation with the king, he hadn't stopped thinking about the prospects of freeing his people. He stammered and tried to answer but found he couldn't. Instead, Chloe spoke up for him.

"I think the general is trying to say thank you, big brother," she said with a smile, which seemed to free General Austin's tongue.

"Yes, milord, thank you. I have wanted to do just as we talked about but couldn't see how. Now, I have options. Thank you, gracious king, I am touched," he replied.

"We can talk about the details later, General, but for now know that the people of Andraya are in your debt. We also absolve you, and the men who fought at your side, of their crimes against our people. As such, you and those you choose, are free as of this moment," William said, once again to a cheering crowd.

"Moving on, I have decided that the entire army shall be given a month's leave, on a rotation. We will work out whom and when but for now they shall all be told a long due rest is coming," William continued.

This time it was the Andrayan Rangers and troops that were in the crowd who cheered loudly.

“Thank you, brother,” Chloe replied with a smile, “I think I agree with you;, I could use a rest, too.”

William couldn’t help noticing how much attention his sister was giving, and receiving, from General Austin who sat at her side.

“Finally, this year we shall have two festivals instead of the one tax festival. During the regular tax festival, we shall all celebrate by only requiring five percent taxes from the people. The second shall be done to celebrate our victory, and to honor those who died in service to their people,” he said, to a reply of “here, here” from everyone in the room.

“My friends,” the king continued, “I believe it is time we all take a moment to remember those who didn’t make it back to their homes. This was a conflict, born of hate, and driven by ego. Let us never forget those men and women who died to once again allow us to live free. To never forget those who pledged their lives to that belief, and to the tragedy we find in their loss. There is no justice for the innocent if there is no penalty for the guilty.

“Now let us enjoy ourselves for we have a lot to do tomorrow. But tonight we celebrate!” he said to cheers from everyone assembled.

The music quickly started, and as William took his seat again, he looked at the smiling faces around him. Each one of his friends, new and old, was happy. His feud with the Lianthus family was over. The people of Andraya could now enjoy a hard and long fought peace. Now they truly could consider themselves free.

The End

Appendix

Artillian Sea
N
ELAND
XANTHOR
ESTUARY
BYWAY
CZARIANA
FARROW
BARUTH
HAROTH
PARINTH
REBEL MEETING POINT
ELVIN
KINGDOM OF LAYENI
ROTHAR
MOUNTAINS
ANDRAYA
GOLAMEED
LAKE ARLENE

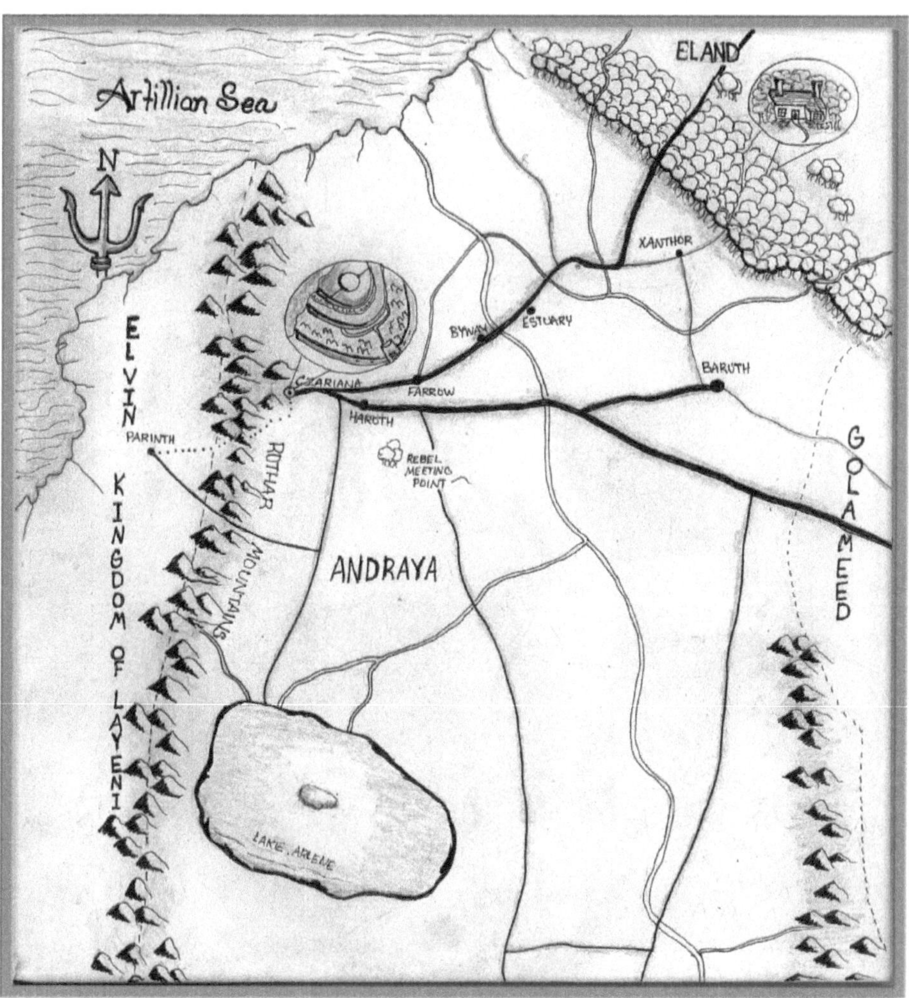

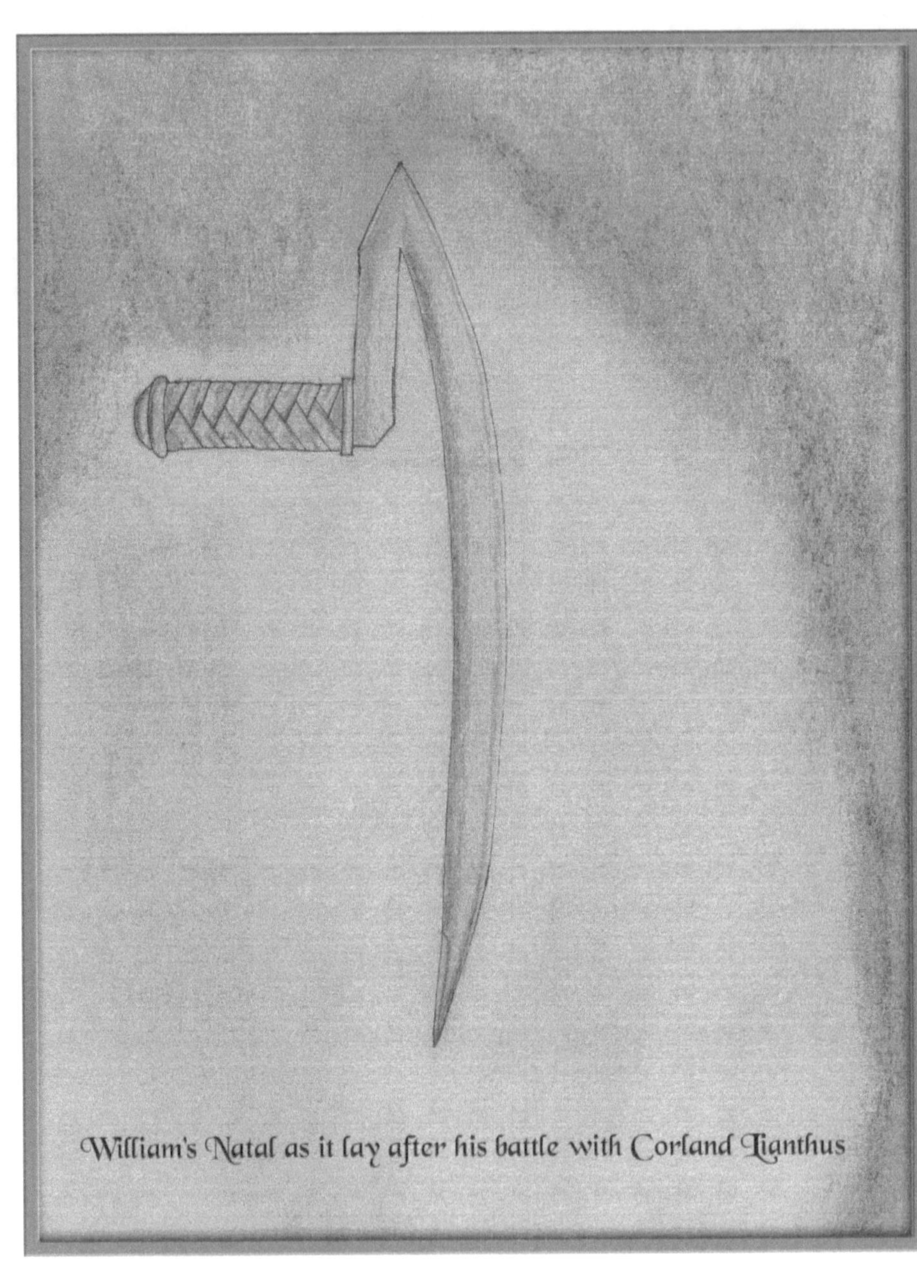

William's Natal as it lay after his battle with Corland Lianthus

Character List

The Duthain Royal Family

- **William Duthain –** First Elected Ruler and King of Andraya
- **Emma Duthain –** Queen of Andraya
- **Logan Duthain –** First Born Son, Prince of Andraya, Commander of the Night Hawk
- **Ashton Duthain –** Second Son, Prince of Andraya, Captain of the Runners
- **Czaria Duthain –** Youngest Child, Princess of Andraya
- **Chloe Duthain –** William's younger sister, Princess of Andraya, Leader of the Rangers.
- **Domitus –** William and Chloe's birth father
- **Czaria -** William and Chloe's birth mother. Passed away in their youth
- **Bachand Duthain –** William and Chloe's adopted father from Parinth
- **Muria Duthain –** William and Chloe's adopted mother from Parinth

The Lianthus Royal Family

- **Corland Lianthus –** Former Ruler of Andraya
- **Elissiana Lianthus –** Former Queen of Andraya
- **Marcus Lianthus –** Former Prince of Andraya, King of Eland through marriage.

The Adrayan Court and Military Leaders

- **Declan –** General of Andrayan Troops, William's cousin
- **Brody –** Prime Minister of Andraya, William's best friend
- **Shade –** Brody's Son, Captain and Commander of the Andrayan archers
- **Violet –** Head servant, Unattributed advisor
- **Minister Reese –** Community Works
- **Minister Finlay –** Agriculture
- **Minister Tobias –** Development, Master Blacksmith
- **Minister Eva –** Arts
- **Minister Payton –** Education
- **Minister Dominic –** Commerce
- **James Blackwell –** Gunnery Sergeant
- **Charlie Bennet –** Second in command of the Night Hawk
- **Owen Surehand –** City Engineer
- **Nathan Glassman –** Apprentice Engineer, Journeyman Glassblower.

Key Layeni/Parinth Citizenry

- **Pethoras Tianvor –** King of Layeni
- **Liddia Yamenus –** Brody's adopted mother
- **Beorn Uramitys –** Declan's Custodian, Parinth's Weapon Smith
- **Narooth Tanian –** Leader of the Parinth Council

Friends of Andraya

- **Austin Ironfist –** High General of the Eland Army, commander of the joint Andrayan/Eland troops during the Eland insurrection
- **Ambassador Shihome –** Golameed Ambassador to Andraya
- **Empress Mura'sy –** Golameed Ruler.

Eland Royalty

- **Yelantas Porthanaclies –** High King of Eland
- **Jasmine Porthanaclies –** Queen of Eland, Marcus' wife.

Kingdoms

- **Andraya –** Human Kingdom
- **Layeni –** Elvin Kingdom, West of Andraya
- **Eland –** Human Kingdom, North of Andraya
- **Golameed –** Gnomish Kingdom, East of Andraya

About the Author:

Growing up in rural Manitoba, Cameron's love of nature comes to the fore in a genre rich with life, hard work and a commitment to ones community. After being introduced to the genre of fantasy as a boy, his passion for reading quickly became one of writing.

The feeling of wonder and freedom that came from creating people, places and events of his own imagination quickly took seed in his heart. After years of planning and shaping he succeeded. Welcome to a Kingdom where community, justice and a desire for peace exist. Welcome to Andraya.

www.ingramcontent.com/pod-product-compliance
Lightning Source LLC
Chambersburg PA
CBHW030819310726
48980CB00006B/557/J
9780988024229